For the second time that day, I stared into the werewolf's red eyes, bright with human intelligence though a wildness flickered in their depths.

The stuff of nightmares stared back at me, through me, and called to the beast that lurked within. Finding me out. My body tightened against the urge to flee. To hide.

I waved my dagger to remind the beast, and myself, that I was the one in control. Or at least, I hoped I was. The security lights glimmered off the sharp silver blade, making my point for me.

Flinching, the werewolf averted his massive head. Thank God, I didn't have to bluff this time. Now I was all about the follow through. My doubts faded on a mind-blowing rush of power at the beast's show of fear.

I took a bold step forward.

The beast stumbled backwards, knocked into the bunny cage, and sent the trapped creatures into spastic scuttles.

I had him. We both knew it.

Then I slipped in the bunny blood. I cried out, flailing my hands in the air, trying to regain my balance, but my feet shot out from under me. I crashed to the floor. My head cracked against the linoleum.

I landed in a sprawl under the werewolf's stinking jowls. His foul breath filled my nostrils as stars spun in front of my eyes. My athame flew from my hand, scraped across the floor, and came to rest a few feet away.

I twisted onto my stomach and reached frantically for the hilt. Oh, this was so wrong. My nails dug into the linoleum floor. I inched closer. My breath escaped in a ragged sob. My splayed fingers trembled. An inch. One inch more. So close. But not close enough.

Under My Skin

JUDITH GRAVES

with illustrations by VAL COX

This is a work of fiction. Names, characters, places, and incidents either are the product of the author's imagination or are used fictitiously, and any resemblance to actual persons living or dead, business establishments, events, or locales, is entirely coincidental.

Under My Skin

COPYRIGHT ©2010 by Tracy A. Belsher

Contact Information: info@leapbks.com

Cover Art by *Nicola Martinez*
Interior Art by *Val Cox*

Leap Books, LLC
PO Box 112
Reidsville, NC 27320-0112
Visit us at www.leapbks.com

Publishing History
First Edition, 2010

ISBN-13 978-1-61603-000-1
ISBN-10 1-61603-000-3

LCCN 2009941503

Published in the United States of America

Acknowledgments

There are many individuals who deserve a brand new hybrid vehicle in their driveway for their support, advice, hacking, slashing, and handholding while I wrote this book. So here goes...

Thanks to: My father, a man of few words, and my mother who speaks volumes. Blaise and Brenda for the good times, the encouragement, and the sibling dysfunction that I so love. Grandpa Scott who wrote me into the story of his life. Early readers on Critique Circle and other online crit groups – you helped develop my thick, leathery writer's hide. A howl out to Kitty and Tami for being my virtual sisters and the ultimate critique partners. To Tess for the political correctness cues along the way. Thanks, darling Bev, for all the proofing – and for teaching me how to drive at the ripe old age of 35. You saved my marriage! ;) Jo and Carol, Leeor, Elaine – my ever ready crew of readers. You're fab and you know it! Many thanks to the staff at Holy Cross for cheering me along, and to all my friends and family who took the time to ask how the writing was going. To Val for bringing my characters to life in such a hip, paranormal way. My editor, Susan, gets hugs and chocolate for beating UMS into submission. Laurie – you're a goddess for LEAPing into the unknown. Cheers and a beverage of her choosing to Rosemary Clement-Moore for her kickass books and willingness to read UMS. Finally, hugs and kisses to my crazy labs, Higgins and Willow. And an X-rated embrace to my husband, Shawn, for being my roadie, my BBF, and the finest man I know. Okay, yes, he did come up with a few of the snappy one-liners in UMS. But I'm not telling you which ones. ;)

PRAISE FOR UNDER MY SKIN

"Under My Skin is a roller-coaster romp through a supernatural world filled with scary beasties, otherworldly magic, and characters you'll root for. Eryn is a tough but likable protagonist whose paranormal problems make a compelling story full of mystery, magic, action and romance. A fun and engaging read. I'm looking forward to the sequel."

~**Rosemary Clement-Moore, award-winning author of** *Prom Dates from Hell, Hell Week, Highway to Hell,* **and** *The Splendor Falls*

"Judith Graves sinks claws into you and doesn't let go. Her stories overflow with nail-biting adventures, hot heroes, and equally tasty villains, not to mention wise-cracking heroines you'll love."

~**Kitty Keswick, author of** *Freaksville* **and** *Furry and Freaked*

A Little Van Hexing

I ran like my life depended on it.

Maybe it did.

Running kept me sane. The faster my feet hit the ground, the clearer my father's voice and the more detailed my mother's face became. My parents lived again in those brief moments when my instincts kicked in and the past hitched a ride on my cross trainers. But when I stopped, the memories faded and left an odd emptiness. Like now.

I laid on more speed. Wind roared past my ears and blasted my hair out behind me, proving why my trademark ponytails were both funky and functional. No matter how intense the run, the hunt, the kill, I never had to stress

about a bad hair day. Hey, I was a sixteen-year-old hunter of paranormal creatures. Bad hair was as much of an issue as taking down big bad evil.

And I'd had my share of both. Lecture number 7201 or something—*if flyaway hair obstructs your vision and means the difference between life and death, shave your head.* Oh, my father was full of those hunter tidbits.

I thundered down the mulch-lined trail, crushing pinecones underfoot. Low-lying shrubs, their thinning leaves a patchwork of fall hues, closed in around me, narrowing the trail to shoulder width. Blocked out by thickening woods, the cheerful sunshine no longer glistened on the dew-covered grasses edging the trail. I forged ahead into the gloom. My arms pumped hard as branches sliced at any flesh unprotected by my T-shirt. Tension crept into my shoulders.

Something was up.

Something not so nice.

I did a quick 360, my legs wobbling. Nothing around. But still… I closed my mouth, inhaled through my nose, and trained my sharpened hearing on the woods that engulfed me. Except for fallen leaves rustling in the wind, scuttling across the earth like mice, the woods were quiet. Freaky quiet. The hush that settled over a hunter as his prey strode blithely into range.

Fighting my growing unease, I focused on the wild smells of the forest. Evergreens, sharp and pungent. Rotting leaves. A fox den nearby. I charged down a trail behind Redgrave High, the lead runner in a gym class race.

What was there to be scared of?

In my experience? Plenty.

The eerie quiet triggered my spidey sense. The hairs on the back of my neck stood at attention and saluted. *Danger ahead, capt'n!* I reached beyond my human limits, tapped into my heightened senses. I tilted my head, nostrils flared. I filtered through the earthy scents of the forest for anything out of the ordinary. Anything *extra*ordinary. The breeze at my back brought him to me.

Werewolf. Four o'clock. Part wet dog, part *I've-been-feasting-on-human-flesh-all-night* foulness.

My pulse jolted in my throat. I kept running, eyes forward, scanning the forest, playing it cool for the creature shadowing me.

Why had I let my guard down? Given into my desire for speed and taken such a huge lead? I'd only made it easy for the werewolf to track me. My scent was pure, not mingled with

sweat and deodorant and body spray as it would have been if I'd stayed with the group.

Now, the werewolf knew I wasn't quite human. Nope, I was something *much* more interesting...and tasty. If the deep growl behind me was any indication, he thought I was definitely worth a closer look.

Careful what you wish for, furball. This is one meal that might bite back.

Launching into the air, I grabbed a thick branch arching about eight feet over the trail, pulled my knees to my chest, and swung my body high. The werewolf ran under me like I was a matador's cape. He shook his shaggy head, letting out a burst of enraged huffs as he struggled to slow down. Werewolves were so uncoordinated. Half man, half beast, their scrambled brains and morphing bodies didn't always work in unison.

I scampered up until I was perched among the branches. Slack-jawed, chest heaving, I sucked in gulps of air. Below me the beast paced back toward the tree, grunting and growling.

Thankfully werewolves weren't climbers. The big bad would never get me up here. I hoped he wouldn't try to ram the tree trunk to knock me out. I hated when that happened.

Safe for the moment, I peered down at the ghoulish, bulbous shapes outlined under his fur. This was no proper change from man to wolf, like with my species, the wolven. Wolven were born, not made. We were paranormal, sure, but still a part of nature, a natural occurrence. Werewolves, not so much. Created with dark magic, their humanity died the moment they were turned. Whoever made this werewolf

hadn't taken any time to give the poor thing a few paranorm life lessons.

His bones kept shifting, as if he were uncertain which form to assume, man or beast. Raw patches of leathery human skin appeared all over his body as he molted and then grew black fur over and over. Shapeshifters often took years to control their abilities—if they didn't go stark raving mad first. This one was a newbie. Making stupid mistakes. No self-control. Sloppy.

Did my new buddy have any friends? I scanned the woods. Surprisingly, there was no hint of other weres. No dark shapes pacing in the shrubbery. Highly unusual. Werewolves worked in packs, serving under a more powerful paranorm, like a vamp or demon. According to the Council, Redgrave was paranorm free. So this werewolf must be a rogue. Whatever he was, his presence didn't totally shock me. After all, if there weren't any rogues in the paranorm world, my father and his hunters would have been out of jobs long ago.

How was I going to get myself out of this one? I was in gym class, for god's sake. I couldn't stay in this tree forever. And in my sweats and T-shirt, I was hardly prepared to duke it out with a werewolf. I didn't have a bit of silver on me.

But *he* didn't know that.

Like my dad always said, when you've got nothing, act like you could care less. I let go of the branch, dropped to the ground, and straightened to my full height, my feet firmly planted, my stance confident.

"Scouting for prey in the middle of the afternoon?" I asked as if amused by his folly.

He staggered toward me, tilting his massive head, apparently questioning my sanity. His grizzly snout trembled, a thick line of drool hung from his jowls. Clearly, he expected to make quick work of me.

I held my ground, chin high. "Let me guess, you're one of those early-bird-gets-the-worm kind of werewolves, right? Too bad I always carry my trusty athame with me." I patted the back of my sweats for effect. "The blade is solid silver."

His ragged ears flattened against his head, and his steps faltered.

"Yup," I breezed, "it's an oldie but a goody, at least three hundred years old."

The beast shuddered. Ahh…now I had him. With ritual daggers, the older, the better. All the more infused with magic. And a silver athame would be extremely deadly.

So deadly, even I wouldn't be able to hold it if my father hadn't forged a rosewood hilt to protect my hands. Silver was deadly to werewolves and wolven alike. For me it wasn't so bad—being half human gave me some immunity, but the blade could do serious damage if I wasn't careful. I'd had more than my share of nasty silver burns during my training in wielding the dagger.

The werewolf's glowing, freaky red eyes narrowed as I moved my hand to my back again as if to grasp a dagger tucked into my sweat pants.

"Did I mention it was cursed?" I kept my tone light and conversational. We were getting to be good buds, me and the beast. "Yup, by a Dutch witch, and we all know how potent they are. Nothing like a little *Van Hexing* for good measure."

The werewolf snorted. The scent radiating from him told me that, though he was new, he understood an athame's power. Interesting. If he'd seen one before or had been warned about them, maybe this town had some witchy action going on. So much for Redgrave—the small, super-duper *normal* town Sebastian had sent me to live in—being off the paranorm map.

"Quit your huffing. It won't do you any good." I grinned as I brought my hand up as if to wield the dagger. "Hold still, this won't hurt a bit."

The werewolf's molt-laden ears twitched, but he didn't move.

Damn. I really wished I *had* brought the athame. The way it sliced and diced. Why had I tucked it under my mattress for safekeeping? I'm sorry, how could it keep me safe *there* when the danger was *here?* I wouldn't leave home without it again, but seriously I never expected to need a weapon in Redgrave. Huh, I'd gone less than a week before the first paranormal disaster came stalking my heels.

The distant approach of my eleventh-grade gym class, all twenty or so students, broke the stillness of the forest. They were some thirty yards down the trail but to my were-friend and me, thanks to our heightened hearing, their cannoning steps sounded very close indeed. I picked up their laughter and groans as they ran.

Checkmate.

The werewolf had missed his moment, and we both knew it. He couldn't risk an attack in full daylight, close to so many humans. Even rogues weren't totally insane. They might not

follow every teeny little rule, which often brought them to the attention of the Council and hunters like my dad, but rogues were all about self-preservation.

Lips pulled back, gleaming fangs bared as if to say, *We'll meet again*, the werewolf bolted into the thicket and disappeared. My breath left me in a relieved rush. Dropping my daggerless hand, I bent over with my hands on my knees. Okay, rogue werewolf roaming the woods—that was a surprise. I straightened, sucking in air, taking in the werewolf's lingering stench, imprinting him on my mind. If I needed to, I could track him on the memory of his scent alone. Judging from this foolish daylight excursion, he was one I'd have to track down before he gave someone all the proof they needed that, although Santa Claus was a myth, beasties like *him* really did exist.

And here I'd thought Redgrave had nothing much to offer a girl like me. Now this was more like it. Possible witch and/or magics flying around, and werewolves. Things were looking up. Being half wolven was kind of cool...sometimes. Thanks to my mom's DNA, I had certain advantages. Advantages I'd never had the chance to explore while taking the drugs my father had created to keep my unpredictable wolven half subdued. Without those drugs I flip-flopped from sheer exhilaration, as I discovered my increasing wolven abilities, to sheer horror. Now, sprouting a nasty case of back hair, a tail, and fangs—some time before graduation—were serious possibilities.

Flying back and forth between treetops, a pair of crows cawed, nagging at me for letting the werewolf go. Although I

didn't speak crow, I was pretty sure they were slandering my good name. I glared up at them and called out, "Oh yeah? I know you are, but what am I?" My voice rose, mimicking their screeching, but when the guttural noises coming from my mouth ran a close second to a horror movie screamer, I stopped.

They sounded too much like the cries I'd heard in my nightmares lately. Since my parents' disappearance, I'd been having vivid, gory dreams about losing control, my wolf completely taking over. Being off my father's meds intensified the dreams threefold. But in every dream, right after I'd been stripped of all humanity, my mother appeared, and the disgust in her eyes, the horror on her face haunted me when I woke. I shoved the thought aside. No point in dwelling on the dreams. They'd be after me later anyway.

My sweat-soaked cotton T-shirt absorbed better than

a jumbo-sized tampon and hung off me like deadweight. I fisted the drenched material, fanning it away from my skin, about to resume the race, when the crows fell silent.

A twig snapped in the thicket off the trail.

I spun around and gasped when a tall form veered to my left, running at full speed. Not a werewolf this time, but someone from gym class out to win the race. Low-hanging branches prevented me from seeing much, but my adversary was definitely male. He had a half a foot on me and a lean body. The rotter. Losing because of some local-yokel shortcut was NOT an option. So maybe I was being a bit too competitive. What else was there to do in this town?

Well, besides scare off the occasional werewolf?

I sprinted ahead, caught up, and soon took a slight lead. Staying off the trail, clinging to the shadows, the guy checked me out with a few sideways glances. I couldn't quite contain the extra bounce in my stride or the flirtatious looks I darted back. Something about running with a guy in the woods set my pulse racing in more ways than one. His smooth pace and fluid form told me this was a worthy challenger. For once I actually doubted my chances of winning, but I'd sure give him a good run.

Our pounding feet and rhythmic breathing echoed through the woods. A gap in the trees along the trail finally allowed me to get a good look. He was Native, with high cheekbones, warm tawny skin, a sharp, hawkish nose that looked as if it had been broken more than once. I guesstimated he was a year or two older than me. His dark, shoulder-length hair streamed behind him as he cut a swath through the

brush. Clad in a stretchy black T-shirt, jeans taut around his muscular thighs, he was a modern-day warrior.

Then I spotted it—his jogging buddy. A sleek grey wolf loping at his side, its jaws open in a canine grin. I gaped at them, man and beast moving as one. Lanky and graceful, with shining grey fur and keen amber eyes, the wolf was a beautiful contrast to the werewolf monstrosity I'd seen.

But still, a wolf was a wolf. I hadn't seen anyone at Redgrave High who looked as if they could inspire the loyalty of a wolf. Wolves shied away from human contact. Whatever bonds we'd had in the past, back in the caveman days, things had changed. Man had turned on wolf. Demonizing them in fairytales, slaughtering them, forcing wolves to seek out new territory.

That kind of betrayal wasn't something any creature forgot. And it was all for nothing. The wolves were never the problem.

So maybe this guy with a wolf at his side wasn't from gym class. Probably not a good thing.

Too absorbed in staring at my opponents, I failed to watch my footing on the uneven cedar chips. The path twisted. I didn't. My sneaker snagged on a piece of deadwood. I staggered and lost my stride. My feet kicked dirt and leaves into the air as I crashed against the rough bark of a tree and struggled to stay upright. Hissing, I pushed off the tree and pitched forward.

My challenger whooped. An unrestrained battle cry at the advantage my fumble gave him. He leapt ahead, devouring the trail, leaving me in his dust. His wolf-dog

barked in excitement.

Swearing, I straightened and managed a burst of speed. I decided to worry about the German shepherd on 'roids after I ran his buff master into the ground. The trail widened as the poplar trees thinned near the edge of the woods. In the urgency of the moment, chasing after the shadowy forms darting through the trees, my mind was blank. For a split second I ran without thought or piercing memory. I ran for the thrill.

By the time I reached the tree line, I couldn't see the guy or his dog anywhere. I must have overtaken them when they were hidden by the trees. Adrenaline rushing through me, I bolted into the clearing, tore through the school field, and ate up the last few feet. I leapt into the air and hurtled the finish line of faded orange pylons in the ultimate victory-is-mine gesture.

I swung back to gloat, but my rival was gone. The empty field of yellowing grass and ankle-busting gopher holes seemed to laugh at me. I spun in a slow circle, scanning the edge of the woods, but saw no one.

That odd, empty feeling I got when I couldn't remember the exact sound of my mother's laughter or the precise shade of blue in my father's eyes was back. I released my breath slowly. Only now I was missing someone I didn't even know.

"All right, Eryn!" Brit, possibly Redgrave High's only goth chick and, therefore, total social leper, bolted from the crowd of gym-challenged kids and other spectators waiting at the finish line. Over the last few days, we had latched on to each other out of self-preservation. There was geek safety in

geek numbers. "The new girl kicks butt. You're way ahead of everyone." She seemed to get a vicarious thrill at the thought.

"Not everyone," I said, scanning the tree line over her head. "This guy came out of nowhere. He was all over me."

I wish.

"Who?" Brit stretched to her full five-foot height and peered across the field. "There's only you. You're the first one back."

"A huge, rather yummy-looking guy was right behind me. He rushed me from way off the trail, totally cheated." I didn't tell her about my run-in with the werewolf or my chat with the crows. High school was bad enough without everyone thinking I was Looney Tunes. *I* might know about the paranormal world, and hunters certainly did, but 99.9 percent of the human population had no freaking clue what monsters lurked in the shadows. "Are you blind? He was pretty hard to miss. Way taller than me, probably six four, and he was with a wolf, a huge greyish-silver wolf."

Brit blinked at me from behind a dark veil of overgrown bangs. "All I saw was you gunning for the finish line." Her black-rimmed eyes glittered with interest. A few of her lashes, heavy with mascara, clung together at the corners of her eyes, but she didn't seem to notice. Brit, in all her wannabe-shocking glory, must have

been used to whatever inconveniences her goth uniform caused. I would have given up at the thought of lacing those knee-high Doc Martens.

"Rewind a sec." Brit spun her finger in the air counter-clockwise. "Did you say *wolf*? There's only one guy in town who thinks wolves are Littlest-Pet-Shop material. Alec Delacroix. He's hot all right, but all that heat's fried his brain. You don't want to go there."

"I don't?" But the image of long dark hair, broad shoulders, and powerful thighs had already registered on my but-I-really-think-I-do-want-to-go-there interest meter.

Alec Delacroix.

Now there was a nice romantic name for a potential boyfriend—one who certainly didn't seem to fit the average psycho profile. And I'd seen a few psychos in my day. Mainly members of my mother's extended family. They'd drop in unannounced and threaten to kill me—the usual we-want-the-half-breed-dead-because-we're-afraid-she-might-start-a-trend type thing. Of course, after my dad revealed his latest anti-paranorm cocktail, they wanted us *all* dead.

Hunters, guys like my dad, served a useful, if occasionally disturbing, purpose in their elimination of the paranorm rogues. They took care of the deranged and careless, the werewolves, wolven, vamps, or demons who had lost control, given into their baser instincts, and threatened exposure of the paranormal world. For centuries my mother's people, the wolven, a race of humans who could turn and assume wolf form, had avoided confrontations with hunters. But after Dad agreed to help my mother in her quest to become human, the

"If you think *I'm* weird"—Brit waved her hand dismissively at my second-too-late protest—"and most people do, Alec is way beyond any obsessive-compulsive, medical-nightmare stuff I've got. His whole family is crazy." She leaned into my shoulder. "They think the town is full of monsters, some kind of werewolves or something. That's why they tame them, the real wolves, so they can help sniff out the bad ones."

She checked out my reaction. "Nice, eh?"

I hoped I looked suitably impressed. At her words all the air had siphoned out of my lungs.

Alec was a hunter?

No, he couldn't be.

Hunters didn't go around advertising their existence. The Hunter Council would have shut them down long ago. The truth had to be hidden. It was law. The paranormal world, circling humankind like animals with their prey, must remain secret.

Besides, no hunter could survive that kind of exposure, no matter how well trained. There would be questions from the townspeople. The police. Maybe even a few lit torches and pitchfork-carrying mobs threatening to run them out of town. Not to mention they'd be easy pickings for any paranorms out for a little revenge.

The practice of using wolves as trackers was archaic, way beyond old school. Mom had fought that kind of bestial slavery for years. The Hunter Council had a policy against it now—Mom's crowning achievement. She'd had pretty

extreme views on animal rights—ideas that had rubbed off on me—and I could hear the lecture she'd have given me about Alec and his wolf. His having a pet wolf might become a bone of contention between us, but I could educate Alec about the wolf's right to run wild. If he'd felt half the sizzle of attraction that I had during our run, he'd soon see things my way.

I couldn't be this interested in a guy and have him turn out to be one of those the-world-and-all-its-creatures-are-mine-to-dominate cavemen. The fates weren't that cruel.

Were they?

But if Alec really was a hunter, chances were he'd despise me once he found out I was part wolven. Hunters and paranorms didn't mix. I was a rarity. So why was I even entertaining the notion of a hunter as a boyfriend?

No, he couldn't be a hunter. It was a rumor. Small town gossip-mill stuff.

But what if it wasn't?

What if Alec had been out there in the woods because he'd been tracking the werewolf who'd wanted me for a bite-sized snack? My instinctive response was to charge back to the woods to help, but I was under strict orders by the Hunter Council to avoid all paranorm interactions.

To lay low.

To blend.

So, I had two options. I could:

A.   *Avoid contact with Alec and his possibly hunter family at all costs—a.k.a. bury head in sand and hope for best.*

Or…

B.   *Do some sniffing around, get to the bottom of the rumors about Alec's werewolf-nabbing hobby, and perhaps engage in a battle to the death once the Hunter Council heard I had outed myself.*

Yup. Plan A it was. Boring and safe and totally against my instincts, so it must be what the Hunter Council would want me to do. Staying-out-of-it girl I would be. For now.

Groans rang out across the field as Mr. Riggs led the rest of our class to the finish line of pylons. Then he jogged over to where Brit and I awaited the okay to go back into the school and change.

"Nice work, McCain," he said, using my last name in the usual manner of gym teachers and drill sergeants from every war film I'd ever seen. "You play basketball? Got the height."

"Ah, no."

"Volleyball?"

"No-o-o." I wrinkled my nose. "I don't do team sports." I didn't like any sport. Period. End of discussion. The running thing was a fluke.

Guys, still panting from the run, gave me The Look,

checking out my long go-go-gadget legs. Like I cared. They were midgets-in-training anyway. I straightened from the slight stoop I usually adopted to mask an inch or two and stood proud of my five feet eleven inches. In this case, it served as an unspoken shutdown.

Defeated, they regrouped and sauntered over to a cluster of simpering girls to pursue more approachable fare. Their collective testosterone level proved overwhelming, and a girl squealed as a fight broke out between the beefier guys.

A smile tugged at my lips. My pulse raced, and I debated joining the scuffle. Or at least grabbing the guys and knocking their heads together. Wouldn't that scare the crap out of everyone? I struggled to keep from laughing.

The grin slipped from my mouth. I was enjoying the fight a bit too much. *Like a wolven would.* I deliberately slowed my heart rate and distanced myself. Sometimes all the changes happening to me physically and to my soul were just plain scary.

"Thompson! Povich!" Mr. Riggs bellowed, charging at the brawling mass of elbows and fists. "Drop and give me twenty."

With loud groans, the guys fell to the ground and assumed the position, but their arms shook by the tenth push-up. Ick, how painful and embarrassing.

I bet Alec wouldn't have any trouble.

Must. Stop. Thinking. About. Hot. Hunter.

The rest of the class ambled to the gym entrance, but I hung back. Over the field, the sun hung afternoon-low while the pale outline of the full moon crept higher in the

sky. Whether in full daylight or in the dead of night, the full moon fascinated me. I could stare, fixated, at that glowing orb and lose all track of time. Though she called to me, the moon didn't command me in any way.

Unlike werewolves, wolven—able to turn at will—weren't ruled by lunar phases, but had an instinctive respect for the moon's power. A crazy madness ran through all paranorms at the full moon. Even humans experienced stronger emotions during the full moon. They became quick to anger, to love, and to give into impulses—though at a much lower intensity than paranorms. Maybe that explained my connection with the guy in the forest.

I looked back at the woods.

I couldn't shake the feeling that he was there.

Watching.

Har-De-Freaking Har

At the rusting metal doors, I balked. I hated locker rooms.

Brit gave me a shove, and we plunged into the ripe-smelling buffet of all things laid bare. I wove through girls in various stages of dress, opened my locker, and grabbed my backpack. A gossip session started in the far corner. Dark looks, sent my way, made the topic of conversation pretty obvious.

I ignored the muffled giggles and rifled through my stuff for my black socks. No way was I wearing glowing white anklets for the rest of the day—not with jeans I'd outgrown by half an inch.

Brit claimed a spot on the glossy wooden bench. Close,

20

but not overstepping our tentative friendship boundaries.

I wondered if she was hanging around to see what I'd do next. New to town. Rambling about racing a guy with a pet wolf. Freakishly tall—a nice foil for her pocket Venus self. Yup, my entertainment value must be pretty high, although I could have saved her the trouble—I was nothing special. Not much, anyway.

So far, I'd exhibited few of my mother's wolven traits except for being a bit stronger and faster than the average kid. I wasn't sure how much Sebastian, my father's ex-Hunter-Council boss, knew about my wolven side or that my father had been controlling it with drugs. But he must not have thought I was a threat to the general public, or he never would have sent me to Redgrave to live with my uncle after the funeral.

The funeral where we'd buried… No. *My parents were dead.* At least, that's what I was supposed to tell everyone. Even my father's brother who had taken me into his home and who had looked so lost when we lowered the coffins into the ground.

Not that I wasn't lost too.

But Uncle Marcus wasn't as good at hiding his emotions. He hadn't grown up the way I had. Tracking the paranormal creatures that go bump in the night, wondering when it would be *my* turn to cling to the shadows. To be hunted.

I gave a disgusted snort and wiggled my feet free from my cross trainers so I could get changed. Was I the only one who thought the plan—sending me to live with my uncle in the middle of small-town northern Alberta—was stamped

certifiably insane?

Getting cast off the island-that-was-my-life wasn't my idea. I was merely following Sebastian's "suggestion." If I wanted to find out the truth about what had happened to my parents, I had to lay low, stay out of trouble—*my* kind of trouble—and wait. Well, fine. I'd do as my father's ex-boss wanted for now. But it might get a whole lot of innocent humans killed.

So much for the Hunter Council's code of conduct. *Humans first.* But then, I wasn't really human, so maybe I, and the destruction I could cause, didn't count.

How ironic that Marcus and his family thought my dad had owned a pharmaceutical company and dabbled in chemicals all day. If they only knew what kind of chemicals he'd mucked around with. I'd been weaned on every batch of anti-paranorm juice my dad created, and one of them must have done the job. I hadn't shown many signs of being like my mother. Thanks to good ol' dad, I was a chemically induced anomaly, a half wolven who couldn't turn. No one knew what would happen if my wolvenness decided to kick in despite Dad's manipulations.

I could be lethal. Stronger than any other of my kind. Or…I could be a drooling idiot with excessive back hair and a hankering for raw meat. Oh, the horror! But if I did start to turn, I'd be feared by hunter and wolven alike. So Sebastian decided I'd be safer living in an area with limited paranorm activity.

Apparently he had Redgrave all wrong.

After less than a week in town, I'd encountered a rogue

werewolf/hot hunter combo. I was back among the paranorms whether he wanted it or not.

A locker door slammed shut like a gunshot. I jumped, putting a hand to my chest, my heart pounding. I'd been so skittish lately—nightmares, lack of sleep, the moon's pull—the fates were against me.

Brit raised an eyebrow at my performance, so I shrugged. "Haven't had my coffee yet today. I'm a bit jumpy."

"I thought *having* coffee was supposed to give you the jumpies," Brit said, "not *not* having any."

I smiled weakly as I fished through my backpack. Luckily, I found my socks before the cursed extra pocket in my backpack, the one that ate every cool pair of sunglasses I owned, could suck them into oblivion. While gathering up my clothes, I spotted a girl sitting on the other side of the locker room, crying. She had bloodred hair and the saddest face I'd ever seen.

"What's up with her?" I asked Brit, who glanced over at the girl and grimaced.

"Olivia used to be the most popular girl at Redgrave High. But her boyfriend split town, and she's been a train wreck ever since. She keeps telling everyone Travis wouldn't have left without her, but..." Brit grabbed a crayon-sized coal black eyeliner pencil out of her backpack and rimmed her eyes without a mirror. "The guy had a track record, if you know what I mean. A textbook case of relationship A.D.D. But Olivia's in denial."

I avoided looking at the girl again to give her some privacy—not that she seemed to care. Everyone's attention

was divided between the pitiful spectacle she made and my shiny newness, but she seemed oblivious.

"I guess you're wondering why I didn't join in the class sweatfest?" Brit said out of nowhere, although I hadn't been wondering at all.

I'd been obsessing over my own weirdness—skipping out of a gym class run didn't seem so interesting in comparison to missing parents, werewolf attacks, and increasing superhuman strength.

"It's a medical-type deal. Want me to read you the doctor's note?"

I didn't, especially if she had something contagious, but Brit was the first student to acknowledge my existence since I'd started at Redgrave High. I owed her mild interest at least. I shrugged, which was all the invitation she needed. She launched into a complex review of her medical history, a rare condition wherein physical exhaustion caused seizures.

I tuned out the boring bits.

Comments from the opposite bench shifted from new-girl-mocking snorts to new-girl-and-school-hypochondriac-unite shrieks of laughter.

Har-de-freaking har.

Brit continued. "I have to show up for gym class to get the credits, but I don't actually do anything. Well, sometimes Mr. Riggs has me keep score, which I like. I'm good with numbers..."

I tried to keep up, but my attention wasn't the greatest. I bided my time. After quick glances at the exposed few inches at the bottoms of the bathroom stalls, my heart sank. They

were all taken, and the doors stayed firmly shut.

I'd have to change in front of everyone.

Brit rambled on, unfazed when I spun, faced the lockers, and quickly stripped off my gym clothes. I worked into my resisting jeans and slid the denim up my legs. A cross-hatching of scars, some red and swollen, others faded to fine white lines, marred the smooth skin at the tops of my thighs. I yanked the jeans over my hips before the other girls noticed.

Self-mutilation, survivor's guilt—whatever the shrinks labeled it—I didn't cut myself.

Anymore.

I was better now.

But my skin bore evidence that I hadn't always been level-headed.

"...we can go to the mall, well, it barely gets mall status, there's like ten shops. Or we could go for coffee. I know this great coffee house," Brit said. "Hello, Eryn? You listening?"

"Of course, coffee, sure thing. I like coffee." I gave an amiable nod, but all I could think about was the werewolf, the hunter Alec.

And my voice echoing through the woods.

I know you are, but what am I?

Gothic Pixie on a Mission

What am I doing? I asked myself for the gajilianth time as I eased my bedroom window open and crept onto the second story roof at precisely one o'clock in the morning. High in the overcast night sky, the moon glowed through heavy clouds.

From my perch on the shingled roof, I stared down at the neighbor's dog, Cujo, a female yellow Labrador, chained to a tree. Day and night she barked, keeping up a steady drone, driving me crazy. Why did people get pets if they were going to cast them out of the house? Didn't they know dogs were pack animals? All she wanted was to be with her people. I debated on busting out poor Cujo, but I had to avoid trouble, and I couldn't get close to her without sending her into a

barking frenzy. Dogs went nuts around me. They sensed I wasn't quite human.

"Maybe another time," I murmured as I scanned the street.

A ghostly fog had settled on the quiet town, muting the streetlights. Row upon row of the same model houses, each had identical stone siding, eerily perfect manicured lawns, and curving slate walkways. My uncle, real estate lawyer extraordinaire, had chosen to settle in Cowley Heights, the most affluent, if tragically carbon-copied neighborhood in Redgrave. In fact, the whole town suffered from a serious

lack of *oomph*. Hard to believe a werewolf was roaming these freshly mowed, about-to-be-seriously-snowed-on lawns.

Again I asked myself, *Why bother going on a hunt?* Alec Delacroix and his family could surely take down one rogue, if all the town gossip about Redgrave's infamous werewolf hunting family was to be believed.

But it was either this or toss and turn in bed for hours, fighting off nightmares, listening to the dog barking incessantly outside while Marcus snored inside. Plus I couldn't take the risk that the lumbering werewolf who had attacked me in the woods might suddenly grab a few brain cells and track me to my uncle's place.

How would I explain that one? It wasn't exactly like having a cuddly puppy follow you home from school—unless you defined cuddly puppies as having three-inch-long claws and bloodstained, yellowed teeth.

The moon was nearing its full-orb glory, increasing my restlessness. My mother had always downplayed its effect on her wolven brethren, but now that I was unfettered by my father's drugs, even a small influence from the moon might push me over the edge. I clenched my fists, arms rigid at my side. I hoped tonight's hunt wouldn't be a bust. I needed the physical outlet. Give me one measly paranorm. I'd bludgeon first, ask questions later.

Although they didn't know it, my aunt and uncle had taken a big risk bringing me into their home, their lives. Besides possibly putting them in a crapload of paranormal danger, I could be a bad influence on Paige, my cousin.

Not.

Paige, a pretty, popular senior at Redgrave High, had likely cut her teeth on Ouija boards when other kids were gnawing building blocks. My uncle and aunt really lucked out on the crapshoot called parenthood. And now they'd inherited me. But with a daughter like Paige, what was not-quite-human compared to really unholy?

Under my olive canvas jacket, the weight of my silver athame rested in the leather holster my mother had made for me long ago. I straightened to ease the pressure. Though the silver wasn't touching my skin, its power worked through my long-sleeved cotton T-shirt, warming my flesh. Mom hated the hunter weapon of choice, but then she was full wolven and could barely glance at an athame without snarling.

I lowered the bedroom window, careful to keep the weather stripping from squealing against the frame. I left my window open a crack so I could get back into my room without waking Paige, whose room was next to mine. Her window remained dark, her curtains unmoving. So far, so good. She hadn't heard me. Not that she could hear anything over Marcus's snoring.

My uncle's thunderous drone offended my keen hearing in a constant nightly assault. Even stuffing cotton balls in my ears wouldn't help. I wasn't used to all the static noise I could pick up now. But it would take more than my uncle's log sawing to make me want to stifle my growing wolven abilities.

No, the day I'd run out of the anti-wolven drugs my father had developed had been the best day of my life.

It had also been the worst—the day I'd found out my parents were gone. Disappeared.

Ever since, I'd had to abide by the Hunter Council's rules. Had to follow Sebastian's plan, telling people my parents were dead, so the Council could do their job and find out what really happened. But I might never know, might spend the rest of my life not knowing if my parents were alive or dead. And all because my mother had wanted to follow her dream of being human.

Human?

How dumb was that?

Tears stung my eyes. I sucked in a breath, muscles rigid. Time to put my wolven strength to the test. I charged from the roof, arms flailing, legs tight to my body. But I'd put too much into the jump. I landed hard. My knees buckled at impact. Moaning, I cupped my jaw. Crap. I'd bitten the edge of my tongue. As the blinding pain subsided, I stood upright, swiping dried grass from my jeans, the taste of my own blood sharp in my mouth. I glanced around. Had anyone seen my swan dive? Well, besides Cujo, whose barks had grown more persistent and shrill since I'd hit the ground. Thankfully, the neighbors were used to ignoring her.

I inhaled deeply, my lips parting so that I could taste the night air as well as smell it. In seconds I picked up the foul, thin thread of the werewolf's scent, musky and rotten.

I stared down the street. The lights, the cars, the road turned grainy and out of focus. I stumbled, squinting hard, and then blinked frantically against the stinging in my eyes. The burn quickly faded, and my vision cleared. I could see… everything.

Blanketing darkness lifted as if the night had been blasted

out by floodlights. The night seemed like a page out of a graphic novel. Colors were super-saturated. My jacket looked a deep forest green. I had zoom lenses for eyes. I could focus on a single tree branch and inspect every knot and scratch on its surface. Wouldn't that be handy come exam time? Heart racing, I started down the road.

What would my parents think of me now—charging after a werewolf, using wolven vision and strength? If I'd had all this months ago, I wouldn't have needed to hunt with my father's crew always looking out for me. I could have gone on skirmishes alone. My stomach knotted. I might have been able to protect my parents.

I charged down the pavement. I couldn't go back and change things, but one thing was certain...this beast was mine.

The stench was strongest on Foulton Drive, also laughably known as Redgrave's downtown. The street ran from one end of town to the other, with the majority of shops, banks, and town service buildings gathered near the middle, but not one car passed as I walked down the sidewalk. Redgrave sidewalks rolled up at nine sharp. No 24-hour grocery chains or fast food joints here—the total opposite of living in Vancouver where even bookstores were open until midnight.

The mist clung to the werewolf's scent, thickening it, making it raunchier—if that were possible. I paused at the corner of Foulton and Cornerbrook. A lamppost to my left was plastered with flyers. I stepped closer, peering at the pages, some typed and others handwritten. All had pictures of...pets. Missing pets. Dogs, cats, and even little bunnies.

No wonder I hadn't startled any dogs during my trek through Redgrave backyards. One rogue werewolf couldn't have turned them all into Scooby snacks, could he?

Then it started—a clamor of animals, like a zoo gone mad. I flinched at the assault. I struggled to filter the sounds, the shrill screech of birds, yips of puppies, and yowls of kittens. I froze, scanning the empty street.

There. Down a block and across the pothole-scarred road.

I focused in. While wonder-vision was fun, I had the sneaking suspicion if I overused that particular skill, my eyes might start to cross and stay crossed forever.

The display window at Polly's Pet Emporium had been shattered, broken glass littered the sidewalk, and an amber glow from the store's security lighting spilled onto the street.

I shook my head, returning my vision from wolven-zoom to normal. No sirens wailed in the distance. Where were all the cops in this town? Was crime so nonexistent they didn't even respond when a store alarm tripped?

I jogged down the block debating my next move. I *had* promised the Hunter Council I would lay low. In exchange, they'd promised to find my parents. Keeping the Council happy was my only shot at uncovering the truth.

Wasn't my fault they hadn't done their research about Redgrave. Rather than the small, quiet northern town they thought they'd chosen, turned out Redgrave had big bad freakage. Surely the Council wouldn't want me to play all damsel-in-a-mess and sit on the sidelines while a rogue werewolf ran wild? Besides, how hard could it be to take

down one itty-bitty werewolf? I'd helped Dad and his hunters drop a whole pack in a few hours.

I crossed the road and stepped cautiously over the jagged glass protruding from the window frame. Glass crunched under my shoes, the sound as explosive as a land mine. I froze, holding my breath.

When nothing charged at me from the pet shop's glowing interior, I crept farther inside.

Ugh. I wasn't sure what stunk worse—the ripe-smelling werewolf on his haunches, leaning over a bunny cage, or the fear blasting from the bunnies dodging his seeking hands.

My breath came fast and hard. I panted lightly, working for control. My inner wolf licked its chops at the heady scent of fear rippling through all the animals in the store but recoiled at the unsportsmanlike tactics. Where was the fun in slaughter? Where was the thrill of the hunt? The chase?

I whipped out my athame and held it high. My hand shook with a blend of exhilaration and blind terror.

I cleared my throat.

Once.

Twice.

Too busy crunching on Peter Rabbit, the werewolf didn't hear me over his own bloodlust.

"How much is that beastie in the window?" I belted out an old wolven favorite in my very un-*American-Idol*-worthy singing voice. That oughta get his attention. "The one eating bunnies for sale?" I sang, mucking around with the lyrics.

The werewolf's dark form stilled. His morphed hand, sporting a mix of human fingers and bestial claws, opened. A

lucky bunny dropped from his grip to land unharmed on the blood-spattered floor. It scurried under some metal shelving, its pale fur stained crimson.

A snarl of annoyance rumbled in the werewolf's throat as it shoved its forearms off the cage, dropped to all fours, and turned to face me. For the second time that day, I stared into the werewolf's red eyes, bright with human intelligence though a wildness flickered in their depths. The stuff of nightmares stared back at me, through me, and called to the beast that lurked within. Finding me out. My body tightened against the urge to flee. To hide.

I waved my dagger to remind the beast, and myself, that I was the one in control. Or at least, I hoped I was. The security lights glimmered off the sharp silver blade, making my point for me.

Flinching, the werewolf averted his massive head. Thank God, I didn't have to bluff this time. Now I was all about the follow-through. My doubts faded on a mind-blowing rush of power at the beast's show of fear.

I took a bold step forward.

The beast stumbled backwards, knocked into the bunny cage, and sent the trapped creatures into spastic scuttles.

I had him. We both knew it.

But then I slipped in the bunny blood and crashed to the floor. I cried out, flailing my hands in the air, trying to regain my balance, but my feet shot out from under me. My head cracked against the linoleum.

I landed in a sprawl under the werewolf's stinking jowls. His foul breath filled my nostrils as stars spun in front of my

eyes. My athame flew from my hand, scraped across the floor, and came to rest a few feet away, its momentum slowed by a rack of jerky treats. I twisted onto my stomach and reached frantically for the hilt. Oh, this was so wrong. My nails dug into the linoleum floor. I inched closer. My breath escaped in a ragged sob. My splayed fingers trembled. An inch. One inch more. So close. But not close enough.

A heavy paw planted itself on my back.

I couldn't breathe.

I couldn't move. Claws dug into my jacket.

I craned my neck and stared up at canine lips as they slowly twisted to form a maliciously human grin. A thick line of bloody drool wavered inches from my face. I shook my head from side to side, trying to avoid the drool. It struck my neck with a heavy splat, running down my neck to the floor.

And so the hunter became the prey. Irony really sucked the big one.

A shot rang out. My body seized. Breath clogged in my throat.

The animals in the store fell quiet.

Above me the beast's grin extended, but the light died in his eyes as a thick pool of black blood formed in the center of his forehead. My nose crinkled as the battery-acid fumes of silver meeting werewolf lit into the air. His breath left him in a rattling gasp. With a thud he toppled onto me, all two hundred pounds of suddenly human deadweight.

Not how I envisioned my first encounter with a naked guy.

"Get him off her!" The voice was familiar, but I'd never

heard it so authoritative.

Two sets of hiking boots rushed to my side, carefully avoiding the bunny blood. The werewolf's weight eased as my rescuers grunted and heaved the guy's body off me. Lungs free to expand, I gulped in waves of ripe pet store air. Air curdled by the panicked frenzy of caged animals.

I pushed my chest off the floor with shaking arms and raised my head. A slick gush of werewolf blood ran down my neck.

I blinked in shock. "Brit?"

My only friend at Redgrave High stood before me, an uncertain smile on her face. Wearing yellow plaid cargo pants tucked into her usual Doc Martens, a black leather coat belted at the waist, and a skull-covered scarf tied artfully around her neck, Brit looked like a gothic pixie on a mission.

Strong hands lifted me to my feet.

"Well, *that* looked embarrassing—falling on your butt in front of a werewolf you thought you had in the bag. Everyone agree?" The question, with its sharp bite, distracted me from Brit's gothic-superhero-to-the-rescue stance.

A guy stood next to me, a crowbar slung over his shoulder, staring at me with suspicious, dark eyes. He was tall, lean, and looked a lot like my new and highly untouchable crush, Alec. But his nose wasn't as hawkish, and his hair was way shorter.

"I'm fine, thanks for asking." I frowned up at him. "No broken bones or puncture wounds. Don't worry about me."

He ignored me. "What's she doing hunting on our turf?"

His gaze flicked behind me. I was being held upright by someone. A very tall, strong someone. My pulse raced. A

solid muscled chest pressed against my back. Thighs shifted against mine. A delicious heat built up between us. Slowly I lifted my chin. My breath caught in my throat. I stared into the most intense brown eyes I'd ever seen. Alec.

"You sure you're okay?" He turned me in his arms, studying my expression.

Completely ignoring the goose egg throbbing to life on the back of my head, I nodded. *Uh-huh. Yup. More than okay. Deliriously fantastic, in fact.*

I didn't say the words out loud, but Alec's amused expression suggested he'd guessed why I couldn't converse like a normal person.

Was it lame for a girl to swoon at a guy's feet?

I didn't get the chance to find out.

"It's Ethan," said the guy who looked like Alec—but had none of his special brand of hotness—as he pulled on Alec's arm until he released me. The two of them walked over to the body that lay on the floor a few feet from where I'd fallen.

The werewolf had morphed into his human form after he died. Just like in the movies. Unlike in the movies, however, his body wasn't clean and unmarked as if he'd been born again. When a werewolf died and resumed its human form, it bore all signs of the physical beating it had taken. Skin peppered with deep purple bruises. Bones jutting out at odd angles. In this case, the bullet wound was a clean entry. A single pool of blood trickled down his cheek, but the exit....

Brit tossed her coat over his naked torso and stared down at the dead boy's face, her expression bleak. Tears welled in the corners of her black-rimmed eyes.

"Matt." She reached out for Alec's almost look-alike. "I think I'm going to be sick."

Matt guided her quickly to a far corner of the store. I blocked out the sounds of her retching and Matt's soothing words. I frowned. Brit and the guys walked, stalked, and tracked like hunters, but getting sick after a kill was the mark of an amateur—or someone far too emotionally involved. What was the deal with Brit? Hadn't she told me she couldn't even run? How was that NOT a requirement for a member of a hunter crew?

Alec knelt by the boy's head. "Ethan Macleod. He went missing about a month ago. The last full moon." He met my frown with one of his own. "The third werewolf we've taken down in as many months."

I wished the rumors weren't true, that the Delacroix weren't tracking werewolves, that no one in Redgrave had seen the things Alec and his crew had.

But the proof was lying on the floor in front of us. If Redgrave had paranorms working over the young, the vulnerable, turning them into werewolves, I had to be very careful what I said around the Delacroix. A group like this probably wouldn't be jumping for joy if they found out I was half-

paranorm.

Ethan's body began to tremble. Alec stepped back. A faint white glow radiated through his bruised flesh, building until rays of light shot from his eyes.

The energy inside Ethan grew. His body radiated so much light Alec covered his eyes behind the crook of his arm. In the corner, Matt turned his back to Ethan, shielding Brit with his body. I'd never witnessed the entire process of a paranorm's passing, although I'd tried many times while hunting with my father. In the end, again, the light won.

I squeezed my eyes shut against the terrible burning white light. Heat waves vibrated in the air. Sweat beaded on my forehead. A muted rumble, like thunder from a vast distance. Then silence.

I opened my eyes a few seconds later. No light. No Ethan. Just Brit's coat flattening to the floor. It settled across a long black burn where Ethan's body used to be. That was one good thing about the paranormal world. It took care of its own. Even Ethan, a human so recently turned into a werewolf, left no untidy traces behind.

Alec was the first to move, breaking the hush that had fallen over us. He scooped up my athame and approached me, casually flipping the dagger from hand to hand. His full lips formed an impressed whistle, making his high cheekbones flash into prominence.

My gaze skimmed over his broad shoulders. I hoped my mental drooling wasn't obvious.

"Some heavy-duty sigils carved here." His thumb traced the magical symbols. "This is old magic. German?" He

handed it to me, blade first.

My fingers brushed his as I grasped the dagger by the hilt. The touch was electric and had nothing to do with the athame's infused power.

Alec raised an eyebrow. Had he noticed my reluctance to grasp the silver blade? I pointed to one of the more identifiable hex signs. "Dutch."

Alec nodded slowly. "Nice." He folded his arms across his chest. "How did you get your hands on something that powerful?"

I shrugged. "My dad collected magical things."

"Magical things can come in handy," Alec said, his expression thoughtful. "So your dad was a hunter?"

"Yup," I said shortly. "Yours?"

Alec observed me, quiet for a long moment, before answering in the same let's-drop-the-subject, shall-we? tone, "Yup."

I turned away, my lips twisting in a quick grin. So we both had daddy issues. How lovely. I walked around the smoldering black outline on the floor, pretending to be fascinated with how deep the burn had etched into the linoleum.

Brit returned, looking clammy and pale—breakable. She picked her way around the blood puddles, careful not to stare at the marked floor. Matt scooped up her coat, shook it out, and tried to drape it over her shoulders, but she pushed it back at him.

"Sorry." Matt grimaced. "We'll toss it later." He put his arm around her instead.

"Give it here," Alec said. He looped the coat through the

rifle strap over his shoulder so it hung at his waist. Seeing Alec and Matt side by side, their resemblance struck me anew. "Are you brothers?"

"You think?" Matt rolled his eyes.

Guess he was sick of hearing the you-look-like-your-brother thing. Or maybe he thought it was lame that I'd stated the obvious. Either way, he really didn't seem to like me much.

"Mathieu's the youngest. He's got attitude enough for the both of us." Alec shot Matt a glare and adjusted the rifle higher on his shoulder.

I glanced at the weapon. "Thanks for the silver-bullet rescue."

Alec shrugged. "Like I said, magical things come in handy."

"Nothing magical about the hours you spend at the shooting range we set up on the ranch." Matt snorted. "Alec's a crack shot."

"You guys train, you hunt. I get that." I frowned at the motley crew. "But how come the whole town knows about your little were-chasing hobby, but the Hunter Council has no idea your crew exists?"

"We don't function under Council jurisdiction," Alec said flatly. "We haven't for a long time. Not since our father died and they did nothing to help us track his paranorm killer."

His frustration mirrored my own. We had more than daddy issues in common. We both had reason to hate the Hunter Council. Except in my case, Sebastian was helping

me find information about my parents. At least, I hoped he was. The possibility my laying low in Redgrave was a huge mistake haunted my days as much as wolven nightmares haunted my sleep.

Alec shot me a dark look. "And don't bother quoting regulations to us." He studied my face. "You're not exactly following protocol either."

"No, I'm not." I wasn't supposed to be within striking distance of a paranorm, and here I was standing over a scorch mark. But I didn't need him to remind me of that. I blew a strand of hair off my face. "I kind of stumbled onto this one. If you have the town covered," I said with a shrug, "then you've got it covered, right? You don't need me getting in your way." Plus I couldn't afford to get tangled up in their crazy, lawless hunts—I had a nose to keep clean and a head to keep low.

"Look, I'm sorry about your friend," I said, my glance taking in all of them. "But like you said, I'm not acting in a hunter capacity."

Matt shot Alec a look, then jerked his head toward the shattered store window.

Alec nodded. "We'd better take off. Redgrave cops are slow to respond, but they *will* show up…eventually." He held out a hand to me. "Let's go."

I almost reached out and put my hand in his.

But I hesitated.

I took a step back. My mind, clearer now that I was on my feet and the danger was over, raced full speed ahead. Brit had warned me about Alec, said his whole family was crazy,

and yet here she was—hunting with them.

It didn't make sense. Knowing she'd lied hurt. This was why I didn't get close to humans. They always let you down. At least with paranorms, you knew where you stood.

I brushed past Alec's outstretched hand and bolted through the window.

I ran.

All the way home.

I wasn't crying.

The wind was in my eyes.

My, What Big Teeth You Have

Second period the next morning, Brit sat a few desks away from me, trying to make eye contact—which I ignored. I wasn't quite ready to talk with her yet, but physics was killing me. I almost caved and asked her to translate.

My brain could handle the big-picture concepts all right, but they fixed in my mind with all the gumption of a sticky note. At exam time everything came unglued.

Brit was really into it though. My dad would have loved her. She waved her hand in the air at every question, even the rhetorical ones.

After forty solid minutes of physics hell, Mr. Phillips gave up with a sigh. "Read chapter ten for the last few minutes of class," he said. He shuffled behind his desk and sat at his computer looking very Mr.-Potato-Head-Goes-to-School,

complete with bow tie. He soon lost interest in pretending to monitor us from his spudly throne, and, courtesy of the reflection in the window behind his chair, everyone could see that he was absorbed in reading his e-mail.

The class broke into conversation. Well, except for Brit. She actually opened her textbook. So bookish, but I knew she was a hunter too. Toiling around in the human and paranormal worlds, keeping the town safe from all things ghoulish, ever wearing one of the smiling skull T-shirts she'd silkscreened in art class.

Pretty impressive.

Now I understood why she'd warned me away from Alec—she thought I was just another new girl, unaware of the paranormal world. She was trying to keep me safe from all the doom and gloom hanging around in Redgrave. But her lying to me about Alec still rankled.

I gave up on my physics textbook and started sketching in the margins of my notebook. The last thing I needed was to get involved with whatever hunter activities Brit and the Delacroix boys had going. I couldn't afford to mess up my chances with the Council. If they found out I'd been involved in a takedown, they might renege on their promise.

I couldn't risk that. I had to know what happened to Mom and Dad. I needed the truth. How ironic. The last thing my father ever said to me was on that very topic. He'd been trying to dig into the truth about my cutting.

Poor Dad. He'd been beyond confused when the counselor at my old school told him I was cutting myself. (I hadn't always been so cautious in school locker rooms.)

Why would I do such a thing? He never once thought his experimenting on me might have failed, that I might be developing some latent wolven traits. That I might be torn, battling the two sides of myself, human and beaten-down wolven, on my own. That I wasn't sure which was stronger.

If I'd told her the truth, Mom would have understood. Admitting you had a fascination with blood was the first step to accepting your wolven nature. She would have nodded and agreed to a just-between-us-girls talk, and then ratted me out to Dad the moment I walked away. Eventually, she would have made him see things were happening to me. Wolven things. I couldn't have handled another round of blood tests, or any more doses of my father's own special blend of drugs and their unknown side-effects.

No, it was better they believed the lies I told them. How I didn't fit in, couldn't make friends, and took my sadness out on my flesh. And they believed me, because they wanted to believe.

They didn't know I had discovered red. The most beautiful color. Alive. Warm.

Each line I etched into my skin, each bloodletting, had been a release, setting a bit of the beast free. I savored the faint tang in the air as my blood flowed. After a while, I could smell it on others—from the teeny tiniest wounds. I hadn't picked up a blade in months, but if I focused, kind of like cupping your ear to catch a sound out of reach, I could tap into my heightened awareness. In this room alone, the boy in the third row near Brit had an almost healed scrape and a torn hangnail.

A rush of saliva filled my mouth. I drank it down.

A deadish feeling settled in my stomach like I'd swallowed a femur. I gave a shocked snort. Well, that *was* a common enough hazard for my brethren. Wolven were known for choking on their food.

I shifted in my chair. Who knew what I was turning into thanks to my father's drugs? I could end up like that werewolf last night, scarfing down bunnies.

I dry-heaved.

No, I couldn't help the young, but keen, hunters of Redgrave.

I'd only put them in more danger.

Eyes burning, I scratched through the smiley face I'd drawn with thick angry strokes. Two-inch-long fangs protruded obscenely through its grin. Underneath I'd written the name Delacroix in gothic swirly letters. My pen sliced deep, rending a few pages from my notebook. The sound brought me back to the classroom. Had anyone noticed my near wig-out? My head bowed when I met curious gazes. Especially Brit's. Her eyes widened with suppressed laughter.

"Don't worry. They won't bite. But I might." The husky voice caused my muscles to tighten in shock. The snap of teeth and a cool rush of air against my neck had me frozen in my seat.

What? Those were fighting words—wolven words—spoken on a honeyed tongue. Lovely. Werewolf, hunter, and perhaps wolven all in the same week. And they'd said Redgrave was a dull town.

Although I'd proven my nose for the red stuff was still

47

keen, I didn't have my mother's ability to scent her brethren. I fell back on the quick and dirty identification methods dad taught me before I even started on solid foods. First off, direct eye contact made wolven nervous, sparked their fight-or-flight response.

I gave it a shot. A sharp glance over my shoulder established the guy lived up to his smooth voice. Dark shaggy hair, silver-grey eyes. A chiseled jaw. He was a bit on the lean side but, as he shifted forward, the greedy material of his shirt

clung to his muscular shoulders like a jealous ex-girlfriend. This guy was Greek god material. An instant mental montage of all things sexual gyrated through my brain complete with bow-chicka-wah-wah mood music. The warm glow in his eyes said the experience might be mutual.

For a girl previously known as the ice queen, I was sparking my share of attention in this town.

"Ummm. You smell delicious." He met my gaze, held it,

and inhaled deeply.

Grey—his eyes were grey mist, clouds rolling in over the mountains. Wonderful, now all I needed was a truck analogy and I'd be writing a country song. I forced myself to relax, to control the fluttering of my heart. I'd been around eye candy before. Looks and wolven were a given—all wild things had a natural beauty—but this guy was too refined, his features too perfect. Wolven were catastrophically sexy in a rugged sort of way.

More like Alec.

Rats.

And I'd been doing so well at not thinking about him. Why did I always go for the road less traveled? Why get stupid over a guy who could only complicate my life and possibly want to kill me once he found out I was half paranorm? Did I need any more stress?

My new friend's glance flicked to my sketch. "Delacroix?" He read aloud, his brow furrowed. "Have those guys been sniffing around you?"

My fingers squeezed my mechanical pencil, popping off the little white eraser. It pinged against the desk next to mine, earning me a glare from the girl sitting there. "Have they been *what*?"

He made a face. "I'm just saying, if I were you, new to town, not up on the gossip, I'd watch my back around the Delacroix. That family is dangerous."

How ironic, first Brit and now Redgrave High's resident hottie warning me against Alec, but for entirely different reasons. Brit had wanted to save me from heartache. This guy

Forget Alec.

Forget everything.

I took a slow breath and surrendered to the soothing balm of harmless flirtation.

"So what are you? The Big Bad Wolf of Redgrave High? Protecting the innocent new girls in town from the Delacroix?" I spun around. My desk creaked, drawing more interest from the class than a fire alarm.

"Exactly." He shook his head to toss his dark bangs out of his eyes.

"My, what big teeth you have." I smirked, aware we had an audience. Play-by-play whispers snaked across the room.

"All the better to bite you with, my dear," he said. "Sadly, we know how that story ended. Not so good from the wolf's perspective." He leaned over his desk. "I'm Wade, and you are…?"

A twitching mass of hormones at your feet. "Eryn," I said over the bell's harsh peal. For once, students didn't bolt for the hall. Instead they wavered, watching us.

Wade angled his chin. "What's with the paparazzi?"

I shrugged, then eyed the students shooting us furtive looks. "I've got New-Girl-itis. The doctors say it should pass any day. No lasting effects. I guess you don't get a lot of newbies around here."

"Well, there was one new kid a few years ago. I think they ran him out of town. Angry mob. Torches. The usual. After that…." Wade stroked his chin, pretending to be stumped.

I chuckled.

"Ah, I made you laugh. And you, diseased and near death, an almost impossible feat. You must really like me."

I bit the inside of my cheek to keep from grinning like an idiot. He was over the top, but I liked his easygoing attitude, the way he lightened my mood. Plus, he was definitely not a hunter.

"Have I been in a coma? Why haven't I seen you in this class before?" I blurted.

"And just like that, I'm busted," Wade said, charmingly shamefaced. "I don't have physics until next semester. The guys said there was a real hottie in this class." He glanced at the girls hovering near the door, and his gaze lingered over a few pretty faces. "I thought I'd drop by and see for myself. Phillips has no idea who's in his class." His attention shifted to Mr. Phillips, still sitting at his computer. "His online girlfriend sucks up a lot of his time, as you can see."

While the scoop on Mr. Phillips and his cyber girlfriend was entertaining, I couldn't help but feel let down. Wade wasn't interested in me? The flirting killed time while he trolled for girls? Disappointment made me crabby.

"Don't be a sexist pig or anything," I said. "Last time I checked, this wasn't a harem. You might have more luck in chemistry. It's down the hall."

I gathered my books and untangled my long legs from under the desk. The class, as if released from a spell, shuffled toward the door. Brit-the-Brainiac, like a store greeter, smiled at kids passing her desk, but waved them by while she glared bullets at me and Wade. The others didn't even notice her as they filed out of the room sideways, crablike, to keep me and

Wade in their view.

Wade jumped to his feet, blocking my attempt to pass him. "I don't think *chemistry* will be a problem," he said, a teasing light in his grey eyes.

"Nice line." I murmured. "Use it often?"

"Never. You're the one and only. Maybe *my* one and only."

"Wow." I snorted. "The soul mate card. You really think you have girls figured out, don't you?"

"Girls, yes," he deadpanned. "You? Now that could take a lifetime. I'm game if you are."

At eye level, I stared directly at his sculpted lips as they formed the flirtatious words and then slanted into a sexy grin. We stood pressed together for a few glorious seconds. My insides quivered. And tingled. And yeah, he certainly did have big, I-give-good-love-bites teeth.

At least Wade stood a few inches taller than me. A minimum requirement for potential love interests in my book. His presence crowded, demanded a response. We were as close as we could get in public, yet he was too far away. I wanted us to sink into each other. Wade inhaled and his chest rose, pushing against mine. I shivered at the curl of sensations winding around me, binding me, making me lean against him.

"Eryn, a moment, please." Mr. Philips came out of nowhere, shattering the moment.

Wade and I flinched as if firecrackers had exploded between us. My heart thumped erratically in my chest. I let my breath out slowly. I hadn't realized I'd been holding it.

Mr. Phillips nodded a dismissal at Wade and, taking my arm, led me to the front of the room. "There's someone I'd like you to meet."

And it has to be now?

Brit stood there, clutching her books like a shield, her eyes following Wade. Something flickered in their depths. Suspicion? Hatred? When her gaze turned to me, she flatlined her lips as if I were a child she was about to scold.

"Ah, we've already…" I began, still a bit dazed.

Brit shushed me with a shake of her head. Explanations must be wasted on Mr. Phillips, because if he'd paid attention to his students, he'd have noticed Brit and I hung out by each other's desks every day. Well, until today.

I spotted a large manila envelope, emblazoned with my name and practically glowing, on his solid oak desk. My cumulative file. The educational equivalent of a criminal record. I'd become all too familiar with my file's bulk when I'd made the shrink rounds at my old school.

I cringed. *So much for a clean slate.* By now I was probably on a teacher-rotated suicide watch, with the schedule posted in the staff room.

"If this is about what happened last year…" Mortified, I shot a look over my shoulder, but Wade had already left. My late, great fondness for box cutters remained safely filed away.

"Obviously *physics* didn't happen for you last year," Mr. Philips said in his Gregorian-chant-like tone—another reason I was failing his class. "Things will be different here at Redgrave High. You see, Eryn, we believe in our students. We believe in their potential…" He eased into full-lecture mode.

It took five long minutes of teacher rhetoric before Mr. Phillips outlined his plan. It was pretty straightforward. Either Brit tutored me in physics, or I couldn't take the class.

"Oh, I can so totally do that," Brit agreed.

I glared at her, but couldn't really object. Brit had a brain, and I needed to borrow it. We agreed to meet every day after school for one hour.

"What're you doing for lunch?" Brit asked as we left the room. "We're starved," she said, pointing from her bright smile to the skull on her T-shirt who did indeed look famished.

I didn't laugh. Not only had she lied to me about Alec, but she'd been giving me the evil eye for talking to Wade. Apparently to Brit, friendship meant running my life. No, thank you.

She grabbed my arm as I turned away. "Look, I know I screwed up, but I can explain." She pressed her lips together, then sighed impatiently. "But you have to hang with me for more than five seconds, or the whole let-me-spill-my-guts thing doesn't work. Besides, I had no idea you were a hunter yesterday. I was only trying to nix your interest in Alec before you got hurt." She crossed her arms. "You can't tell me you haven't been creative with the truth a time or two. All hunters lie."

She had a point. I'd lied so much in my lifetime, it was hard to believe anyone ever told the truth. I would have done the same thing in her place, protected a friend from certain heartache—a clueless human girl with no paranormal knowledge would get chewed up and spit out by a hunter.

"You talk, I'll eat," I said finally. But I couldn't stomach

the thought of the bologna sandwich Sammi had stuffed in my backpack. My uncle's wife pseudo-parented a tad too hard, first with overdecorating my room and then with making my lunches like I was six. Besides, wilted lettuce never did appeal. For the last week I'd been hanging out in the library at lunch, munching on a granola bar. My way of avoiding a lonely table in the cafeteria while the whole school watched me eat.

"How's the cafeteria food? I haven't tried it yet."

Brit studied me. "I think you're ready."

"For what?"

"Clogged arteries." She started down the hall, her heavy boots clunking loudly enough for an entire military parade. "We'd better go together. I can point out the least toxic items on the menu. But first there's something important you've got to see. I think it will put last night into perspective for you."

As we rounded the corner, a skinny blonde slammed into Brit knocking her against the wall.

"Sorry," the girl tossed over her shoulder, barely breaking stride.

Brit pushed away from the locker she'd crashed into. Strands of her straight black hair, charged with static, floated around her head. With her flying hair, goth clothes, and super-pale foundation, Brit had a kind of Bride of Frankenstein look going on. But I suppose the real Bride of Franky was probably taller.

I fought back a grin.

"You okay?" I scooped up her backpack, surprised at the weight. She must have crammed every textbook for the whole year inside.

"Yeah." She glowered down the hallway. "There goes your new boyfriend's usual type. Wade likes them blonde, brainless, and with boobs out to here." She held her hands at a physically impossible distance from her chest, then glanced at the front of my shirt and shrugged.

I resisted the urge to roll my shoulders back and stick out my chest. Not that it would make much difference. I'd even put in extra effort this morning and worn a padded bra to fill out Paige's hand-me-down shirt. Regrettably, the bra slipped around because I had nothing to hold it in place. I'd definitely gotten shafted in the boobage department.

Brit led me down the hall and paused at a six-foot-high trophy cabinet outside the gymnasium. Sports trophies, banners, and photos decorated the glass shelving. She pointed to a section featuring Redgrave's community hockey league.

"Here are the guys from our school who made the town team." Brit pointed to a group shot of guys in hockey gear. They stood in a rink, helmets at their hips, their hair mussed and smiles wide. "Recognize anyone?"

I stepped closer to the glass to scan the faces. I gestured to a familiar face in the middle. "There's Wade." Oh, he looked amazing in all that extra shoulder padding.

Brit rolled her eyes. "Anyone *else?*"

I slid my finger along the glass and studied each face. At the last one, my finger stopped. "That's the guy from last night. Ethan." How happy he looked in that photo. How cute and cool. How dead he'd looked on the pet shop floor.

"What if I told you that he"—she jabbed her finger at a short guy in the middle of the photo—"and he"—at the tall

blond on the end—"were the two werewolves we took down before you moved here?"

I examined the picture again. Three out of the six guys pictured had turned into werewolves? No wonder Alec had sounded so bitter last night. The kills his crew had made couldn't have been easy. These beasts were once kids they knew, went to school with, grew up with, but now they were taking them down.

I turned away from the confident, grinning guys in the picture to face Brit.

"Okay," I said. "So someone's targeting Redgrave High, that's obvious. Why hasn't anyone done anything about it? Paranorm activity or not, the police should be involved by now."

Brit patted me on the back. "You know, I thought you'd never get there. Well done. And now for the whopper." She leaned closer, her gaze holding mine as she spoke her next words. "My dad's a cop on the force and was almost fired for asking those questions. Guess whose father is the chief of police? Wade's. And he's pointing the finger at Matt and Alec."

I pursed my lips. "Oh. That's ironic. Now you want to blame Wade's father for the rumors about the Delacroix?" I gave Brit an are-you-feeling-the-irony look. "The same rumors you used to keep me away from Alec? And Wade warned me to stay away from Alec because his family is dangerous." I crossed my arms. "There's a lot of finger pointing going on with you guys, and I don't like being in the middle. I just got to town."

"Yeah," Brit said, nodding. "Don't you think it's interesting that all this started right before you showed up? Like maybe there's a reason you're here?

I frowned. "And what would that be?"

"To help us." Brit dragged me a bit further down the hall. I let her pull me along, a bit dazed by her logic.

"Here we are," Brit announced. "Let's eat before the big reveal. I can't unload Redgrave's secrets on an empty stomach."

My mouth watered on cue.

The weight of grease thickened the air in the crowded cafeteria. My stomach rumbled again, loudly. Brit laughed and handed me a tray.

The long line started way back at the dessert coolers, which was fine by me. I loaded my tray with goodies.

"I hate you," Brit said, eyeing my chocolate pudding, donut, and huge brownie. "How do you stay thin, eating like that? I've been on a diet since fifth grade. Have you seen me in shorts?" She pinched her thighs. "I've so-o-o got to get rid of these."

"I'm sure it'll catch up with me someday." I shrugged and shuffled forward as the line advanced. "Oh, look." I skipped toward the steaming grill behind the coolers. "Cheeseburgers!" My hollow stomach rumbled. Hmm…maybe I had been eating more than usual. Please, not another growth spurt.

All eyes were on us as we weaved through chairs to find a table along a row of windows. I plastered on a fake smile. Shouldn't there be a time limit for staring at the new girl? We plopped down our trays, and, between my rabid bites of greasy burger, the crowd went on to inspect some other

poor schmuck who thought legwarmers really had made a comeback. I quizzed Brit about everything to do with Redgrave, except its paranormal badness.

"No, we don't have a recycling program and, yes, I think we need one." Brit rolled her eyes. "Would you stop trying to distract me?" She drowned a fry in the mountain of ketchup she'd poured on her cafeteria tray and became very businesslike as she fired out the details. "I thought you'd want to know all about the Redgrave situation after last night's close call. *We* thought you'd be eager to get more field experience. Banish a few weres. Wage a few battles."

"Not really," I hedged. "I'm trying to cut down."

Brit laughed as she drenched another fry. "Guess what? Diets don't work. You can't quit cold turkey. It's a lifestyle thing."

I laughed. Giving up hunting wasn't quite like cutting back on carbs, but I appreciated the comparison. I mashed my fork down into my brownie square, flattening it. Alec's concern about the number of weres being created was valid, and I could see why he might have asked Brit to approach me, but I was in no position to help.

"Someone has to be controlling the werewolves." Brit's tone shifted from flippant to full-on military briefing. I liked her better when she was being all sarcastic rather than inundating me with facts as if I were already a part of the crew. "Only a strong paranorm could control a pack of werewolves. There are too many for these to be rogues. They weren't the victims of a random biter. They're a pack. We could use a hand tracking them down."

I ignored her last comment and removed a slimy pickle from my third burger. "I don't know. You guys seem like a pretty tight team. I'm sure you can handle it." I shrugged as if I'd lost interest and groped for a change of subject. Wade's sculpted features flashed through my mind. "Now, why don't you give me some information that might help me out?"

Brit cocked a brow.

"Wade details. I want them all. Where does he hang out? How old is he? What about girls?" I asked.

Brit choked on her drink. "Oh, he's into girls. You thought he was gay? Wade might be a lot of things, but gay isn't one of them."

I sighed. After the hard flirting we'd done in physics class, I was pretty sure Wade was interested in more than being my shopping buddy. "No, I meant, what about girlfriends?"

Brit shook her head. "Haven't you heard a thing I've been saying? Wade's our top suspect." At my pleading look, Brit sighed. "Okay, I give. He goes out with a girl for a few dates, and that's it. He hasn't had a steady relationship, and he hates girls who cling." She paused. "Especially Paige. She's always trying to latch her tentacles around him. They went out for like a minute last year. She barely survived when he brushed her off. She's been psycho ever since."

"Paige McCain?" I asked, but I already knew the answer.

"The one and only." Brit slurped the last of her drink and then shot me a questioning glance. "You know her?"

"Unfortunately." I shared a bathroom with her every morning—I expected the toilet to be booby-trapped every time I used it. Paige wasn't the sharing sort. "So you're saying

you think Wade's a paranorm because he dates a lot?" I shook my head. "Sorry, first you warn me off Alec, and then you end up being one of his hunting crew. THEN you warn me off Wade, because he's good looking and all the girls like him. Do you see my hesitation here?"

Brit blinked at me. "There's more to it than that."

"Oh, I'm sure there is, but you know what, Brit?" I stole one of her cold fries. "I don't want to know. Last night was last night. A onetime thing. I've got other things I'm dealing with." I looked over Brit's shoulder and winced as I spotted Paige headed in our direction. Coming to the cafeteria had been a mistake. I hid my face behind a napkin.

"Uh… What are you doing?"

"Shhhh." I lowered the napkin so I could peek over it. "She's coming this way."

"Who?" Brit craned her neck.

"Paige," I rasped. "I don't want her to see me. I do not feel like sparring with Rose Harry's baby at the moment."

"Huh?"

"Haven't you ever seen that old horror film? A woman gives birth to this demon/child thing. Anyway, that's my cousin, Paige, remember her? You were saying how nice and psycho she is."

I peeked around my napkin. Paige glided down the aisle with all the attitude of a red-carpet diva, accompanied by two cookie-cutter friends, equally blonde and perky. They followed a step behind Paige like good little peons should. I ducked back behind the napkin and spun it in different directions to get the most face-hiding coverage.

I stared at the floor, horrified, as a trio of cute shoes (shoes I could never wear because what was cute in a size six was fashion blasphemy in a size ten) cat-walked up the aisle and stopped at our table.

Brit cleared her throat, so I lowered my napkin and said, "You know, Brit, you're right. These really are made of recycled paper." I handed it to her. "There's a little doohickey stamp on each one. It's barely visible."

Brit contemplated the napkin while Paige and her groupies regarded us with loathing. Unless the sneers on their faces were supposed to be model-like pouts. Better yet, it could have been gas. I sucked back a snort of laughter. This was one cluster of girls I wouldn't try too hard to save from a perfectly good werewolf munching.

"Oh, Paige, how great to see you here." I tried to ignore Brit, who let me know what she thought of my recycling cover story by wiping her nose with the napkin, before crumpling it and tossing it over her shoulder.

I rested my arm along the back of the chair next to me and acted as if the possibility of running into Paige at the school we both attended had never occurred to me and wasn't one of the reasons I'd avoided the cafeteria until now.

"Brit and I were discussing the benefits of using recycled

products. Fascinating stuff," I said. "Wanna join us?" I nudged one of the empty chairs at our table with my foot, and it scraped along the floor in a noisy invitation.

"What? Are you kidding?" Paige's face puckered. "I'm not here for a social visit, cousin." She spit out the last word as if saying it might bring on a contagious disease. "Frankly, I'm surprised you got up the nerve to eat lunch outside of the library. But since you did, I thought it only fair to warn you. You guys better stay away from my table. Don't get any ideas. Just because we're related doesn't mean I have to introduce you to my friends."

"Duh." I snorted. "I've been here for a week already, Paige, and this is the first time you've spoken to me in public. I think I got the message." I rolled my eyes at Brit. "Paige likes to state the obvious." I spoke behind my hand. "She gets it from her mother."

Brit smacked her palm on the table and let out a bark of laughter. Even Paige's groupies snickered. Maybe they'd had Mrs. McCain for kindergarten too.

Paige shut them up with a glare.

The blondest one tried to redeem herself. She eyed my shirt. "Hey, Paige, isn't that the top we bought at the thrift store when we were shopping for Halloween costumes? You planned to dress up like a scarecrow, remember?"

Paige gave the girl an approving smile. "Why, Michelle, you're right. I couldn't bring myself to wear it. I mean, eww, someone else sweated in that shirt." She shuddered. "I was hoping no one would notice, for Eryn's sake." She shot me a pitying glance. "But now it's out of the bag. You see, Eryn lost

all her luggage at the airport, so she has to wear clothes I give her. Isn't that sad? I'll tell you all about my loser cousin when we get to our table. Everyone's got to hear this." She linked arms with the girls and walked away without another word.

They joined a table overflowing with half a dozen other girls, more like THEM, the would-be-cheerleader type. Redgrave High barely had the population for a basketball team, let alone frills such as girls bouncing around in micro-mini skirts. Paige's brood giggled and whispered behind their hands, and, from their glances in our direction, I could tell she was filling everyone in on her woeful little cousin. Why were helpless little Dodo birds extinct while girls like that walked the earth? Seriously, they rendered the entire feminist movement moot.

I turned back to Brit. "Is it just me, or do you feel unclean?"

She grimaced. "I can't believe you guys are related." Her jaw dropped. "And good lord, you live with Mrs. McCain."

"She's my aunt." I hastened to make the information easier to digest. "By marriage. She's married to my father's brother. And usually Sammi's not that bad."

"Sammi? She has a first name?" Brit laughed. "Isn't it weird how you don't think of teachers having first names? Man, I still have nightmares about her kindergarten class. I can't imagine living with her." Brit finished off her pudding and cleaned out the plastic container with her finger. "Why don't you live at home with your parents?"

Ouch. Family issues. A direct hit. Good thing I was used to analysis. Otherwise I would have told Brit where to go with

her probing questions and what to do when she got there. I swallowed hard. This was it. Once I said the words, there'd be weirdness. She'd feel sorry for me, I'd feel sorry for myself, and we'd slip into a pity spiral.

"My parents are dead." I pushed my tray aside, appetite gone.

A look of sadness crossed Brit's face. She started to speak, then stopped, and reached for her backpack.

"Then we have even more in common." She plunked her backpack over her shoulder. "My brother died in a car crash four months ago. They found his car wrapped around a light post on Main Street at two o'clock in the morning. Wade's father said it was a cut-and-dried case. Said Blake was driving under the influence." Her face settled into harsh lines. "Only my brother didn't drink. He wouldn't, not after growing up like we did."

I leaned back from the rage she spitballed across the table. Anger seeped from her pores and darkened her scent from its normal citrusy glow to a dank odor.

"Guess who else is in that hockey team picture I showed you? Blake, my brother. Every werewolf we take down, I think it's going to be him."

I sucked in a startled breath. So that's why she'd been so devastated when Ethan turned back into his human form last night. She'd thought the beast might be her brother. I couldn't imagine hunting under that kind of emotional turmoil.

"Brit, I'm sorry about your brother. I really am. But I don't think my help is the kind you need right now.

"Well, I do," Brit said simply. "And so does Alec."

I sighed. Then snorted. "What about your boyfriend, Matt? He doesn't want me around."

Brit waved her hand. "You leave Matt to me. Next period, biology," she said with false cheerfulness as if we'd been discussing the weather. "We get Mr. Riggs again—imagine a gym teacher and a bio teacher all rolled into one. Aren't we lucky?" She picked up her tray. "He's a real stickler about being on time. Every minute you're late is worth ten push-ups. And the only push-ups I like are the leather corset kind you get online." Her laughter bordered on hysteria.

Oh, this was so getting personal. Brit was in the exact same situation as I was. Both searching for the truth, both afraid of what we'd find. I knew how much she hurt. How confused and sad she felt. Wasn't I grasping at Sebastian's offer of help the same way Brit was grasping at me?

How could I possibly tell her I couldn't help now?

I WAS BORN THIS WAY. WHAT'S YOUR EXCUSE?

Brit's revelation about her brother haunted me the rest of the day. We spoke no more about it, but she expected me to join Alec's crew. She didn't get why I hadn't immediately announced I was in like sin.

She didn't know how much I had to hide.

I stewed over my current predicament on the walk home.

Sebastian had warned me to stay out of trouble and avoid paranorms. But he hadn't said anything about paranorms finding me. I had no rules of engagement to follow. I wasn't officially under the Council's control, because I wasn't officially a hunter. Could I put my parents at risk by helping Alec's crew with Redgrave's werewolf infestation?

Would the crew welcome me into their inner circle if they knew I was half wolven? It would be hard enough for a group of hunters to accept a full-blooded wolven in their midst, someone who could turn into a wolf at will, someone who retained certain wolfie abilities in human form—speed, agility, heightened senses, strength.

I hadn't shifted yet. No one knew if I had it in me, or if I'd be able to shift back.

I was only half wolven, but I'd been taking my father's drugs for years. And then I'd stopped taking them—ripped the bandage off so to speak. Now I was jumping off buildings, sniffing out werewolves, experiencing pangs of bloodlust.

Ugh. High school wasn't supposed to be this complicated. I should be worried about who to ask to the Harvest Moon Dance at the end of the month—not concerned for the souls of every person in Redgrave. But I wouldn't be able to live with myself if I didn't at least try. For now, I'd stay on the sidelines and observe, keeping my wolven eyes open to help Brit and the crew. But I had to keep my nose clean, keep Alec at a distance, and avoid Wade. Easy enough, right?

I could do it all. I didn't have much of a choice. Now if only I were ready for that stupid physics exam next week.

The neighbor's yellow Lab heralded my arrival with a few extra-shrill barks. I plodded up my uncle's porch stairs and shouldered my way through the front door, marveling that I didn't need a key. No one in Redgrave locked their doors. Given the werewolf activity, people in this town were overly optimistic. If they only knew. By the time the werewolves were done with this town, people would be installing deadbolts

and security systems, maybe having priests bless their homes.

Aunt Sammi cornered me in the hall as I tiptoed past the kitchen. I'd hoped to sneak up to my room and hide, but I couldn't very well knock her over to get there, even if she was a foot shorter. In her cotton-candy-pink sweater set and black dress pants, with her sleek, auburn chin-length hair, she looked fresh and perky. Very kindergarten teacherish.

"Eryn. There's the girl we've been waiting for." She smiled at me as if I were a five year old on the first day of school rather than the niece who'd been living with her for a week. "Marcus and I were deciding what to make for dinner. Since Paige is at a friend's, you can be the swing vote." She opened her arms wide for a hug.

She was the huggy type.

Normally I wasn't, but this once I wanted to fall into Sammi's arms and cry. Instead, I leaned back on my heels, feeling mean as Sammi flushed. Her arms dropped to her sides, her welcoming, big-toothed smile collapsed.

So I had some tough decisions to make. That wasn't an excuse for letting my guard down in front of my human relatives. What choice did I have but to act normal, even if it felt like playing dead?

Brit was right. Hunters lied. We lied to the people around us, and we lied to ourselves. Every time a norm tried to make an honest connection with us, we could only return their kindness with a con, an angle that would protect them from the paranorm world. The REAL world. I was my hunter father's *half-wolven* daughter. I had even more to lie about. I had to hide my wolven nature—my very self—by building a

lopsided wall of untruths between me and everyone else.

"Is that Eryn?" Uncle Marcus' hulking form filled the kitchen doorway, as well as the silence that had settled between us. Sammi and Marcus stood together, presenting a united front, even though Sammi only came up to his shoulder. Marcus was tall like my dad, but spongy through the middle. He had none of my father's commanding presence. He did, however, look every bit the successful real estate lawyer. Well-fed and indulged. I studied their identical, innocent expressions. Had they been talking about me, their problem child?

"Hey, kiddo, how was school?" Marcus asked, loosening his tie, his rounded face carefully casual.

I shrugged. What else could I do? Get into the nitty-gritty details? Tell him, *I'm flunking physics and I found out werewolves are terrorizing the town and my only friend is trying to exterminate them?* Not unless I wanted a tête-à-tête with every psychologist from here to Toronto.

"That good, eh?" Marcus and Sammi exchanged a look.

Sammi rolled her finger in the air like a movie director as if prompting Marcus to keep up the conversation.

"About dinner. What do you feel like tonight?" Marcus asked, sniffling a bit. "Italian?" He held up a box of pasta, rattling the contents. Then he heaved in a breath and let out an enormous sneeze.

"Goodness." Sammi patted him on the arm.

"There I go again," Marcus said with a laugh, swiping at his puffy eyes. "I swear it's as if I'm allergic to you, Eryn. Same thing when I met your mother."

I grimaced. Unfortunately, that was true. Marcus *was* allergic to dogs. Poor guy, I'd been setting him off ever since I moved in, even though I tried to keep my distance.

I gave a weak laugh. "Probably our shampoo. Dad hootched up a special formula for Mom and me."

"Whatever formula it is"—Sammi reached up to pat my thick, dark locks, but dropped her hand abruptly as if remembering my anti-hug reaction—"it's fantastic. I don't think I've ever seen such beautiful, healthy hair. Have you, honey?"

When Marcus didn't say anything, Sammi elbowed him. Hard.

"No, I have not." Marcus glared at her and rubbed his ribs. He looked at me. "Your hair is very pretty, so don't mind me. I know beauty comes at a price." He held a finger under his nose to hold off another sneeze.

I mentally sighed. They were always like this. Trying too hard. They meant well, but I wasn't sure I could keep up happy family pretences tonight. My talk with Brit had left me raw.

"If Italian doesn't appeal, how about we check out that new Chinese place downtown?" Sammi said, the wide smile pasted on her face again. The restaurant was right beside Polly's Pet Emporium. I couldn't eat there without gagging over the memory of last night and Ethan's all-you-can-eat bunny buffet.

I put a hand to my stomach. "I don't feel very good." Not a complete lie. My stomach had been in knots since my doomsday chat with Brit. "You guys do whatever and if I feel

up to it, I'll fend for myself later."

Didn't I always?

I took a step forward, forcing Sammi to lean back into Marcus. That gap in the hall was all I needed to escape up the stairs.

"Your luggage finally arrived from the airport," Marcus called after me. "It went all the way to Montana before they tracked it and shipped it here. I picked it up at the bus depot this morning. One bag, right? It's on your bed."

"Thanks." Halfway up the stairs I turned and looked down at them.

Marcus had his arm around Sammi's shoulders. They presented a united front of concern, and confusion about how to handle this strange girl they'd been asked to care for. I almost went back downstairs.

Then Marcus released another deafening sneeze.

So I kept climbing…one stair at a time.

In my room, lime green walls closed in on me like a fly slowly being digested alive by one of those creepy Venus Flytrap plants. If that wasn't scary enough, my bed, complete with heart-shaped pillows and eye-popping, daisy print comforter, looked more conducive to an epileptic fit than an invitation to snooze. No wonder I hadn't been sleeping.

Then I saw it. There in the middle of the bed. A little bit of home.

I hopped onto the springy mattress and hugged my suitcase. The suitcase I thought I'd lost forever, shipped off to Tunisia or some other exotic destination. I'd have felt really dumb if Paige had walked into my room at that moment,

but in my world, luggage was okay to hug. It didn't have any expectations.

I'd wrapped a green headband around its handle so I would recognize it on the airport's baggage-conveyor-belt thingy with so many similar black cases. The cotton material was almost completely ripped off. The hard plastic case had a new dent in the side and grease stains on it. The thing had been on an adventure, that was clear.

But it was *mine*.

I snapped the latches and flipped back the lid.

My own stuff. I ran a hand over my favorite *I was born this way. What's your excuse?* T-shirt. No more borrowing from Paige and being subjected to public humiliation when she told everyone I was wearing her castoffs. No more suffering through Sammi's impromptu visits to the mall. Shopping always made me cranky. Especially clothes shopping, a time honored mother-daughter thing. With Sammi and Paige, I turned into the orphaned third wheel.

I dug through the bag looking for the good stuff—my treasures—the few books and photos I had brought from home that I couldn't live without. Eager to imprint myself on Sammi's lime green guest room, I propped a picture of my parents on the nightstand. I'd taken the photo of them after we'd made the long hike up Rundle Mountain.

Dad, impressive despite a layer of grime from the hike, looked too brawny to be the owner of a major pharmaceutical company—kind of a giveaway, really. Mom stood with an arm around his waist, and they faced the camera with adrenaline-charged grins.

In wolven form, Mom was strong and graceful, but in human guise, she was achingly beautiful. At least I had some of her looks: the dark hair and the hazel eyes accented with flecks of gold. I was thin and more than passably pretty, a watered-down version of Mom. Her tanned skin, dark hair, and delicate build gave her a timeless beauty. The dust-jacket photos her fellow treehugging readers fawned over, moody black and whites, couldn't quite capture it—although they sold a ton of her save-the-animal-world-it's-not-too-late books.

I gripped the glass frame and stared down at my parents' faces, glowing with joy, exuding life. A part of me, the raw, gaping, hole-in-my-heart part, refused to believe they were dead. They were alive here in my hands. Jubilant, with no idea what the future had in store. No clue it would all go so wrong.

Mom had always hated having her picture taken. Believed bits of your soul would be captured on film, lost forever to those brief flashes of light and shadow. Now plastic-framed pieces of my parents' souls were all that kept me sane.

They'd wanted what they thought would be the best life for me. I understood their motives, but I questioned their methods. I shouldn't have been a lab rat. I should have only been Eryn. Their child. No matter how noble their intentions, my parents had made a huge mistake in messing around with my wolven abilities, denying me my birthright.

But I still loved them.

They were my parents.

I blinked back tears and placed the photo on the bedside

table. Better to unpack than unravel. Since nothing I owned needed a hanger, I loaded up the dresser. I shoved my disemboweled suitcase under the bed and sat cross-legged in the middle of the spongy mattress.

The pungent smell of frying onions drifted up the stairs to my room.

Onions always made me cry.

I lay down and buried my face in a pillow.

My tears drowned the daisies.

I stood alone in a mountain clearing, dressed for a hike in my boots, cargo pants, and long-sleeved shirt, a backpack heavy on my shoulders. I walked through long-stemmed wild flowers in brilliant shades—fuchsia, purplish blue, and mustard yellow, their sweet scents blending—nature's perfume. The drone of honeybees and other insects harmonized with the gentle swoosh of the breeze bending the tall grass.

I was safe.

And then I wasn't.

Clouds, brooding and dark, gathered over the mountains. Thunder rumbled in the distance. A fat drop of rain struck my face and ran down my cheek like a single, devastating tear. I ducked into the dense shrubs edging the clearing, scanning the grass.

They would come.

They always did.

They were here.

Charging from the shrubs across the field, a large grey wolf bolted through the grass. He howled out to his mate. A jet-black wolf, her coat in stark relief against the fading sun, stepped gracefully into the clearing, howled in answer, and rushed to him. When she was midway through the clearing, the first shot rang out.

I cupped my mouth, screaming into my shaking hands, terrified to leave the safety of the shrubs. I should help them. Why did I never try to help them? Why was I frozen here, unable to move?

The female wolf advanced, her wound forcing her into an awkward lope. She fell. Heedless of the danger, the male wolf raced to her side. He stood above her, keening low in his throat. The second round took him down. He staggered and fell to the earth—nose to nose with his lifeless mate. A gentle mist descended from the heavens.

God…no…they were my parents. And they were dead.

I dropped to the earth, sobbing.

Violent tremors of grief rocked my body.

Long moments passed.

I stilled. I waited to wake, for this was where the dream always ended—where I woke to fear and guilt.

But this time, something was different. I held my breath and listened. Only the whistle of the wind broke the silence.

I gasped when a hand rested on my shoulder.

"We have to hurry, child," a woman's voice said. "They're coming."

The hair on my neck quivered. I was kneeling on the dust-covered plank floor of a rustic cabin. I peered through murky

lighting filtered through a smoky haze. No, not a cabin—a house. A historic home, filled with antiques still in their prime, except for the heavy film of dust coating each surface. A vacuum-tube radio of solid cherry wood shaped like a church window, a cast iron stove in the corner, colored-glass jars and bottles in a curio cabinet.

I stood and brushed the dust from my pants, coughing as I inhaled some of the fine grit.

She thrust a wet rag into my hand. "Breathe through this. It will keep the sand out."

I pressed the rag to cover my mouth and nose. She was right. It was easier to breathe now.

"Where am I?" I asked through the cloth.

"Ah, child, the question is: when are you?" The woman's sad smile lightened grey eyes that shone above hollowed cheeks. Her gaze mesmerized despite her fine features smudged with dust, the collarbone that jutted through the lace at her neck.

She glanced from my cargo pants, my T-shirt, and backpack to her own muslin dress. Ankle length, pleated. Her dark hair wrapped around her head in an intricate braid. The weight of all that hair too much for that slim neck. Forget the mint-condition antiques in the house, our clothes alone screamed that we were from different times, different worlds.

The woman circled her hands in the air, drawing ancient symbols with smooth movements. Gesture magic. A witch, working a spell.

Odd how I didn't feel panicked. My pulse beat steady. Her magic settled over me like a shroud. My body, light. There…but not really.

"You are cloaked. They cannot see or hear you," the woman said. "Nor will they catch your scent." Her eyes darkened. "What happens here is in the past. No deed can stop it. What you see has already come to pass." She gripped my arms, her fingers strong. "You are my witness. The only hope for my boy. I risked more than I should have to bring you here. Don't fail me."

With that the witch spun to face the door at the end of the parlor. The pine slab splintered, the wood was sucked out and up into the air. Outside, thick red sand swirled the entire height of the gaping entrance. The world had submerged into a sandy sea.

A tall, dark form filled the doorway. The wind carried the

smell of decay and rotting flesh. Slow-cooked death with all the trimmings.

"I know you're in there, witch," a deep voice roared. "Come see what I've got for you." The man reached an arm out into the dust and then shoved a young man into the room.

He was around my age, nearing eighteen. Tall, dark haired, thin, one hand shading his eyes from the dim glow of the Tiffany lamp. He staggered about the room as if blind, his feet scuffing in the dust. He sniffed the air, then almost fell over when he zeroed in on the witch.

His lips pulled back in a snarl.

A groan of agony ripped through him. His jaw unhinged like a snake's, opening wide. From his gaping mouth the smell of death filled the air, rancid. His incisors extended into fangs.

A vampire.

My pulse raced. I dove between him and the witch, holding my hands out to block his approach. He walked through me. Through my very being. I gagged as darkness permeated my flesh and drifted out my back. I didn't exist. Not in this time, not here and now. The witch was right. I could do nothing.

"Feed, boy." The man leaned his shoulder against the doorframe and crossed his legs at the ankle, nonchalant and at ease. His fedora slanted above his harsh, but deadly attractive, face. Under his long overcoat a silver sheriff's badge glinted on his lapel.

He took a long drag from a smoking cigar. Then he grinned, fangs exposed.

Another vamp. The boy's sire, eager to watch his fledgling's first kill.

I spun. Screamed a warning. I bolted, grabbing at the boy's arm, but my fingers slipped through air. I clawed at his back, my hands sinking through his cool flesh. I toppled forward, bursting through mother and child as if I'd tried to lean on a wall of fog.

I backed away, my body shaking.

The boy dragged the witch into his embrace.

"My son," she said. "If you need, then I will provide."

"Noo..." I screamed again, my throat burning with the force of it. Sand settled on my tongue.

With a guttural moan the boy sank his fangs into his mother's neck. He fed, a sickening slurping, his Adam's apple bobbing up and down as he gulped and gasped. The witch weakened. The two collapsed in a tangle of limbs.

I clapped my hands over my ears, trying to muffle the slurps and sighs of his hunger, her death.

The witch's eyes fluttered open, met and held mine, while her son drained the blood from her body. "You see how he cursed my boy? Do you see?"

I forced myself past the disgust, the fear—to a place of calm. I had to for the witch's sake.

I crept closer. His muscular shoulders, lean hips, shaggy brown hair were all familiar. I reared back. Bile rose in my throat. No. It couldn't be...

The young vampire ripped his fangs from his mother's ravaged neck.

Wade stared beyond me to face the sheriff, guilt marred his too-perfect face. Blood dripped down his chin. His mother, dead at his feet.

Piercing barks rang in my ears. I woke, struggling for breath and coughing up red dust. It spattered my daisy print pillowcase like blood.

Gasping, I swiped a hand across my mouth. I reached for the lamp on my bedside table and flicked it on. A shape, like a band of smoke and blacker than the shadows in the corner of my bedroom, slipped out the inch-wide gap under my window.

Heart pounding, I surged from clinging sheets and slammed the window down in its frame, turned the rusted lock home, and muffled the barking of the Lab next door.

Vampire mist. I'd only experienced it once before, while on a hunt with my father's crew, but you remembered things like a strange smoke that moved with a mind of its own.

Panic clawed at me. I struggled for breath, trying to shake off the dream—the vision of Wade at his mother's throat. I swallowed hard and backed away from the window. Shivering, I wrapped my arms around myself, clutching at the sides of my tank top, my nails digging into my waist.

Earlier, when I'd come upstairs…that window had been shut.

"Wade Gervais is a vampire," I announced as I balanced my backpack on a stack of book bags draped over an empty cafeteria chair. Alec, Brit, and Matt looked up from their Taco Tuesday specials, all wearing the same dumbfounded expression. "And I'm thinking his father, the chief of police,

is really his sire. Definitely old. Definitely powerful."

Brit and Matt glanced from me to Alec, who bit deliberately into his taco, chewed thoughtfully, and then said, "What an entrance. Have a seat, and let's all keep our voices down, shall we?"

I sighed, grabbed an empty chair from the table behind me, and sat down with the crew.

Alec pushed his empty tray aside and leaned his forearms on the table. Muscles bulged under his black long-sleeved hoodie, but I tried not to notice.

"Wade and his father are paranorms. We all agree on that. But vampires?" Alec laced his fingers together and shook his head. "They don't fit the profile, Eryn. They walk in full sunlight. And there's been no sign of vampire activity in Redgrave. Vampires spread like a plague, killing and infecting people until their nest outgrows a town and they're forced to move on."

Brit patted my shoulder. "Really good effort though." She gave me an encouraging smile, her black-rimmed eyes bright with excitement. "I'm so glad you decided to help us."

Matt snorted. "We had to save her from a bunny-brained werewolf, she doesn't even know about vamps and daylight, and you're glad she's going to *help* us. Nice." He scraped back his chair, crossed a leg over his knee, and tapped his shoe.

"Don't be so hostile." Brit shoved his foot off his knee. "Eryn's new at hunting, she told us that already. We have time to bring her up to speed."

"Do we?"

"Your mother will help."

I frowned. What did their mother have to do with this? She knew they were hunters? While I appreciated that the Delacroix boys ran their crew much like my father had run his—with close family involved, usually a hunter no-no—the Wade situation took precedence. I waved my hand in Brit's face. "I'm sorry, could we include me in the conversation *about me*, please?"

Brit grimaced. "Sorry."

I took a calming breath. "I know it goes against every bit of vamp lore, but these guys are up and moving in the daylight hours. I don't know how it's possible—but they're vamps. I'd stake my life on it."

"Stake your life?" Matt sneered. "Oh, that's cute."

"Enough!" I slammed my palm on the table, my chest tight with anger. "You guys don't know what you're up against."

The three of them regarded me while kids at other tables turned to stare at us, apparently fascinated by the sight of the new girl hanging with the town outcasts.

Alec's expression darkened.

"Temper, temper." Matt tsk-tsked. He turned to Brit. "She's quite the hothead. I'm thinking she might be too much of a liability." An I-told-you-so smile tugged at his lips.

Brit put her hand over mine. Did she feel it tremble? My beast had woken up wild from my dreams. I wasn't quite myself.

"Why do you think they're vampires?" Brit's voice was hesitant—as if she was afraid my answer would prove Matt right.

I drew in a steadying breath. I'd had one of the freakiest experiences of my life when Wade's witchy mom took me back in time, and I wasn't going to let Matt's resentment stop me from warning this fledgling crew what they were up against.

"I have kind of a sleeping disorder," I said, formulating my words carefully. "I inherited it from my mother." That at least was true. Wolven did have active dream lives. The expression "let sleeping dogs lie" originated from wolven lore. It was dangerous to wake a wolven, their dreams were so real, so blood- and battle-filled, that being jarred awake made it difficult for them to tell friend from foe.

Brit regarded me with an encouraging expression, while Alec's face remained neutral. I couldn't tell what he was thinking. He probably thought I was a complete headcase. Matt certainly did. I could read him like the cover of a tabloid on display at the grocery store. REDGRAVE'S NEW GIRL IS LOCO!

"I get these extremely vivid dreams." I forced myself to continue. "But last night..." I struggled against the images flashing through my mind, Wade, his father, the blood. "Last night I dreamt about Wade in a house filled with sand. I think it was in the 1930s, like the Dust Bowl era, you know? But he was a vampire—newly made. And he had been turned against his will, by an old, powerful vampire wearing a sheriff's badge. Then he was...forced to feed on his own mother."

"Eww, that's sick." Brit scrunched up her face.

I shuddered. "Yeah, it was." I glanced at Alec.

He gave away nothing, but kept his body still—listening and observing.

"Wade's mom was a witch," I said, then broke off. Somehow I couldn't tell them that she'd brought me through time, had meant for me to see what happened between her and her son. I was still trying to figure out why she'd done it. How had she known about me? How could I help Wade when I didn't understand all the things that were going on with me?

Matt scraped his chair closer to the table and leaned over his food tray, a look of grudging respect on his face. Finally I'd captured his attention. "We know a bit about witch lore. There are a few who work with our mother. Witches don't often birth males." He glanced at his brother. "It's rare, right?"

Frowning, Alec tapped his plastic fork against his bottle of iced tea. "Usually they have one child. A girl. When a witch dies, all her powers go to her young." He met my gaze. "Male witches, or warlocks, are more powerful than their female counterparts. In the old days witches killed their sons at birth. Warlocks have a thing for the dark arts." He grimaced, then exchanged a look with Matt that I couldn't quite interpret. "Maybe guys weren't meant to have that kind of power—it corrupts."

"So if Eryn's dream was a replay of an actual event," Brit said, "Wade might have super-witchy power."

"Power enough for Wade and his sire to walk in daylight," I said, relieved they were finally getting my rather substantial point. "Which means more than enough power to control a pack of werewolves. But if I'm right, why are a couple of übervamps hanging out in Redgrave?"

"Good question," Alec said, an unmistakable glint of

respect in his gaze. He glanced at his watch and stood. "Okay, we've got two more classes, and then we'll meet after school and head to our ranch."

I shifted in my chair. Alec's commanding tone rankled, as did his assumption I would blindly follow where he led. If he thought I was his to order around, he was sadly mistaken. I had enough people trying to control my life. I hoped I wouldn't regret my little sharing session with Alec's crew. I scratched behind my ear in frustration.

"My mother should be able to contact her friends and get us some more information." Alec rested his hands on the back of his chair. "We can check Eryn's story out." With a sharp scraping sound, he slid the chair home, tucking it under the table.

"Check my story out?" I jumped to my feet. Who did he think he was? Insulted, I bared my teeth at him.

Alec caught my fierce expression and did a double take.

I swallowed my ego and concentrated on relaxing my lips.

"Don't get your back up, Eryn." Alec lowered his voice. "I've seen a lot of things hunting. We all have. Things that aren't supposed to exist or contradict everything we thought we knew about the paranormal world. So could a vampire retain his inherited witch powers?" He shrugged. "That's likely Wade's situation. But we can't risk screwing this up, doing anything drastic, until we're absolutely certain."

Ugh. Why did he have to sound so in control and logical—and right? My beast was eager for battle, even if only a verbal butt-kicking. But I couldn't fault Alec's logic.

If the situation were reversed and the crew started spouting off about dreams and witches and vampires, I'd do a bit of investigating on my own before I made any hasty decisions.

I held out my hand to stop them from leaving. "I'm all for fact checking, but I don't think you're seeing the big picture." I paused, striving for that concise, authoritative tone Alec used. But my words came out a bit panicky. "I need you guys to believe me, and I need you to hurry. When I woke up from the dream last night, something black and nasty, like a thick smog, was slipping out my window. Only I hadn't left my window open. I think Wade pulled the vamp mist thing and paid me a visit, which means he has access to my uncle's house. Not good. I won't have him threatening my family."

"Your *family*?" Alec asked. "What about the threat he poses to you?" Something dangerous flickered in his brown eyes. He glanced around the cafeteria as if scouting for Wade. He looked like he wanted to do some serious damage to his living/dead person.

I was about to shrug off Alec's words. I was wolven. I could probably hold my own with Wade. Maybe. But the crew didn't know that, so I had to be a good-little-scared-human. At the same time I didn't want them fighting Wade. He'd be way too strong for them.

"Vampires." Matt snorted. "Always stalking chicks, lurking in their bedrooms. They're so predictable. Pervy," he said, making a face. "But predictable."

Brit slapped Matt's shoulder as my words sunk in. "OMG! He can get into her house? That's against the rules, isn't it?" She paused. "Uh-oh."

"Uh-oh, what?" Alec bit out.

"Paige." Brit's eyes were wide. "She must have invited Wade in. For a date? To make out?"

I grimaced at the thought of Paige making out with *anyone* in the house I now lived in. "I thought they went out *last* year?"

"Doesn't matter when she said the words." Matt fished his backpack from under the pile. "We're talking vampires, not salad dressing. Once a vamp is invited into your house, there's no expiration date."

Lovely. I started a list of things to pick up after school. Crucifixes, holy water. Oh, and lots of freaking garlic. I choked back the tide of hysterical laughter threatening to leap from my throat. I had to pull it together. Losing it in the cafeteria wasn't going to inspire confidence.

Alec slung his pack over his shoulder, moving with angry jerks. "We'll have to move fast. Mom's friends might be able to help us set up a barrier or a banishing spell. But until then, I'm going to give Wade a little message. Vampire or not, he needs to know Eryn is off limits." He strode away from the table, leaving us in a charged silence.

"You had to throw in the Wade's-stalking-me-while-I-sleep bit." Matt shot me a frustrated glance. "Let's hope he doesn't do anything stupid. Alec on a mission is a scary thing."

As Alec started for the exit, my stomach dropped. So much for not getting involved. My body suddenly felt 100 pounds heavier, like a huge weight had jumped on my shoulders for the mother of all piggyback rides.

After giving me a helpless look, Brit followed the guys.

I could only stand there and watch them go.

A few hours later, the last bell of the day rang. I threw my books into my locker, hesitated, but then tucked my physics text into my backpack. No point in taking the others. Except for physics, I was holding my own. I'd always had trouble with science, but some sadistic part of me wouldn't rest until I'd at least passed the subjects my father had excelled at.

I slammed my locker shut and started down the hall. What was I thinking? How could I be stressing over a stupid physics class when I should be tracking werewolves, or at least worrying about Wade and his vampy stalking? Only a few weeks out of my father's strict training schedule and hunter practices took a backseat to theories I'd seen debunked a million times.

A bitter wind blew across the parking lot as I pushed through the entryway doors. I tucked my chin into my jacket collar and blew against the material to warm my cheeks. Since morning, the temperature had taken a nosedive. Good-bye, rainy Vancouver winters. Hello freakin' frostbite. I'd take the rain any day.

"Eryn, wait up." Brit joined me on the steps overlooking the parking lot. Her black skull T-shirt offered little protection against the chill. Not that she seemed to notice the cold. Redgrave kids didn't. They had some built-in tolerance to the low temperatures, or maybe the longer you lived in Redgrave, the more leathery your hide became.

"I can't believe it's only October," I whined, my toes

numb. I added boots to my list of must haves.

"Wait till it starts getting dark at three o'clock," Brit said. She blew on her cupped hands as she scanned the parking lot. "Alec went to get the truck." She shot me a preemptive look. "And don't tell me you're not coming to the ranch with us. If there's anyone who can find out about Wade and his father, it's Marie."

I quirked a brow. "And Marie is…?"

"Alec's mom." She spun in an impatient circle. "Matt had to stop at the garage, didn't he? I swear he loves that mechanics class a bit too much, you know? It's unhealthy." She rolled her eyes. "Alec hates waiting around for him."

Brit glanced beyond the concrete stairs to the nearly empty parking lot, looking for Alec. Her lips formed a silent *Ohhhhh*. I turned to see what had her attention. A red sports car cruised past. An old classic with a custom paint job. Sunlight reflected off its polished chrome surface and zapped my eyes. Someone sure spent a bundle on their toys.

"There goes our monster-on-campus," Brit said. "Bet he's nice and warm in that baby. Not that vampires need heat, being dead and everything."

Wade.

I should have guessed.

Everything about him was smooth. His car was no exception. It screamed, "Hey, sweet thing, wanna go for a ride?" Like it had read my thoughts, the car screeched to a halt and reversed. Wade cranked the driver's window down by hand.

"Can I give you ladies a lift?" he called. His grin

emphasized his chiseled jaw and white teeth.

Brit crossed her arms. "Do the syllables 'ne-' and 'ver' mean anything to you?"

"Not really." Wade shrugged. "What about you, Eryn?" he asked, a challenge in his eyes. "Or are you one of those girls who lets their friends make their decisions for them?" He rested his arm on the open window, waiting.

Oh, a low blow, and it struck with pinpoint accuracy. How did he know I hated people telling me what to do?

"Unh…" I stammered. I wanted to rush down the steps and hop into his hot little car. Equally as gripping came the urge to give him the brush off, but good. Scenes played through my mind. Most ended with Wade's fangs tearing a hole in my throat. But wouldn't going with him serve two purposes? I'd be making my own decisions, and I'd have the perfect opportunity to pick Wade's brain to find out what he and his father were up to in Redgrave. I could handle a vamp, even a witchy one…couldn't I?

While I hedged the question, ignoring Brit's you're-not-seriously-considering-getting-into-that-car expression, a rusted Ford pickup barreled around the corner. A flash of dark eyes pierced through the truck's mud-splattered windshield.

Alec.

He glanced from Brit and me to Wade's suave little car below our perch on the steps. The truck lurched forward at full speed, back tires squealing and smoking.

So much for not doing anything drastic.

"Look out!" I hollered, taking a frantic step toward the impending wreckage, holding my hands out as if I could stop

Wade ducked back inside, his gaze fixed on his rearview mirror. He tried to move, gears grinding, but it was too late. *Crunch.* The pickup's massive grill devoured the trunk of Wade's car. Wade's head cracked against the steering wheel, then ricocheted back against the headrest.

A microsecond of frozen silence, then pandemonium as screaming students converged on the mangled vehicles from all directions.

I started down the steps, looking for signs of life from either vehicle. "Brit, get help!"

"I can't run," Brit said, near tears.

It took me a second to process her words, then I stopped, remembering her get-out-of-gym-free doctor's note. "Are you serious?"

She bobbleheaded her agreement.

"What kind of hunter are you?" I ground out in her ear.

"It's complicated." Brit's voice wavered.

I sighed harshly and started toward the scene.

"Don't!" Brit grabbed my arm. "Wait for Alec."

"Wait for Alec?" I rasped. "Did you see what he did? What if I'm wrong about Wade? What if Alec attacked an innocent human?" I pulled from her grip. "Get help. Call 9-1-1!" I bolted down the steps and ran around the hood of Wade's car. I yanked on the driver's door handle, but it refused to open. Wolven strength built in my hands. Too many witnesses. I couldn't rip the door from its metal frame. I gasped with relief when I spotted a large silver button on the handle. I pushed on it with both thumbs and pulled for

all I was worth. The door swung open. I stumbled backwards. Damn relic.

I hesitated. What if the crash had propelled Wade into full vamp mode? I bent over and peeked inside, half expecting the hideous slack-jawed, fanged vamp from my dream to fly out at me. But Wade, fragile, human Wade, still gripped the wheel, his head lolling back at a dangerous angle.

"Wade? Answer me." I waved my hand in front of his dazed eyes. "How many fingers?" The vision test seemed appropriate. Wasn't that what movie doctors did?

Wade groaned and knocked my hand away. With slow, cautious movements, he arched his back and rolled his head from side to side. Blood oozed from his hairline and streaked down his face.

A crimson line to his lips that I wanted to lick off his face.

I shifted closer, entranced by the minty scent rising from his blood. Hunger pangs twisted my stomach as if I hadn't eaten for weeks. I pressed myself against his body. My lips parted. I sighed against his warm skin. Wade turned his face up for me, like he wanted me to take his lifeblood, feed on his flesh.

I almost fell for it.

Vamp thrall.

I gasped, fighting his seductive glamour. His grey eyes stared into mine. Mesmerizing. Inviting…

Don't forget devilish. The voice of reason brought me back from the brink.

And evil.

Wade had killed and feasted on his own mother. He'd invaded my room, haunted my dreams. I'd seen his very creation, his downfall.

I cringed away from the car like Superman cowering from kryptonite. Propelled backward, I stumbled on the concrete. The beast in me writhed in protest, outraged, my gut in knots. I doubled over with shock. Risked a glance at the crowd. Where the hell was Brit? I hoped she'd made it into the school for help. Maybe Redgrave police came equipped with nets and tranquilizer darts for random cases of students going *Canis lupus.*

I breathed hard through my nose to expel the pennies-in-a-jar scent of blood from my greedy nasal cavities. Once the scent of blood faded, the pains in my stomach ebbed. I straightened, my stomach muscles tight, but at least I could move again.

Wade swung his legs out of the vehicle.

"Don't. You're hurt." I bolted forward, held out a hand to stop him.

He stood in a fluid motion. "It's nothing, a scratch."

"Oh really?" A dry laugh forced its way out of my throat. A scratch hadn't set my wolven hunger into overdrive. I frowned, staring up at Wade. Not a smidge of red stuff visible on his attractive face.

Wade swiped a hand across his forehead, lifting his hair to reveal a small cut, already clotting over.

What the—?

"You all right, Wade?" The deep voice at my back distracted me from Wade's one-second-it-looked-life-

threatening-the-next-it-wasn't wound. The desire to chow down at the Wade Deli had ebbed, but it left me drained. Bile flooded my mouth. I swallowed it back.

"I didn't see your antique parked there." Alec smirked. "Does your grandmother know you're driving her car?"

The crowd tittered. Wade glared over my shoulder, teeth bared.

"Alec," he said with a sneer. "I should have known. You're lucky my father hasn't thrown your whole family in jail."

Ooh, nasty. I whirled around into a wall of chest. The rush I'd felt when Alec and I raced through the woods was back. His proximity made my heart stutter, my insides quiver. I forgot about Wade and the crowd of students—forgot my first name and date of birth. Alec in full rage was potent, elemental. My wolven hormones surged into overdrive.

"You all right?" Alec grabbed my arms. "Did he touch you?" He stared down at my face. His gaze settled on my lips.

Wade grabbed Alec by the arm, jerked him away, and then thrust himself between us.

"Eryn's fine. And I intend to keep her that way," Wade said with a snarl.

"You?" Alec laughed. He pressed close to Wade, his voice low. "Is that before or after you suck all the blood from her body?"

Wade's eyes flickered. He leaned closer to Alec. Nose to nose. Bodies as rigid as elevator cables, ready to snap.

Since when did I become the bitch in heat, stirring up the boys? The air was thick with their rage, their passion. It settled over me like a dangerous mood. Bones in my back

shifted, grinding painfully. Skin stretched taunt, heat built under the surface like I'd been chucked in a microwave and roasted from the inside out.

Kids chanted, "Fight, fight, fight," as they encircled the scene. I'd seen fights before, but never when my wolf was this close to the surface and the moon almost full in the sky. Its pale outline blended with the clouds, but it called to me. A fine tremor weakened my legs.

Queasy, I squinched my eyes shut.

IF I WANTED SOMETHING DEAD AROUND MY NECK, I'D GET A FUR COAT

The chanting faded into a charged silence, broken by the periodic scuffle of shoes on pebbled cement and the sickeningly exciting sound of fists hitting flesh. Alec and Wade were duking it out, but I was fighting a battle of my own.

My system had flooded with wolven adrenaline at the first blow. My breath left me in little gasps, my pulse galloped in my chest. Hunter training told me to back Alec up—he was hopelessly overmatched against a vampire, especially one of Wade's witchy persuasion. I shouldn't be frozen on the concrete as if I were pinned, but my she-wolf was thrilled at

being the focus of all that male aggression, and I was afraid to move. Afraid to give in. Crazily, presiding over a battle for my attentions was only fitting. My right.

Barbaric.

Yet breathless excitement coursed through my body. The tingling low in my stomach warned me of danger. I tried not to think about what would happen if I stepped closer and surrounded myself with the jolting scent of rage thick in the air. I focused on less arousing sounds, engines revving in the parking lot, the school secretary's Charlie Brown wah-wah-wah voice making an announcement on the intercom.

Open your eyes. A male voice whispered, curling around me—an invisible embrace.

You know you want to watch.

Wade's voice.

Too close.

In my head.

Vamping around in my thoughts. *Damn.*

I should be freaking about now. So why did I have the urge to strut right up to Wade, press myself against him and… Talk about wrongness.

I squeezed my eyelids together so hard squiggly golden dots appeared. I fought against the seductive invasion. Vampires had influence over the weak, working their specialized, hot and heavy mojo.

Taking a shuddering breath, I forced myself beyond the sultry heat washing over me, through me—to find a way to stop him.

Hmm…yes, stop him from ever looking at another girl.

Everything he desired rested here in me. Fierce possessiveness, wanton, aching need—I gasped at the churning emotions.

Not mine.

Not real.

No wonder Paige obsessed over Wade. I'm sorry, *I* wasn't going to fall for his smoke and mirrors. My eyes flew open as Wade's right fist connected squarely with Alec's nose. A spray of blood sprinkled the concrete as Alec staggered.

Blood. Fresh. Tantalizing. Purely human. Damn, I'd gone from the frying pan directly to the source of the flame. My pulse drummed in my neck. The bad news? That wonderful aroma meant Alec was hurt.

I looked away from the bloody concrete and tried to remember my hunter training, tried to focus on Alec's injuries. No broken bones, just swelling where a clawlike scratch marked his cheek. He swiped a hand under his nose to clear the blood.

A smile hovered on Wade's lips. His eyes glowed. He was taunting Alec, flaunting his strength. With me too, because I couldn't fight his influence and tune out the heady scent of blood at the same time.

I told you the Delacroix were dangerous. Wade's voice again, bold and confident. Only his lips weren't moving. He didn't even look in my direction as he and Alec stalked each other in a wary circle. *Smashing my car, attacking me this way was stupid, Eryn. See how careless they are?*

My breath caught in my throat. Why was he mind-talking as if he knew every doubt I had about the Delacroix? Wade laughed aloud, and a ripple of fear crawled up my

spine. And then it hit me.

Lovely.

Wade could not only enter my bedroom, he could tap into my thoughts. My body tensed as if to run. Pointless. No escape. Wade prowled in my mind like he owned me. My wolf roared in outrage. I couldn't manage them both. Desperate to shut Wade out, my vamp-thralled, beast-wracked brain began regurgitating hunter-vampire rules of engagement. Christian symbols had power. The cross. The rose. Both red with blood. No. There was something else. Something my father told me. That's it! I imagined a solid limestone wall and slammed it to the ground between us.

An unbearable quiet settled over me. How singular and strange. I tamped down the surge of loneliness that begged me to stop fighting and let Wade in. To let him know the wolf, to understand *me*.

Hadn't I already learned my lesson? Though I wouldn't rest until I saw my parents' bodies with my own eyes—whether they were alive…or dead—even they had never understood me.

So why did I expect it from a vamp witch? Or a small town hunter for that matter?

Bitterness strengthened the mental wall between me and Wade as he and Alec circled each other. I'd broken his link, beaten the affect. Barely. I shivered. Why hadn't I paid more attention when my father had bored me with a lecture on visualization techniques and how to use them?

A shove from behind caught me off guard. I stumbled. Brit, and she was panting. The effort to get assistance quickly,

without breaking into a run, had obviously tired her out. She was lucky she hadn't gone all seizure-y and collapsed on the concrete. How in the world did she function as a hunter? Why would Alec let someone with such a disability join his crew? Sure, Brit was smart and a great cheerleader, but she'd mess up a hunt. It didn't make sense.

I held out a hand to steady her.

"I brought reinforcements," she yelled, although she was right beside me.

I flinched and covered my ears as her words screamed through my head. What Brit lacked in speed, she made up for in volume. I'd been concentrating so hard on blocking Wade, I'd forgotten to regulate my hearing to human levels.

Mr. Riggs and Matt shouldered past us and rushed into the middle of the fight. Mr. Riggs wedged himself in front of Wade while Matt grabbed Alec and whispered harshly into his ear as he pulled him away from Wade. I held my breath. Would Alec out Wade? Would Wade say *screw you* to the norm world and out himself? Right there in the Redgrave High parking lot?

A sea of curious faces surrounded the fight. Elbows and shoulders collided as students jostled each other for a better view. They hummed like fallen power lines, ready to do some damage. How blind my mom had been to human failings. One schoolyard squabble revealed their potential for violence. The kids shoving to get a better view proved wolven weren't the only beasts who enjoyed a good brawl.

My breath whooshed out on a relieved sigh as Alec and Wade were forced apart. Chests heaving, each turned away to

inspect his vehicle for damage.

Matt ran his hands over the truck's smashed-in hood, then shot Alec a dark look. Clearly, the brothers would have their own battle over Alec's stunt.

"We were right." Brit's mouth twisted in an ugly grimace. "Wade's paranorm through and through. If he were human, we'd be scraping pieces of his cabbage brain off the dashboard."

I scrunched my face. "Lovely image. And what a way to prove it. I hope Alec has severe whiplash or something." I linked my hands to hide their trembling. "He deserves it for pulling a lame stunt like this. Now's probably not the time to say this, but didn't Matt accuse *me* of being a hothead liability?"

Brit heaved a sigh. "Yeah, how's that for irony? A week ago this wouldn't have happened. But in the last few days Alec has started acting a bit…"

"Out of his mind?" I supplied.

"Unpredictable."

"Hmm," I mumbled, watching Alec run a frustrated hand through his black hair. "In the last few days?"

"Right." Brit cocked an eyebrow at me.

"You mean since I moved to town?"

Brit sighed like my dimness was too much to bear and nodded. Once.

"Ohhhh…." I stared at Alec with renewed curiosity. So I had Alec all twitterpated, did I? I pulled my gaze away from his broad shoulders. All the more reason I should steer clear of the crew. Hunting and flirting went together like a land mine and a clown on a pogo stick.

Mr. Riggs brushed between me and Brit. "Show's over folks. Move along."Everyone groaned in disappointment at his words. "Pick up the pace, or you'll be running suicides after school all next week. Hustle, hustle, hustle." His threat scattered the stragglers.

"Girls," he yelled in our direction. "Wade says you saw the accident. The police will be here soon to take your statements. Don't go running off."

The weight of Wade's and Alec's gazes both pulled me in different ways. A speedy escape would be so good right now. Being held for questioning because I'd witnessed the school's hottest guys smash up their rides and brawl in public wasn't exactly keeping a low profile. Wait till the Hunter Council got a whiff of this.

But I wanted to take off for reasons other than keeping my nose clean. I had issues with uniforms. Doctors, nurses, shrinks in suits. And I wasn't too comfortable with the whole stop-or-I'll-shoot thing cops had going either. After my parents disappeared, the police interviewed me, looking for clues, anything to help them figure out where my parents might have gone or who might have wanted them dead. I told the officers nothing. They were out of their league. No way were they ready for the monsters of my world.

I couldn't believe the way the cops treated me, though. Like *I* was on their list of suspects, me—the kid with the missing parents. The *victim*. I'd woken that morning to find my parents gone. That was all I could tell them. They'd wanted more. They'd asked questions, the same ones over and over. Phrased a hundred different ways. But my story

never changed, because paranormal or not, that was what had happened. My parents had vanished.

The finer details of those few weeks were a blur, lost in a haze of pain and fear, but I no longer had any illusions. Chivalrous cops didn't exist. Today's breed of law enforcement was jaded and suspicious, and generally not so nice. And who knew? In Redgrave they might also be vampires.

I had bitten my fingernails down to ravaged stumps by the time two officers arrived in a police car. It appeared the cops were on a first name basis with Wade. One even patted him on the back as if they were old buddies.

Nepotism, anyone?

Brit wrapped her arms around her waist, her face bleak. "No one messes with the chief's son. He's untouchable. My dad tried to give Wade a speeding ticket once and almost got fired."

I grimaced. "I forgot your dad was a taser toter." Life with a cop would be the ultimate freak out. You would either get away with murder, or you'd have no life of your own. "So Wade's dad is your dad's boss?" I was getting lost in the incestuous nature of Redgrave and its police force.

"Our families used to be real close. Until Blake died." Brit shook her head. "My dad hasn't been the same since."

I frowned, about to ask her for more details, when a cop about my height, overweight and barrel-chested, approached us. He gave Brit a brief glance of acknowledgement before settling his probing gaze on me.

"Eryn McCain?" he asked, pulling a ballpoint pen from a breast pocket monogrammed with the name "Officer Flutie."

I nodded.

"You moved in with Marcus McCain. Is that correct? You're the niece?"

I nodded again, slowly. How did he know that? And what did it have to do with the smash-up-derby I'd witnessed?

"Give your uncle a message for me, will you?" Flutie bared his teeth in a smile. "Tell him the next time he shows up on private property with his group of wing-nut treehuggers, we won't be so accommodating." He flicked his pen with a hard snap of his thumb, stuffed it back into his pocket, and stalked to his cruiser. His partner, who'd been chatting with Wade, joined him. They both glared over at me and Brit before getting in their vehicle.

"Guess he didn't want a statement after all." I shot Brit a questioning look, my stomach tense. "Any idea what that was about?"

She shook her head. "Just 'cause my dad's a cop doesn't mean I understand the way their minds work. Especially Redgrave cops." She looked past me, her expression hard.

A strong hand pressed down on my shoulder. "You see, Eryn." Wade's voice was like velvet—and nails on a chalkboard—as his cool breath fanned along my neck. "If you and Alec's band of merry men are so concerned with bringing down all of Redgrave's bad guys, I'm the least of your worries." He paused and ran his finger down my arm. His touch burned through my jacket like frostbite. "You better start looking in your own backyard."

Wade had clearly been snooping around in my thoughts for a while now. He knew I was worried about him getting

into my uncle's house and that I was thinking of working with Alec's crew.

I took a deep breath and checked my limestone shield, pleased he hadn't found a way around it. Part of me wanted to toss Wade to the ground and stake him with the nearest piece of wood, but part of me, the dark predator trying to claw its way out of me, hungered for Wade. A vampire with witchy powers. A hybrid. Like me. Didn't mean I could trust him. Or anyone.

"Do you mind?" I shrugged the weight of his hand from my shoulder and shoved any sympathy I had for him to a far, isolated corner of my mind. We were not the same. I was on the good-guy side of the line. Wade? Not so much. "If I wanted something dead around my neck, I'd get a fur coat."

"That's what I like about you." He placed a hand to his heart. "You're so honest, it hurts."

Brit took a step forward. "You want to hurt?" She shot a look to her left as Alec and Matt stalked toward us, their expressions fierce. "We can make that happen."

Wade smiled slightly at the crew's united front. His gaze drilled into mine. "Talk to your uncle, Eryn. Ask him how his day went. I'm sure it will be an enlightening conversation." He winked, but before I could respond, he was at the tow truck, climbing inside. His damaged sports car swayed on the hitch, resembling a crushed beer can on a frat boy's head.

Alec glowered as they pulled out of the parking lot. The loose bumper scraped along the concrete and let off sparks. "What did *he* want?"

"I'm not sure I should tell you," I snapped. "You might

go all look-at-me-I'm-a-crazed-berserker again."

"*Berserker*. Now there's a word you don't hear every day." Matt hugged Brit. "But in this case, I agree with Eryn. Brother of mine, you were way out of line. I know you've been weirded out ever since Mom told you—"

At a dark look from Alec, Matt glanced quickly at me and then back at Alec. "Well, you've been edgy lately, but that *doesn't* mean it's okay to act without consulting the rest of us."

"I said I'd give Wade a message," Alec said. "That's sharing information. Besides, now we know for sure Wade's a paranorm. And if Eryn's dream theory holds up, he's possibly a vampire who's able to walk in sunlight." Alec gave me an assessing glance. "But you still haven't told us what Wade said to you."

"Oh, he put the moves on Eryn, but she brushed him off." Brit jumped in with a wave of her hand. "But before that, the police officer pretty much threatened Eryn's uncle. I've never seen him before, so he must be one of Logan's new recruits. I definitely felt negative vibes coming off him, didn't you, Eryn?"

I shrugged. "Aren't negative vibes what cops do best?"

Brit looked a bit forlorn.

Oops. I'd forgotten about Officer Dad. "I have no idea what Flutie was talking about. Something about Marcus and a group of treehuggers. Maybe they protested on private property and the cops got involved." I paused. "Although I've never thought of Marcus as the protest type." Nope, that was more my mother's thing.

"Doesn't sound very paranormal to me," Matt said.

"No, it doesn't," I agreed. "But then Wade came along and made a big deal about it too. Told me we should look in my own backyard for bad guys."

Matt's expression brightened as if he were pleased my family and I were getting blamed for something.

Alec's jaw flexed. "If he's threatening your home, we'd better crank up our security. You know, the best place for you is our ranch, where we can keep an eye on you." He looked trapped, as if the thought of me hiding out at their place held all the thrill of a social dance class in gym.

I didn't want anyone's pity patrol. I could handle Wade myself. "Although I hate to say *no* to that gracious invitation"—I gave a mock bow—"*if* that's what it was, I think I should stick close to home and snoop around. See what the deal is with my uncle. It's got to be freaky and paranormal, or Wade wouldn't have wiped my nose in it."

Brit and Matt exchanged a look. "She's right," they said in unison.

I grinned at them. Only Brit grinned back.

"Hey, Alec!" A big burly guy hopped out of a second tow truck and began unwinding a thick chain. "Let's get you hooked up."

Alec gave the guy a wave.

"Okay," he told me, "we're going to be here a while. Get home, find out whatever you can about the treehugger issue, and wait until we tell you your next move."

"Right." I folded my arms. "Should I hold it if I have to go to the bathroom too? Or are potty breaks something I can make a command decision on?"

"You don't like taking orders. I get it," Alec said, not in the least apologetic. "And I don't like repeating them, or explaining myself. But I'm trying to keep you safe, Eryn." Determination hardened his voice. "You want to go it alone, say the word, and we'll leave you to it."

I swallowed back a mouthful of angry words. Without access to my father's men and resources, I had no way to keep Wade from entering the McCain household. I had more than myself to worry about. I had to keep my family safe. Besides, agreeing to be available when Alec called didn't mean I had to sit on my hands.

When I kept my mouth resolutely shut, Alec continued, "Once we get to the ranch, we'll find out how to keep Wade out of your house tonight, and *every* night. I promise."

But what about my mind? I wanted to shout the question at Alec, but the crew didn't need the additional stress of knowing Wade was trying to influence me with telepathy. Vampire mind games were individual and very personal. Part of their lure was the senders' absolute understanding of their prey. They knew exactly what buttons to push.

And Wade was certainly pushing ones I never knew I had.

Brit gave me a supportive smile. "Marie will know how to stop him. We'll be in touch." She paused. "Are the McCains religious? Do they have any crucifixes at home? Your athame is super cool and everything, but it's not going to help with Wade."

I blinked. I hadn't thought of that. For so long my athame had been my major defense, but then my father's cell

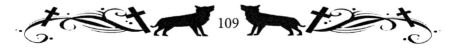

of hunters had been focused on rogue werewolves and wolven.

"Crucifixes? I don't know." I couldn't remember seeing any religious symbols on Sammi's trendily painted walls. Generic artwork, yes. Crucifixes, no.

Brit fished in her pocket and handed me a small medallion. "Take this. It's St. Anthony. He finds stuff for people who chronically lose things, like I do. Until we bring you some supplies tonight, he's all you've got."

I closed my fingers around the silverplated saint and thanked her through gritted teeth. As soon as the crew left for the truck I dropped the medallion into my backpack. A small reverse imprint scalded my palm, red and itchy—but already fading.

"It's the thought that counts, Eryn," I muttered, knowing Brit would never have given me the medallion if she'd known the pain it would inflict. My aching flesh would be back to normal in minutes, but any kind of silver burn was nasty. A full wolven would have thrown the medallion back in her face. I'd be in a lot more pain if the thing had been solid silver.

I started toward home. Now to figure out what kind of trouble my dear Uncle Marcus was into. *Crap.* I was starting to think of my uncle's place as *home*, which meant on some level—I cared. A lot.

So not good.

A Little Knowledge is a Dangerous Thing

Twenty minutes later, I shuffled down the narrow lane behind Marcus's house, cringing at the ever-present barks and snarls from the neighbor's yellow Lab. I couldn't blame it for raging against the world, at the mercy of a higher power. *You and me, Cujo. We're in the same stinking boat.* If only I could string up the dog's owner, along with Sebastian, the guy pulling *my* leash. Now that would be the day. I pictured Mr. Philips droning on and on in physics-speak about the karmic laws of nature while Sebastian sat at a school desk, bungee cords strapping him in. And me, with the *bwahaha* evil giggles. Holding a can of gasoline and a match.

All too soon my payback fantasy went up in smoke.

As I reached the whitewashed gate, muffled grunts and clanging came from inside the McCain's detached double garage. My neck hairs vibrated like stage speakers at a deathgrind concert.

Not good.

Someone was inside, rummaging through my uncle's things. Someone dared to threaten my home. My people. My pack.

Inhaling, I picked up familiar scents drifting from the house, the garage. Sammi's baby-powder cleanliness, Paige's cotton-candy perfume, and Marcus with his lemony cologne. And then some lingering car exhaust.

I opened the gate and sprinted along the narrow path bordering the fence. Silent but fast, my feet skimmed the ground. At the garage I pressed my back to the grey vinyl siding and slunk along until I reached the narrow window. I peered inside, but a shelf filled with birdseed and ceramic flowerpots blocked my view. I ducked under the windowsill and crept along until I reached the side access door. Behind the thick wood, metal clanged and the occasional whispered curse came from inside.

I sniffed around the doorframe, tried to get a lock on the scent. Werewolf? Or human? All I got was the nose-hair-burning fumes of paint thinner.

Damn Sammi and her furniture restoration projects. She'd been working in the garage all week, refinishing an old church pew for the porch.

I let my backpack slip from my shoulders to land softly

on the grass. I lifted the edge of my sweater. My fingers curled around the rosewood handle of my athame, warm from the leather shoulder holster I'd started to consider a wardrobe standard. I whipped out the dagger and held it high, ready to plunge it deep into whoever, or whatever, skulked inside.

I took a deep breath. Pivoting on my back foot, I struck the wooden door with a solid side kick that ripped it from its hinges. It slammed down onto the garage's concrete floor, sending a cloud of sawdust into the air.

I paused. Silence. Did I scare them off, or were they lying in wait? Pulse thudding in my ear, I crept forward and peered through the empty doorframe.

My uncle's startled, pain-filled face stared up at me from under the mangled door. His mouth gaped open, and he let out a deep groan.

I shot a quick glance around the garage. Only Marcus. On the floor. Under the door. No signs of a struggle or an intruder.

Craptastic.

"Marcus?" I angled my body away from him and swiftly tucked my athame into its holster. I adjusted my sweater over the silver dagger, then yanked the heavy wooden slab off my uncle's chest.

"Eryn, is that you?" he asked. *Whew.* He was so dazed he hadn't noticed my dagger or that I'd tossed the door aside like an empty pizza box.

"Yeah, it's me," I mumbled as I pulled him to his feet. "What hurts?" At least he wasn't bleeding. I would have smelled it the instant he was injured. "Anything broken?"

"Nothing. I'm fine." Wobbling, he pushed my hands away. "This is what I get for putting off cleaning the garage for so long."

Berating myself for panicking like an amateur and endangering a human, I dusted off his plaid, collared shirt and talked fast. I'd discovered people were more inclined to swallow the lies you fed them if you didn't give them time to chew on your words.

"Wow," I said, blinking innocently. "That was some wind. Came out of nowhere and blew the door right in. I walked into the yard and saw the whole thing."

Marcus harrumphed, patted himself down, and rubbed a spot on his lower back. "Wind did that?" He eyed the trees, visible through the now-open garage. Not one branch swayed with even the gentlest of breezes. The sun hung low in the sky. A beautiful fall afternoon.

I couldn't get a break. "Yup. Maybe it was a mini twister. Remember when you picked me up at the airport, and it was so windy it almost knocked me over?" I fabricated on the fly. "Didn't you tell me that you get a lot of tornados around here?"

"Not that I recall, although we do get the occasional twister." He swung his head around to run his gaze over his black Volkswagen. Luckily, it was parked far enough from the side door to have escaped harm.

I shrugged, waving a hand. "Maybe that was a dream I had. Sometimes they're scary-real, you know?"

"Tornadoes?"

"No, dreams." I tilted my head and gave him a concerned

frown. "Are you sure you're okay? I bet you fell pretty hard."

Marcus studied me for a long moment. My stomach dropped. He didn't believe me.

"You know, Eryn," Marcus said, his voice slow and deliberate, "I'm experiencing a fairly strong feeling of déjà vu." He heaved the wooden door upright and propped it in the doorframe. Bits of sawdust and dirt sprinkled the floor. "Your father had a habit of busting down doors too."

"Seriously?" My father hadn't told me much of his life before he joined the Council. "He busted down doors?" Dad was strong for a human, but he didn't have superhero strength.

Marcus nodded. "Personally, I think he watched too many action movies. He had a thing for kicking in doors and *saving* us from Lord knows what. Back then Liam's exploits were our parents' problem, but if this is going to be a habit, tell me now so I can add an allowance for new doors to our monthly household budget."

I grimaced and stared at my shoes. "I guess the apple doesn't fall far from the tree then, does it?" I balanced my weight on the outer edges of my Mary Janes before adding, "I heard someone in the garage and just reacted. Before I knew it, I'd kicked the door in. It won't happen again, I promise." I lifted my chin to scrutinize Marcus's expression, praying he hadn't witnessed my zooped-up strength.

He stood there, hands on his hips. Plainly shocked, but not because he suspected I was Supergirl.

"Let me get this straight," he said. "You thought there was a *thief* in our garage—and you expected to do what? Beat him into submission with your homework? You barely bring

any home with you anyway." He swiped ineffectually at a dark grease stain spreading on his navy dress pants.

While the thought of Marcus worrying about my safety eased some of the sting of the no-one-wants-you-here vibe I'd been getting from Paige since I moved in, I couldn't help but feel a bit miffed at the homework jibe. I was a hunter and wolven to boot—I so didn't need to slam villains with textbooks. "I've been training with Dad since I was a kid. Martial arts and self defense." *And tracking werewolves and strange nasty things that go bite in the night and aren't supposed to exist.*

"You know, you even sound like your father. I never understood how someone that brilliant could be such a thrill seeker. Let me tell *you* what I used to tell *him*. A little knowledge is a dangerous thing, especially when it comes to that Rambo nonsense Liam was so fond of. It can give you a false sense of confidence. Make you take risks."

"I don't take risks," I protested, ignoring Marcus's disbelieving snort. "But I did flatten you with a door." My cheeky grin had no effect on him.

Marcus walked over to the door he'd propped up and then shot a look at my skinny (but toned!) arms in my wool sweater as if speculating how much I could bench press—and wondering how in the world I had managed to lift the solid slab of wood.

"So you know a few moves and you think you're pretty tough," he said. "None of that does any good if the other guy has a gun. The next time you think you've stumbled onto a crime scene, walk away and call 9-1-1. That's an order."

I winced. I really hated that word.

Marcus's lips twisted. "Make that the request of a concerned uncle."

I smiled and held out a hand. "You've got a deal," I lied.

Marcus stepped into the doorway and frowned. "Those hinges must have been rusted right out. You ripped them from the door jamb." He strode over to a worktable and sorted through a bin of nuts and bolts. The grating clang of metal on metal rang through the garage. I rolled my eyes. So *that* was the commotion I'd heard. Talk about overreacting.

"I think I have a few extras in here somewhere." He gave a long sigh. "This is so what I needed after today."

"What happened today?" I plucked a metal washer out of the bin and slipped it onto my finger like a ring.

"Harbinger Properties happened." Marcus found two hinges and set them aside.

Harbinger? Didn't that mean impending-badness-on-the-way or something? Not the typical publicity-buzz name most executives chose.

At my silence, Marcus glanced at me. "Haven't you seen the commercials?" He adopted a deep voice-over tone. "*The future is here. The future is now.*"

"Uh…no. I haven't." I dropped the washer back in the bin, willing my heebie-jeebies to go away, but they didn't. They got worse.

"A few months ago a group of ranchers came to the office." Marcus lifted a stack of sandpaper and peeked beneath it. "They'd all been offered a substantial amount of money from Harbinger to sell their land. As in immediately."

He paused. "Where's my hammer?" He shoved a rusted old bicycle chain and a clump of soiled rags out of the way. "Thing is," he continued, "they don't want to sell. So they told the Harbinger sales rep to get stuffed. Next thing they knew, their cows were attacked in their fields. Horses were found slashed to death."

The disgust and horror on my uncle's face told me all I needed to know.

No way was Marcus involved. I ground my back molars, miffed at how easily Wade had made me doubt my own.

As a wolven, I should have put more faith in my kin, my pack.

A good man in the middle of something much darker than he could ever imagine. I had to keep Marcus safe. Harbinger Properties was the real evil. I had to uncover their plan. Without kicking in any more of Marcus's doors, if I could help it.

"And let me guess, Harbinger is throwing some muscle around?"

"Exactly. Buildings look as if they'd been hit with a wrecking ball. Legally we have no proof the developer is trying to scare people into selling. All I can do to help is file complaints." Marcus harrumphed. "Lot of good *that's* done." His slightly rounded chin tightened.

"But why would anyone buy up ranches out here? No offense, but this is the frozen North, not Vancouver oceanfront."

Marcus laughed. "You're right. I can't figure it out. We're the last town before miles of bush straight to the North Pole."

I raised a brow. *The North Pole? Since when?*

"A small exaggeration," Marcus conceded. He leaned his hip on the worktable and crossed his arms. "But we *are* at the edge of civilization. At first I thought maybe the company was searching for oil, but if the government hasn't found it yet, it doesn't exist."

"Okay," I said slowly, thinking aloud. "If you and the ranchers are only filing complaints about Harbinger and fighting them the great paper way, why did Officer Flutie want me to pass along a message to you?"

Marcus uncrossed his arms when I paused dramatically.

"A friendly, not-so-friendly warning to stay off private property?"

Uncle Marcus pushed away from the worktable so hard it banged against the wall and knocked a hammer off a shelf. He avoided my curious gaze. "Ah, there's my hammer." He picked up the tool and the two hinges and strode to the door. "When did you see Flutie?" he asked over his shoulder, super casual like.

He was so hiding something. "I witnessed a fender bender at the school today, and he showed up to make the report. But he never even asked me about the accident, wanted to know if I was your niece. Then he told me to give you that message." I smirked, just a little, and folded my arms across my chest as he had moments ago. "So what did you do?" I paused. "Kick down a door, maybe?"

Marcus flushed. "Something like that. We held a protest this morning, but it got a little out of hand." His tone was dismissive, like getting out of hand was something he dealt

with on a daily basis at his *oh, so dangerous* real estate law firm.

I didn't buy it for a minute.

He glanced at his watch. "It's getting late. Let's cover up that hole and fix the door before Sammi gets home. It could snow any day now, and I might not have time to clean up this mess until the weekend."

He wasn't going to tell me anything else, so I let it go and went along with his conversation shutdown. I'd probably find out more on my own anyway. We spent the next hour working on the door. When it was securely fastened again, and no fresh air was circulating through the garage, Marcus began to sneeze.

As I eased my way out of his allergy zone, the automatic garage door opener rattled and jerked into action.

Sammi pulled in and hopped out of her car. "Hey, guys." She gave us a curious look and a smile. "What's up?"

I waited for Marcus to rat me out and tell her about my recent garage redecorating, but he gave me a deliberately casual glance. "Oh, we're hanging out. Let me help you with that." He rushed to help Sammi remove a heavy box of binders from the backseat.

"I've got to get started on my homework," I said over the *How was your day dear? Good how was yours?* conversation they had slipped into, and left Marcus to explain his sawdust-covered clothes and grease-stained cheeks.

In my room I sprawled on my springy mattress, hands behind my head, and gazed at the ceiling. Cujo was barking her fool head off again, and it took all my strength to keep from jumping out the window, hurdling the six-foot fence, and freeing the poor thing. I imagined myself kneeling beside her, patting her fur, hugging her tight—giving her all the affection she'd been denied. Miraculously, the barking outside paused momentarily.

I sat up at the silence, my vision a bit blurry, my head aching.

Whoa, had I done that? Had I communicated with the dog from this distance? I tilted my head and listened.

The barking started up again, sharper and louder than before.

I groaned and sank back down onto my pillow. I didn't think anything could be worse than the time my father recorded a banshee wail and blared the track over and over to trap the banshee with its own call.

Evaluating the last two day's events, I couldn't help but wonder if the Hunter Council had known all about the level of paranorm activity in Redgrave. And about the Delacroix. If throwing me into the mix was some sort of test to see what my father had created. Or maybe to see whether I'd fight the town's growing damnation, or if I'd accelerate the process by joining Wade and Logan.

Maybe Sebastian had been in on it from the beginning. Had he been working for the Council when he sent me away, before I could start asking questions about my parents? After all, Redgrave had been his suggestion. How could I have

trusted the man who was responsible for my father being cast out of the Council?

Now I was torn between a vamp-witch and a green-but-keen hunter crew determined to take him down. Only thing was...I didn't want to see Wade get hurt. I freaked at the thought of Wade entering my uncle's house again, but not because I was afraid to take Wade on. When the time came—would I fight Wade off? Or would I welcome his darkness?

The grating tone of my cell phone, muffled by my backpack, provided a timely distraction. I dug through the mess and snagged the phone on the fourth ring.

"Are you alone?" Brit's voice, intense and worried.

I propped myself on my elbow and glanced around the lime green room. "Why? Shouldn't I be?" From Brit's tone, I expected to see Wade in his vamp mist form or a demonic face in my bedroom window. But all was normal as far as I could tell.

Brit sighed loudly in my ear.

"I mean are you good to talk? About...you know... stuff?"

Relieved no immediate paranormal visitors lurked outside, I relaxed back onto my pillows. "Yeah, what's up? You guys draw a *Vamps Keep Out* sign for Wade?"

A pause. Not where I wanted to hear one.

"Brit?" I sat up again. My heart raced. "You did figure out a way to keep Wade from entering the house, right? Alec's mom came up with something?"

"Well, not exactly."

"What does that mean?" I put a hand to my aching

forehead.

"Matt was right. You can't retract an invitation once a vampire's been invited."

I groaned.

"However, Marie knows a witch. A very powerful witch." Brit sounded starstruck. "Kate's also the coolest person I know. You should see how many piercings she has and her tats...anyway, once we told her about your dream and Wade inheriting his mom's power, well, that changed the rules a bit."

"Fine, Kate's the good witch of the north. But did she say the rules changed in a beneficial way?"

"Yes." Brit's voice was decisive. "His witchy talent makes him stronger than the usual vampire, but it also makes him more susceptible to magic." Brit paused again. "At least we hope so. Kate put a misdirection spell on him. Basically every time he tries to go to your house, he should get directed elsewhere and forget where he was headed in the first place."

I held the phone away from my ear and stared at it for a second, then spoke. "You're giving Wade a bad sense of direction. And that's supposed to save *my life*?"

"Don't worry. Matt's been tailing Wade to make sure the spell is working. So far he hasn't made any moves toward your end of town. Alec's stocking up on anti-vampire gadgets, a water gun that shoots holy water, stuff like that, and then he's going to watch your place all night."

"He's going to *watch it*? From where?" I pictured Alec miles away with some high-tech binoculars.

"Hello? From right out front. He'll park near your house

and do regular patrols around the area." I heard the grin in Brit's voice. "You know, like a stakeout."

"A stakeout to fake out a vampire," I said, not amused.

"Yup. Personally, I believe it's impossible to overmilk vampire puns."

I walked to my bedroom window and pushed aside the daisy print curtain. Sure enough, a vehicle was pulling to a stop on the dimly lit street across from the house. Once the driver killed his lights, I made out Alec's dark hair sliding over his broad shoulders as he leaned forward in the seat. Without conscious effort, my vision blurred for a second, then narrowed, and cut through the twilight to circle in on Alec.

So maybe I was spying, cheating—using my vision to see things I shouldn't. Like the tension in Alec's body as he scanned the street. Worried Wade would get to me. How cramped he seemed in the tiny hatchback with his knees pressed against the steering wheel. His truck probably undrivable after he'd turned it into a slinky-mobile by smashing it into Wade's car.

He shot a look at my room, a look a human wouldn't be able to see. I stepped away from the window, but the heat in Alec's eyes drew me back to the glass. The curve of my cheek warmed, my lips tingled as he stared up at me, backlit by my bedroom light. He waited to see what I'd do.

I was tempted to raise the window, jump off the ledge, and run to him. My fingers searched for the latch, but then froze. How quickly would his interest cool if he saw me tossing doors around? Or if he knew Wade had slipped into my thoughts? If the Delacroix were as versed in vamp lore as I

thought they were, Alec would know that a vampire can only enter a mind already susceptible to darkness. A soul walking the fine line between good and evil.

"Eryn…earth to Eryn. Are you still there?" Brit's yell startled me. I let the curtain fall, watching through the lace as Alec turned away. Eyes forward, he huddled low in his seat and pulled his coat collar up around his chin.

"Sorry, Alec's parked outside. Is he really going to stay there all night? That's crazy. It'll be freezing and uncomfortable. There's got to be another way."

"It's just for one night, until we know the spell is working. If Wade doesn't show, you should be fine. Now if *Alec* wants in your room?" Brit laughed. "You're on your own."

I closed my eyes against the sudden rush of heat low in my stomach. What *would* I do if Alec appeared at my window? Wanting in? Wanting me?

What were these guys doing to me?

When I remained silent, Brit sighed. "Don't have a hissy fit. I was joking. Since I think I've covered everything, I'll let you go. I know you're going to be wigging about Wade and everything, but don't forget to study for that physics exam tomorrow."

I was so sick of tests it wasn't even funny.

A PEEPING PAIGE

I alternated between studying my textbook and skulking at the window studying Alec's shadowy form in his car. By 11:07 p.m., I'd skimmed over the corresponding formula and sample questions until my eyes crossed. *Thwack.* I closed my textbook and bailed on Sir Isaac Newton's third law of motion. It was making me seasick.

I stretched with a groan. I had zero understanding of Brit's love of textbook education. I preferred to learn what I needed through trial and error, *living* life—not reading about it.

I flicked off my desk lamp and crept to the window as I had a dozen times since Alec's arrival.

Even in the low lighting of the neighborhood porches,

I could easily make out the little hatchback. The driver door opened, and Alec slipped from the vehicle. In long strides, he crossed the street to my uncle's house. For a second he paused on the lawn and stared up at me. His gaze bored into me. My heart jolted in an erratic beat. I sliced my gaze away and pressed a hand to my stomach, trying to calm its schoolgirl flips. When I regained control, he was gone. His third patrol so far.

I traced delicate lacework ice crystals on the cool glass. I knew I should stay inside, not attract attention to myself by helping Alec patrol. But I was going loopy sitting around while someone else hunted the bad guys.

I flicked the latch and opened the window. I told myself I was only furthering my education. Putting Newton's theory to the test. *For every action there is an equal and opposite reaction.* Therefore, since Alec went on a patrol to protect *me*, *I* was sneaking out of the house to protect *him*.

This time my rooftop exit was graceful, no running jump. I hesitated at the edge. I couldn't look down without wooziness. I dealt with heights when I had to, but it didn't mean I enjoyed the experience. I closed my eyes, took a deep breath, and stepped off. Air rushed over my body. My stomach dropped as I plummeted to the ground. I landed on both feet and barely registered the impact. My very existence, my wolven abilities, my extra-human strength—all added up to some major laws-of-physics rule breaking. Paranorms would have rocked old Newton's world. Or maybe he had known about them but spent his life trying to find some scientific way to explain their existence.

Like my dad.

Forcing the thought aside, I sprinted around the corner where Alec had slipped out of view. Taking in sharp gusts of air, I sniffed out his scent on the night breeze. There. Tantalizing with spicy undertones. So different from Wade's crisp mint. I followed Alec's invisible trail. He had climbed the fence to our backyard.

Away from the glow of house lights, this side of the garage was in complete darkness except for the small flashlight Alec panned back and forth like a windshield washer. He paused at the hedges lining the yard.

I snuck up behind him.

"You think a guy like Wade hides in shrubbery?" I asked.

He gasped, then spun to face me. The flashlight burned into my retinas like a laser eye surgery disaster. I threw up a hand to block the brilliant beam.

"Do you mind?" I retreated a few steps.

He lowered the light to illuminate the grass between us. "Where did you come from?"

I shrugged. "I snuck out." I blinked hard, not mentioning exactly *how*. "I couldn't sit around while you were out here patrolling. Besides, I guess the spell worked. No sign of Wade, not even a smidge of vamp mist."

Alec pulled a cell phone out of his pocket. The green glowing screen lit his face. "Matt said Wade keeps driving around town in circles. He starts for this subdivision but ends up back at his house."

"That's gotta be frustrating for him." I grinned through my unease. The last thing I wanted was for Alec to see through

my bravado to the heebie-jeebies settling in my gut, warning me no spell, no matter how powerful the witch who cast it, would stop Wade.

Or prevent me from making a huge mistake if I let him in.

Alec's broad shoulders jerked in an impatient shrug. "As long as it keeps him away from you, I could care less if his fangs get twisted."

My heart tripped at his words. Was he jealous? Or merely concerned for my safety?

He gave me an assessing look. "Did you ask your uncle about that cop today?"

"Yeah, Marcus is representing a group of ranchers being run off their land. He's lodged complaints and started protests. My guess is the property developer bought off Wade's dad, because Marcus said the cops are doing zilch to stop the scare tactics."

Alec peeked around the garage toward the house. "So why did Wade want you to check into Marcus?" He paused, then tipped his flashlight up to my face. "What's the name of the developer?"

I squinted back at him through the harsh light.

"Would you stop that?" I shoved his hand down and tried to ignore the warming shivers that flooded me whenever we touched. "The developer? Hmmm…it was this really ominous sounding phrase, you know? Harbinger something."

Alec gave a dry laugh, opened the back gate, and slipped into the alley. I trailed in his wake.

"What's so funny?" I stood in the open gateway as Alec

checked out the access lane, his stance alert though the night was quiet.

"The developer didn't have to pay Logan off. He *is* Harbinger. Logan owns the company."

I frowned. "Are you sure? Isn't that like a conflict of interest or something?"

Alec shrugged. "Maybe, but it's not common knowledge."

"Then how do you know he owns it?"

Sculpted lips slanted into a sarcastic smile. "Because Harbinger tried to buy our ranch a few years ago. Back then, Logan wasn't so hush-hush about his controlling interest in the company. My dad had it out with him more than once before...."

"Before he died?" I asked, then flinched as pain flickered in Alec's eyes. I had to steel myself for the anguish that knotted the air around Alec each time he mentioned his dad. He'd told me the Hunter Council had done nothing to track his dad's killer, but knowing Alec and Matt, there had to be a whole lot more to the story. Stillness settled in my body...a hush, a fear. What if a rogue wolven had killed Alec's father? How would Alec ever accept me?

"How did your father die exactly? What got him?"

The light in Alec's hand flashed upward. "What got him?" he echoed, his expression harsh.

I so knew that look. I'd glimpsed it in my reflection many times. The look of someone whose pain was eating them up inside, but who'd never let it show.

Choking on the lump of sorrow jammed in my throat, I cupped a hand over my mouth. "God, that was rude," I

mumbled against my fingers. "Forget I asked it."

"No, it's okay. I've got nothing to hide." Alec straightened as if bracing himself for my reaction. "I'm warning you, this will make me sound like a mystical native. Cue the ceremonial drums and flutes playing in the distance." He shook his head. "I hate that stereotype." He met my eyes in the darkness. "Ever heard of a Windigo?"

I shook my head.

"It's a Cree myth, passed on by my mother's people, the Métis. The Windigo is a wicked creature, half-man, half-beast that lives only in the North. It loves the cold because its heart is made of ice."

He did sound all mystic. His words, the tone of his voice—I could almost hear the drone of war drums. But he wasn't just sharing a bit of cultural folklore.

"Windigos feed on human flesh. The more they eat, the bigger they get and the more they kill."

"And that thing...the Windigo," I struggled to sound out the unfamiliar word, "killed your dad?"

"Yeah. My father was a good hunter, did everything by the book. The Hunter Council told him to go after it, to use my mom's knowledge of the legend to take it down." Alec's lips twisted. "Mom appealed to the Council, spoke with some top level guy from Vancouver. She insisted that one hunter wasn't enough, no matter how skilled he was. The Council must send help; they'd underestimated the Windigo's trickster ways."

The beam of his flashlight moved over the lawn, residual glow illuminated his set jaw and rigid posture. "But they

didn't send anyone, so my dad went alone. Months passed, he never came back. Some Council guy showed up with a wad of cash. Told her the Council was sorry for our loss. An arrogant puke. Had bodyguards all around him."

Full of himself and surrounded by goons. That sounded an awful lot like my dear friend Sebastian. Mr. Big Bossy Pants, yet intimidated enough by the paranorms to have round-the-clock protection.

"To them, my dad was another casualty in an ongoing war. He'd been assigned a remote outpost. They never expected much action around here and treated it like an isolated incident." His hand formed a fist. He thrust it into his jean pocket.

"So what did you do?" I held my breath.

"Matt and I went after it, and with the help of…friends." Alec smiled, a sharp quirk of his lips. "We killed it. End of story. Like all shapeshifters, as long as pure silver strikes its heart, the Windigo disintegrates."

I jerked back a pace at the mention of a heart full of silver. *We killed it, the end.* Now that was a glossed-over version of one hell of a story. Who were these friends? Brit, the I-can't-run-to-save-my-life girl, and what army? Still, they'd done it. Tracked their father's killer, their own personal monster, and slain it. Visions arose of Alec and Matt spending night after night patrolling for their father's killer. Tracking it. Taking it down.

I wanted to revel in their triumph.

But epiphanies had a way of taking the *reveling* out of *revelation.* I'd been so stupid. That's what I should have been

doing all this time. Tracking my parents. Not toeing the line for Sebastian and the Council. How long did it take for them to get their revenge? A week? Two? I waited for Alec to rub my nose in how efficiently he and Matt had avenged their father's death while I'd wasted months doing nothing for my parents.

But Alec only stared into the night, his gaze unfocused. "You know, before my dad died, I used to want to split town, run off and join the Council's training academy. Become one of their soldiers." He snorted. "But now I know the Council's not much different from Logan—breeding his army, brainwashing the town, sending his minions to fight his battles. Someone has to help the humans who get in his way." Alec gave me a pointed look. "Matt and I will never make the mistake my dad did. We don't go after paranorms alone. We work as a team. We have each other's backs. And when we tell someone to stay inside for their own safety—we expect them to do as they're told."

I grinned. "But I'm not a helpless civilian. I'm part of the crew, remember?"

"I don't know what you are, Eryn." His glance took in my strong, lean form, sending a tingle of awareness through me. "But I knew you wouldn't sit on your hands for long."

A pang of guilt gripped my heart. If only he knew how long I'd done absolutely nothing to find out what happened to my parents, he wouldn't be so impressed.

"You said Harbinger is behind the land grab, and Logan is behind Harbinger. And that means what?" I dug my heels into the frozen earth, needing to feel grounded. "When people

wouldn't sell their land, Logan created a pack of werewolf wise guys to do his dirty work?"

"Looks like."

"And the cops needed a scapegoat, so they blamed your family? Nice." I met his gaze. "How do we prove it?"

"*We* don't." Alec's face softened into a smile. "At least we don't tonight. Get back in the house and stay put. Kate put wards around your house, so you'll be protected inside. Until I'm sure Wade's bedroom stalking days are over, you have to do as I say. I want you safe."

Once again his words hit me hard, but this time it wasn't pain curling low in my stomach. Forget rules. Forget orders. I wanted nothing more than to rattle Alec, to make him lose some of that brooding control. My heart pounded as I took a bold step forward.

"You want me safe?" I sidled up against Alec's warm body. At his swift intake of breath, I smiled, letting the tension build. He smelled of sweet spice and possibilities.

He dipped his head. His lips drifted slowly down to mine. The heat of his breath feathered over my sensitive skin.

I grabbed his coat collar and pulled myself onto my toes, wanting his kiss and wanting it fast. The intensity of the moment fed the wolven yearning for power, for freedom, to feel alive, that rushed through my veins like a tsunami. Alec's lips brushed against mine.

Sweet, but I wanted more. I opened my mouth and drew him in.

Alec groaned low in his throat, then grabbed my arms, and pulled me against him. His kiss was hard, urgent.

His full lower lip brushed against my teeth. I nipped at it. The unexpected deliciousness of his blood flooded my mouth as if I had ripped him open, cutting deep into his flesh. Hunger pangs ripped through my gut. Every cell in my body screamed at me to finish what I'd started. To bite deep, to shred, to tear. To destroy. I shoved Alec away, my heart racing, stomach coiled with hunger.

A streak of blood smeared across his dazed smile.

My nostrils flared. The scent of metal, tantalizing. My wolf surged to the surface.

We stared at each other under the starlight. My chest rose and fell with my gasping breaths. I couldn't lose it, not now. Not with Alec. *Don't think about the blood. Never the blood.*

Alec took a step forward, but I stumbled back, holding my hands up to keep him at bay. He frowned down at me.

"Go to bed, Eryn," he said, his voice husky. "We'll talk tomorrow."

Tomorrow. Yes, tomorrow, when I was more myself and wouldn't want to dig into him as if he were a chocolaty, gooey morsel. Already the distance between us lessened my craving.

I spied movement in my peripheral vision and turned. Curtains swayed at the twin dormer window next to my room.

Paige's bedroom. Her blue eyes, wide with shock, glimmered through the window before she ducked out of view.

A Peeping Paige.

Lovely.

Alec's phone pulsed. He held up a finger, freezing me in place. "What's up?" he said into the phone. He listened for a second.

Alarm flashed in his eyes before he turned away from me, his voice harsh. "Give me details. How close is it?"

I frowned. Still charged with wolven energy, need flared into anger as I observed Alec's rigid shoulders. Something was up, and I'd be damned if he'd shut me out. I focused on the muffled voice replying to Alec.

"Brit checked in," Matt said, his voice tense. "Another male. She spooked him and he bolted. They're about a block from you. I'm on my way to intercept."

"We should have known he'd send his wolves." Alec hunched over his phone and spoke low so I couldn't hear—if I was the human girl he thought I was. Fortunately, I wasn't. "Bring the rifle."

Alec snapped his phone shut, pocketed it, and then turned around, his face expressionless. "Like I said, Eryn, you should get inside."

Was he serious? "Uh, nope." I sidestepped him, opened the gate, and started down the alley, inhaling through my nose and mouth, searching for the werewolf's scent.

"What are you doing?" Alec called at my back. "Wait!"

I concentrated on getting a lock on the beast before Alec saw me sniffing the air like Fido tracking a floating rack of ribs. When the reek of death hit me, I was prepared, able to spin around and face Alec without gagging. A human wouldn't get to enjoy the full stench of werewolf until they were right on top of one.

136

"I heard something back here," I said. "Didn't you?"

"No," Alec said with an exasperated huff, "but Matt said a werewolf is headed this way." Alec lit up the lane of darkened garage doors and garbage bins loaded with trash. "If I can't convince you to get inside, then keep your eyes open and stay close."

Ticked by his domineering tone, I bit back the urge to demonstrate my superior tracking skills by telling him the werewolf was about two hundred feet down the alley, meandering in our direction.

A scuffle and crash resounded behind us. We whirled at the same time, Alec jerking his arms up to block a blow and me baring my teeth in a silent growl.

Yellow eyes gleamed in the distance, twin beams reflecting Alec's light. Alec inched forward, crouched low, but I let out a relieved sigh and tugged on his arm.

"Unless you want a tomato soup bath tonight, I wouldn't bother." At Alec's blank look, I grabbed his hand and pointed his flashlight toward the glowing eyes. "Skunk." The flashlight caught the cat-sized dark form as it ducked under a fence and disappeared. I had scented the stinky little bugger as soon as I'd entered the alley and promptly forgotten about it.

I laughed as Alec wrinkled his nose and tested the air as if he couldn't believe we'd escaped a skunk bath.

An explosion ripped through the night. Gunfire. I jumped, inhaling sharply as the singe of silver penetrating werewolf permeated the air.

Alec looked to the stars and gave a long sigh. "So we're good. Matt got it."

The hair on my arms stood upright. Okay, if Matt had taken down the werewolf, why did my muscles tighten, my ears strain for the slightest sound? Something was wrong. I inhaled again, letting the night air sharpen my senses.

Damn. Another one. How had I missed it?

A single yelp, choked off in the middle, then nothing. Not even the barking from the neighbor's Lab that had been driving me crazy for the last week.

I pivoted sharply and broke into a run, with Alec tailing me.

At the wooden fence surrounding the yellow Lab's yard, I gasped. Boards had been peeled back and shredded as if something large and paranormal had used them for a scratching post. A series of claw marks outlined the perimeter. I leaned closer and sniffed. A putrid stench lingered in the shredded wood fibers. Werewolf.

The grooves around the gap were deep, with five distinct claw marks. Whoa. Either these werewolves were unusually sloppy, leaving evidence like that behind, or they wanted to send us a personal message. Meaning they weren't following the rules.

I stepped through the hole, but Alec pulled me back.

"Wait for Matt, he has the rifle." His voice was a harsh whisper.

"Fine, stay here if you want to." I pulled out my athame. "I can handle a werewolf on my own."

Alec's dark eyes glittered. "Really? You and your fancy butter knife weren't doing so well when we saved you at the pet store."

"That was a fluke." I stood tall, a bit miffed when Alec smirked. He still had a foot on me, and my height didn't intimidate him one bit. "I slipped in bunny blood." Who did he think he was? Making me feel all defensive? Disrespecting my dagger? "There was more than a drop or two on the floor in case you hadn't noticed. We're talking a pool of blood." I paused. "Several pools."

"Oh, I noticed. But if you hadn't been so cocky, you would have walked *around* it the way we did." Alec's disapproving tone clashed with his heated gaze as it traveled from my eyes to my lips and rested there.

I tromped on the sudden urge to tilt my chin invitingly. Just because we both had tempers didn't mean we had to get hot and heavy at life and death moments. His gaze focused over my shoulder as if he expected someone to arrive any second, and I realized what he was up to. Damn him for using my own hormones against me.

"Are you done stalling?" I glanced around pointedly. "Matt's still not here. I'm going in." I placed my hands on either side of the hole and lifted one leg through.

Alec sighed. "You really are going to be the death of me."

"What does that mean?" I shot over my shoulder.

"Nothing." Alec waved me forward. "After you."

Inside the yard, we spotted the Lab's mangled chain and a few tufts of blood-drenched fur. I swallowed hard against a rush of guilt. If only I'd set the dog free when I'd wanted to… This was what came of following someone else's rules.

I didn't like it. Not one bit.

A gust of wind sent the werewolf's scent drifting over the

grass. It had jumped the fence and ducked into the woods that bordered Cowley Heights. But I couldn't give chase, not with Alec around. I was feeling seriously stifled.

"Heya," Brit called breathlessly from the alley side of the splintered fence. Alec and I trotted over and peeked through the gap.

She stood with Matt in the alley, Alec's truck sputtering behind them, the dents punched out, but sounding barely roadworthy.

"We got him." Matt's gaze skimmed over me and then settled on his brother's face. "What's going on?"

He climbed through the fence, followed by Brit.

Alec sighed. "The male wasn't hunting alone. One scooped up a dog."

Matt grabbed Alec's flashlight and cast it over the lawn, the tree, the chain—the blood.

"Ewww…" Brit stopped in her tracks and turned her back to the tree and bloodstained chain. Her chest rose and fell rapidly as if she'd been speed walking and had pushed her limits. A sheen of sweat glistened on her forehead.

Maybe this was too much for her.

I elbowed Alec to bring my concern to his attention, but he ignored me.

"There's bound to be leakage after a kill like that." He eyed the fence boards. "My guess is he jumped the fence over there, attacked the dog, and then busted out here." He rested a hand on my lower back to guide me through the gap in the fence. "Let's pick up the trail."

And that's when Mrs. Lurgen turned on her deck light

and all hell broke loose. She swept out onto her deck, a straw broom held high.

"Who's there?" she called out. "Cujo, where'd you get to? Some guard dog you turned out to be…damn fleabag."

Anger simmered inside me like steam from an espresso machine, ready to scald anyone standing too close. *She* was the one who'd left her dog tied to a tree night after night, helpless and abandoned, unable to escape when the werewolf attacked. *She* was the reason doggie bits were strewn all over her lawn. I wanted to smack her silly, gut her where she stood, and then really let her have it.

Mrs. Lurgen pulled a flashlight from her coat pocket and shined it around the yard, impaling us with its beam as we huddled around her fence. She gasped when she saw Alec. Her right hand twitched in front of her, her face scrunched into a mask of disgust, and then she spit in the air at us before she rushed back into the house.

"What," Brit drawled, "was that?"

"That was the old evil eye," I said, stunned and amused at the same time. "You know, make the sign of the cross, contort your face, and spit at the devil."

We all glanced at Alec.

"Nice. So now I'm Satan." Alec gave me a pained look. "Thanks."

I grinned. "No problem. But we better get out of here before she calls the police."

As we slipped through the fence, a wail of sirens rang in the night. We froze like gophers along the highway, trapped in a barrage of headlights. Two cruisers sped down the alley

from either direction and squealed to a halt a few feet in front of and behind Alec's idling truck.

I groaned. What happened to the delinquent Redgrave cops who didn't even show for the pet shop disaster? I'm sorry, what part of keeping my nose clean didn't I understand? I craned my neck as a cool breeze whipped my hair into my eyes. I cleared my vision and confirmed my suspicion—my uncle's bedroom light was now on. The sirens had penetrated his snoring.

Crappers.

My good friend Officer Flutie bore down on us from one car, while a short, stocky officer came at us from the other. Matt stiffened and exchanged a meaningful glance with Alec. I looked to Brit for strategy cues, but she was no longer beside me.

She was gone. That was weird.

"Where's Br—" I started.

Alec leaned into my shoulder, overwhelming me with his size and presence, forcing me to look up at him. He ever so slightly shook his head.

So I kept quiet, but I wondered how Brit had gotten away without running past one of the cars. Or had she snuck back into Lurgen's yard? Not a smart idea. That woman was on the warpath.

"Well, isn't this a surprise," Flutie said to his partner as they stopped in front of us. "The Delacroix boys and..." He stared at me, his lips pursed in thought. "Marcus McCain's niece. Eryn, wasn't it?"

I nodded.

142

Flutie glanced up at the lights shining from my uncle's windows.

"Does Marcus know you're out this late?" Flutie motioned toward Alec and Matt. "With them?"

I shook my head.

"Looks like he does now." Flutie laughed.

I turned. Marcus was striding down the back alley toward us in his slippers, stumbling over the length of his forest green bathrobe.

Lovely.

Smirking, Flutie folded his arms across his chest and rested them on the expanse of his belly, buttons straining on his standard issue blue shirt. I imagined that if he had a toothpick handy, he'd have been turning it over in his mouth. He seemed like that kind of cop, the rough around the edges, small town, vamp mind-controlled, wish I had a toothpick kind.

I wished he had one, too, so I could stake him with it.

"Officers, what's going on over here?" Marcus began. "We heard the sirens and saw the lights. Then my daughter noticed that my niece wasn't in her room." He pulled his robe tighter around his waist, his face stricken. "We looked through the whole house, but she's not inside. I thought maybe she came out to investigate the goings on here. She does rush into things. Have you seen her? She's tall, with dark hair." He glanced around at the faces watching him. "Looks rather like that girl…"

I gave a halfhearted wave, and Marcus did a double take. "Eryn!" He started toward me. "Thank God, you're all right."

"Not so fast, McCain." Flutie's hand shot out. "We have a situation that needs clearing up, and it involves the girl." His suspicious gaze sliced over to our silent group. "We got a call five minutes ago about a gunshot fired off further down this alley. We were scanning the area when we got another call from Mrs. Lurgen crying her head off about her dog, blood, and the Delacroix boys busting up her fence." He glanced sideways at Marcus. "When Officer Hiels and I arrived at the scene," he said, raising a brow, "your niece was with them."

Officer Hiels? Oh man, no wonder Brit pulled a Houdini. Her dad. Over Flutie's head, Marcus leveled me with a you-have-lots-of-explaining-to-do-young-lady look. Yup, Brit had it right. I, however, had to face the country music. Marcus glanced at Alec's clenched fists and Matt's hounded expression.

"Boys," he said, giving them a nod. "How's your mother doing? I haven't seen her in town for ages."

Flutie dropped his arm and glared at Marcus. "This isn't the time for polite conversation starters. Did you hear what I said? A gun has been fired, a dog has been—" He sliced his gaze to the other officer. "Hiels, get a statement from Mrs. Lurgen. Find out what she thinks happened to her dog."

By now a few curious neighbors had spilled into the alley and crowded around the police cars, trying to hear what we were discussing. They elbowed each other out of the way, jostling for the best view, staring at Alec and Matt with judging eyes. Only I could hear the slanderous words they were muttering to each other. They saw cop cars and the Delacroix boys, and that was all they needed to spark their fear of Marie Delacroix, her strange ways, and her equally

strange boys.

"I can tell you what happened to that poor dog," I said loudly, ignoring Alec's muffled curse as I shrugged off his restraining hand. "Everyone who lives around here knows Mrs. Lurgen has been neglecting that animal. She leaves it tethered to that tree 24/7, letting it bark its head off to get some attention." I stared into the closed faces of the crowd, daring one of them to contradict me. "It was only a matter of time before a bear wandered by searching for an easy meal."

A small murmur of agreement rustled through the crowd. I waved a hand at the leaning fence. "Even a coyote could have knocked through that. It's falling apart."

"That's true," a man called out in a grudging voice. "We had a bear in our yard last year. Jumped the fence to get to our crab apple tree."

I bit back a smile. "Wow. That's interesting. Because the tree that poor neglected Cujo was tethered to?" I blinked innocently. "Overflowing with ripe crab apples."

Flutie sucked in a frustrated breath. "What about the gunfire? Explain that. Everyone knows the Delacroix are hepped up on some fantasy about tracking down creatures of the night."

Amusement flickered in Flutie's eyes. He was enjoying the irony of this moment. The vamp-corrupted police officer pretending there was no such thing as a paranorm. Then Alec's truck, which had been idling unsteadily for some time, let out a belch of backfire—sharp as a gunshot—and died.

The crowd jumped. Then uneasy laughter started.

"There's your gunfire, Officer," Alec spoke for the first

time since the cops had arrived. He jabbed his brother with an elbow. "Matt's been tinkering with her, but she still gives us trouble now and then. I do apologize if the noise startled anyone."

Marcus shouldered past Flutie, but he slipped on the frosty concrete. His arms shot out as he regained his balance, catching Flutie in his bowl-full-of-jelly gut.

The cop let out a whoosh of air.

"Come on, Eryn." Marcus gestured toward home. "Let's get inside. It's freezing out here." He glared at Flutie who rubbed his large belly, practically pouting. "Unless you're going to waste these taxpayers' hard-earned dollars and take these kids in for questioning?"

Flutie glanced at the crowd. Officer Hiels looked like he wanted to do more than question Alec and Matt—like he wanted to string them up in the crab apple tree. But the residents of Cowley Heights were an influential bunch, full of money, and Flutie wouldn't want to upset the town's cash cow.

He waved Hiels back to his cruiser. "Go on back to bed, folks. Nothing to see here. A bear mauling." He saluted the crowd. "You keep your pets inside until we trap that beast, you hear?"

Marcus grabbed my elbow and guided me toward the "safety" of his house, but as I went, the heat of Alec's gaze warmed my back and the evil stench of vampire emanated from Flutie's skin.

After a restless night fighting off dreams where I became the beast and ran wild with a pack of wolves through Redgrave Mall, I woke to twanging vocals.

"I gave her my horse, and she gave me a divorce…"

Country music sobbed from Paige's clock radio in the room next to mine. We shared a wall, and Paige had her radio turned up so loud it sounded like it was under my pillow. I couldn't escape it. The region's only radio station was "Utterly Country," whose mascot was a grotesque play on words, a heifer with a distended pink udder. The stickers were everywhere.

I covered my ears and writhed on the bed until Paige finally gave the offensive machine a solid whack. *Ah, silence.* I kicked off the bed sheets, yawned, stretched, and fell back to sleep, only to waken again a few minutes later to the whizzing of Paige's hair dryer. She was diffuser-attachment crazy, determined to bring forth a perfect spiral from each strand of her naturally curly hair. It would be at least an hour before I could take my turn. I was long past expecting Paige to have consideration for the other members of the household.

An eternity later, Paige stomped down the stairs, and I rushed off to shower. Back in my room I applied a smattering of makeup and pulled my hair into a messy bun. In yesterday's jeans and a wooly sweater, I made for the kitchen in less than fifteen minutes. Girly-girls like Paige wasted so much time.

Marcus sat at the table, his face zombie blank, his gaze fixated on the small flatscreen TV on the maplewood island. His greying brown hair stuck out in all directions. Bedhead—

not out of a jar, but the real thing—and he had on yesterday's clothes. His once properly ironed white dress shirt had fanlike wrinkles, and grease stains blotched the fabric from our garage mishap.

"Hey, you alive?" I frowned at him. He really looked weirded out. "I thought only anxiety-riddled high school kids had that haggard look down to a science." I opened the fridge and grabbed a glass pitcher of orange juice.

"Mr. Dacopha, one of the ranchers, called me last night after all the excitement settled down," Marcus said in a toneless voice, not even looking in my direction. "His son has been missing for days. The chief of police called a press conference this morning and made a plea to the public, asking for anyone with information to contact the station."

"Mr. Dacopha is one of your rancher clients? The ones Harbinger is trying to scare off their land?"

Marcus nodded. Had Brit mentioned the name Dacopha when she'd showed me the picture of the hockey team at school? What if Logan and Wade were branching out? Recruiting their werewolf army corps from outside Wade's hockey team? Or even worse—turning the ranchers' own kids into beasts to scare their parents off their land?

I took a long swig of juice and then clunked the pitcher back down on the rack. The fridge door drifted shut. Plopping down onto one of the island stools, I stared at the TV along with Marcus, but my racing thoughts made it difficult to hear what was said.

As if in a similar state, Marcus lifted the remote and upped the volume. The news camera had focused on the

chief. Wade's father—no, his sire. It weirded me out to see Logan in a twenty-first-century cop uniform, rather than the fedora, long black coat, and shimmering gold badge from my dust bowl dream. But there was no mistaking the vamp who'd turned Wade and forced him to feed off his own mother.

"Our citizens deserve to live their lives in peace," Logan told Mina Clark, the station's cute, perky investigative reporter. Only she didn't look like she was doing much investigating, more like a lot of drooling over Logan. "To settle in Redgrave and raise their children, knowing our town is free of violence. When I get calls from parents concerned for their missing children, I get angry. And that's a good thing, because with the help of my entire police force, I'll bring this town under control." His piercing grey eyes seemed to zero in on me. I squirmed at the impact, the menace in that freaky gaze.

Wasn't it obvious he wasn't human? Couldn't viewers see his plasticky looking skin, the way his lips twisted in an evil-oozing smile for the flashing cameras at the press conference? He'd bring the town under control all right—his control.

Wade's mother's face flashed into my mind, along with her plea, *You're the only one who can help him…* How did Redgrave's simple townsfolk stand a chance against Logan, when a witch who could pull me across time thought *I* was her only hope?

Speaking of *witches*, Paige swept into the kitchen, a sour expression on her face as if she'd bitten into her own brand of poisoned apple.

"Your wife is smoking crack if she thinks I'm going to call you guys every two seconds to let you know I'm alive,"

I grimaced. Too bad Paige's observational skills were only fit for clothing brand names and runway lipstick shades. Otherwise she'd have taken one look at Marcus's rumpled appearance and shell-shocked expression and realized he wasn't in the mood for a bit of diva-child rebellion.

"Excuse me?" Marcus shoved back his chair and stood in wrinkled glory. "If I ever hear you speaking about your *mother* in that tone again, you'll be grounded until the day you graduate." He sniffled, then rubbed at his reddened eyes. "Do I make myself clear?"

Paige's mouth goldfished open and closed for a few seconds, then she sputtered, "Well, what do you expect? *Mother* tells me I have to check in before I head home from school, when I get home, and every hour, on the hour, when I'm out with friends." She threw her hands up, her lavish curls bouncing in angry protest. "And you call that living?"

"I call that survival." Marcus held up his hand, let out a powerful sneeze, and then gestured to the TV. "Watch this, and you'll see why your mother's so concerned." He sat back down with a *thunk*.

"Hey, that's Wade's dad." Paige stared at the screen. She, too, plopped down at the table. "What's going on?"

Marcus shushed her with a sharp hiss and grabbed a tissue from the box he'd started carrying around the house. He spared my hair a dark glance as he blew his nose.

Feeling even more like an outsider, I retreated a few steps to give him some non-doggy-Eryn breathing room and leaned back against the sink.

"As for the ranchers on the outskirts of town," Logan said, his fake smile taking up half his face, "I aim to help with their plight. Someone's been tampering with their crops, their livestock." He shook his head sadly. "We're doing everything we can to find the perpetrators."

For a second the camera focused on Mina Clark's flushed face. Her glazed eyes fixed on Logan like she was hanging on his every word. And she probably was. Authority emanated from Logan in waves as he charmed the gathered press.

"But the ranchers have made themselves easy pickings for the money grabbers in this town," he said. "They're grasping at straws, victims of fear. Hiring lawyers, protesting on private property, or taking vigilante stances won't help the situation." Logan gave the reporter a rapier grin. "Let's leave the law enforcement to the police, where it belongs, and let my men do their job. We know how to keep you safe. Count on it."

The blonde reporter spun to face the camera, her forehead beaded with sweat. "And there you have it, folks," she said, breathless. "The latest from Redgrave's only hope of solving the rash of disappearing children and heinous pet slayings, Police Chief Logan Gervais."

With a sound of disgust, Marcus turned off the TV. "Redgrave's only hope," he repeated. "Now, there's a scary thought."

Logan's Jedi mind tricks deflected off Marcus, which meant his soul was pure, not easily swayed by the vampire's darkness.

Unsurprisingly, his daughter was a different story.

Paige stared at the blackening TV screen and looked forlorn as Logan's face disappeared. At her father's words, she jumped up from the table. "Why do you always do that? Every time someone says anything good about Wade or his father, you try to bring them down." She flipped open a cupboard and slapped a bag of bagels on the counter. "Can't you see he's changing things for us, making Redgrave the best place to live in the whole world?"

I rolled my eyes at her dreamy expression. She sounded like she was talking about a beloved cult leader. Creepy. "I get the lawyer comments, thanks to your protest and the very friendly Officer Flutie," I said, before Paige could continue, "but what did Logan mean by vigilantes?"

Marcus shifted in his chair. "Oh, one of the town's founding families hated the Gervaises on sight. As soon as he took over as chief of police, Marie Delacroix started showing up at town meetings to warn people about him. Said she'd had a vision."

Her face in the fridge, Paige snorted.

"A vision?" I prompted, hoping to find out more about the woman who'd raised her sons to be hunters like their father, despite knowing the dangers they'd face.

"You have to know Marie," Marcus said, clearly at a loss. "She's different. She graduated a few years before we hit high school, but even then there were rumors. Some said she could see ghosts; others said she could tell the future. Then she married an out-of-towner and they pretty much stayed on their ranch." He quirked a brow. "You were with her sons last night after you went out to investigate the alleged shotgun

sound. Have you met them before?"

I swallowed hard. What should I tell Marcus about Alec and Matt? I shot Paige a quick look. She leaned her elbows on the island countertop, her chin propped in her hands, a smirk on her face and waited for my response as well. What had she seen between me and Alec last night?

I answered with a casual shrug, "Yeah, I've seen them around."

Marcus held my gaze for a moment before continuing. "Well, the town's blamed the Delacroix family for years. For everything from droughts in the summer to rainy springs drowning their crops. Now the police are in on it, saying the Delacroix are responsible for the attacks, acting as vigilantes against Harbinger." He caught the bagel Paige tossed to him and began to slice it. "It's common knowledge the Delacroix don't want the town to expand, that they're resistant to increasing the town's population. But who could accuse that family of attacking house pets or kidnapping children to make their point? It's ludicrous."

It certainly was.

Alec's family had been taking the blame for all the freaky stuff going on in Redgrave. Sure the Delacroix were hunters and had thick *I'm-in-the-paranormal-know* skin, but were they ready for an old-fashioned witch hunt? With the police force pointing its corrupt, black-nailed vamp fingers in their direction?

"Morning." Breezing into the kitchen, Sammi gave everyone a brilliant smile. She poured herself some coffee while killing looks from Paige glanced off her as if she were

wearing steel armor instead of a pastel yellow sweater with dancing white lambs. She eyed the bag of bagels and the large serrated bread knife resting beside it. It sat closer to me, but she shot me a quick glance and snatched the knife before I could hand it to her.

"I'll get breakfast started." She deftly halved a bagel and tossed it into the toaster. "You want one, Eryn?"

Every time I got within reach of a knife—Sammi pulled this stuff, with the frantic look, then the tearing it away from my immediate range. "Yeah, thanks, but I *can* handle sharp instruments without the urge to slice and dice, Sammi."

The McCains were well informed on my previous cutting obsession, thanks to the shrink reports they'd asked for when I'd moved to Redgrave. But Sammi was the worst at dealing with it, always hiding cutlery in case I had a setback. Her übervigilance made my nerves fizzle like a mouthful of Pop Rocks.

She didn't respond to the sarcasm in my voice, which didn't surprise me. Sammi tended to ignore outbursts. She did work with five-year-olds all day. I watched her wipe down the blade and carefully return it to the wooden knife rack.

"You know, I shave my legs with a razor every morning. Plenty of opportunity there." I forced a laugh when she cringed at my sharp tone.

"You shave?" Paige glanced sideways at me. "Why bother? It's not like you'll ever have a boyfriend. The guys in this town aren't interested in beanpole headcases."

Unfortunately, Sammi and Marcus had been kind enough to inform Paige of my history as well, thinking she'd

look out for me like a big sister or something. You could kill with that kind of kindness.

"At least I don't have a white moustache." I touched the hairless skin of my upper lip, ripe with the knowledge that Paige had tossed an empty box of facial bleach in the bathroom garbage bin.

Paige's eyes bulged.

"That's enough!" Sammi slammed a pot down on the counter. Everyone jumped and gaped at her. Sammi never yelled. And she never made a scene.

Sammi sighed and tucked a wayward strand of hair behind her ear. When she spoke again, her voice had resumed its usual relaxed tone. "Let's use our inside voices, girls. It's a new day, and we don't want to start with shouting and tearing our hair out, now do we? I was only trying to help you, Eryn, to fix you a nice breakfast. I didn't mean anything when I grabbed the knife. Honest." She shrugged. "But maybe I am guilty of trying too hard."

I hated the hurt look in her eyes. And I'd put it there. Not cool. Ashamed, I glared down at my plain, naked bagel.

"There's cream cheese in here if you want some." Sammi reached for the fridge door, still trying, still reaching for *me*.

That made me feel even worse.

"Yummy, yummy…you can't resist cream cheese." Sammi held up the plastic container, waving it at me.

My stomach growled.

"Thanks." I took the container from her and swiped Marcus' knife off his plate. He gave me a distracted wink. Who knew if he'd even heard our spat? I slathered a heart-

155

stopping amount of cream cheese on my bagel.

Paige watched with a sneer.

We ate breakfast in silence. Luckily, we all ate super fast.

A few minutes later Sammi headed to the front door, her arms overflowing with art supplies, glue, water-based paints, and brushes. "It's papier-mâché day at school, so I have to get there early to set up." She gave Marcus a pointed look and nodded toward a piece of purple construction paper on the table. "Eryn, we have a few new rules. Your uncle will give you the fine details."

The door slammed shut behind her.

Marcus made a face. "She always makes me the bad guy." He picked up the paper. "Okay, girls, this is how it's going to be around here from now on." He read:

1. Call and check in at home—a lot. *(We couldn't call Sammi too much.)*
2. Call 9-1-1 if anything suspicious happens *(a.k.a., don't go kicking in doors. Not that Paige would ever think of such a thing. Why ruin a perfectly good pedicure?*
3. Failure to comply with these and any other additional rules will result in grounding until graduation.
4. Paige must drive Eryn to and from school—no more walking home alone.

"What?" Paige shrieked at that last one. She clearly missed the whole *the family's in danger* part of Marcus's little

rules speech. "It's not bad enough that she goes to my school? Now I have to drive her around? Like one of those, those *car driver* people?" She paused dramatically. "I'm sorry, is there an *I'm such a loser I have to drive my reject cousin to school because my parents are suddenly way overprotective* sign on my forehead?"

At Marcus' sharp look she tossed her hair and started out of the room. "If you're not ready in five minutes, psycho, you'll live to regret it."

"I gotta get a car," I said under my breath. Or a truck or a moped. I didn't have a preference. Anything that got me out of driving with Miss Paigey would be hot wheels in my eyes.

Marcus' sympathetic nod was interrupted by a furious sneeze, followed by a series of three more that he aimed into the crook of his arm. His red, runny nose provided a nice distraction from knife blades and Paige's dull wit.

All this, and I still had a physics exam to pass.

BATHROOM CONFESSIONAL

So much for the mystical powers of my lucky hoodie. The rust-colored cotton one my mom had helped me iron black stars on during my whole aren't-constellations-stellar phase. I was jinxed. For one thing, the drive to school had been far from pleasant. I'd forgotten my iPod and endured Paige's caterwauling along with the redneck cowgirls on the radio. If she wanted me suicidal, her plan was working.

Luckily, she turned down the volume after we rounded the corner and blasted me with a piece of her mind instead.

I almost preferred the country music.

Almost.

"I don't care what kind of loser activities you were up to last night with Alec Delacroix," Paige said, with no preamble.

"But if you think I'm covering for you if you get caught sneaking out of the house…it's not gonna happen."

Ah, so she had seen me with Alec. Houses blurred by as I pressed my lips together and stared out the passenger window, neither confirming nor denying her statement.

"Didn't you hear what my dad just said?" She hit her palm against her pink fuzzy steering wheel cover. "Alec's whole family are suspects in the pet maulings. No way should you be hanging out with the Delacroix."

At first I was touched—Paige truly sounded concerned for me—go figure. Then she continued, "They're creepy with their legends and telling everyone about werewolves in town or whatever it is they're afraid of. And if *you're* seen with them, my family will be crazy by association. Dad's stressed enough as it is."

Okay, so she wasn't worried about *me*, but at least she cared for her family and seemed genuinely concerned about her father. Then she ruined it by saying, "Plus they have it out for Wade. And anyone who can't see how he equals awesomeness—I don't like."

"Speaking of Wade," I said in my best school counselor voice, "isn't it time to move on? Didn't you guys go out like a year ago? And now he dodges you in the hall at school. I mean, it's obvious the guy's not…"

"…that into me?" Paige supplied.

"Right." I beamed. "So you do see it."

"You have no idea how into me Wade really is. Our relationship is private, but if you *must* know…all his passion, his need, he saves for me. No one knows him the way I do."

Hmm. I didn't like the sound of that. Had Wade been sipping on my obnoxious cousin? Up until last night he *had* had unlimited access to the McCain household. Paige's obsession with him would make sense in a nasty vampish way. They usually glamoured their food, cranking up the influence, so their tasty morsels didn't resist the sucking of their blood and stuff.

"Haven't you noticed he's kind of cold?" I meant it literally, but Paige didn't get it. Big surprise.

"Are you kidding? Wade is hot, hot, *hot*. A walking inferno. He gets close to me, and I go up in flames."

"That's what I'm worried about," I muttered as I pictured Paige drinking margaritas in Hell's Fire and Brimstone Pub. All I needed was for Paige to turn vamp. If living with her was hell—as an undead, night-stalking people eater, she'd be really annoying.

Paige careened into the school parking lot and slammed to a lopsided stop at the end of the row. She swung her door wide while I carefully held onto mine and squeezed from her car, trying not to dent the door on the lamppost she'd parked an inch from. This driving together thing wasn't going to last long.

As I squeezed between the door and the post, the wind flicked a piece of paper taped on the rusting steel, and it nicked my cheek. I shoved it out of my face, then cringed when I read the words MISSING: BELOVED PET.

The address was in our neighborhood. The image of Cujo's blood, gleaming wetly on the grass, tightened my throat.

"Paige-a-licious, over here."

She left me without a backward glance and hurried to the blonde clones waving to her from the sidewalk. They quickly gathered in a gossip huddle. I slammed the car door, ignored their glares, and headed into the school.

As soon as I crossed the threshold, kids ran up to me, chattering about Alec and Wade's crash in the parking lot the day before, asking for all the gory details.

Who hit who first? Was there blood? What did the cops do? One guy had it so mixed up, he asked if Alec had pulled a gun on Wade during the fight. I gasped, which some took as confirmation, and voices rose.

Paige and her friends skirted the fringe of the gossipmongers buzzing around me. She gave me a Medusa glare while her blondes questioned the crowd for details, getting the front page news for their drama queen.

"Everyone knows Wade is hot for Eryn," a girl confessed to the blondest of Paige's minions. "I don't know why she's hanging around with that giant, Alec. If I were her, I'd be all over Wade by now."

I shot a glance at my cousin, who'd obviously heard the comment too. Her corkscrew curls quivered. I exited the crowd, weaving through conversations to escape Paige's wrath. The gossip would flow on with or without me.

I hadn't told Paige, or her parents, about yesterday's collision. Apparently her friends hadn't known either, or she would have been inundated with calls last night. And been even nastier to drive with this morning.

The bell pealed. Everyone scattered, including Paige's

minions. Teachers scrambled from the staff room with giant mugs of coffee, while Paige faced me across the emptying foyer, her body rigid with rage.

My leg muscles tensed. Here comes the ridiculous hair pulling and hand slapping. I couldn't imagine anything really physically threatening from Paige. She was such a girly-girl—all about the mind games.

We waited in absolute silence as the hall emptied around us. She'd be the first to break. I whistled the theme song from those classic Clint Eastwood gunslinger movies. Paige's eye twitched. I hoped she'd have a brain hemorrhage right then and there. I let the last note ring through the hall.

"You think I don't see through you?" Paige put on an exaggerated pout and whined, "*Hi, I'm Eryn. Poor little me, my parents died, and I have no friends except for the town's circus freaks.*" She paused. "You know what? Forget what I said earlier. If you want to associate with wackos like Alec and your little goth groupie, Brit—then fine."

She stalked closer, her face blotchy under her thick foundation. "But let me give you a bit of cousinly advice, Eryn. If you want to survive at this school, don't screw with me. Wade is mine, you hear that? Mine!" A stray curl snaked into her eyes, and she blew it back into place with an angry huff.

I was kind of off the Wade bus, considering he turned out to be a vampire-witch serving under a master vamp with a thing for turning local boys into frothing beasts and everything, but Paige didn't have to know that. Not right away.

"Really? 'Cause I'm sensing a major lack of communication between you two." I paused for effect. "Wade's been offering me rides home, looking out for me. I think he even wants—" I pursed my lips and covered them prudishly with my fingers. "Sex." I lowered my hand. "I gotta tell you, having two guys fighting over me yesterday was pretty cool."

Paige's eyes flickered with rage. "This is your last warning. Stay away from Wade. Keep your claws off him, or I'll tell everyone about your cutting habit and how my parents had to take you in to save you from a mental institution."

Whoa! Where did that come from? Like mental institutions even existed outside of computer games and horror movies. I struggled for a comeback, but I had nothing.

Paige's face glowed like someone had plunged a needle full of triumph directly into her make-Eryn's-life-miserable vein. "Remember, hands off," she said, sashaying down the hall. "Or everyone will know what a disturbed psychopath you are."

One nice thing about Paige, she didn't treat me with kid gloves like her parents did. How refreshing.

The morning announcements cackled over the school PA system. Scarier than the thought of a straitjacket was the thought of being late for my physics test—I needed every possible second. I threw my stuff into my locker and ran for the science wing.

I skulked into physics class. Perfect timing. Mr. Phillips, occupied with handing out exam booklets, hadn't seen me enter. Brit gave me a thumbs up, looking impressed. Mr. Phillips' obsession with punctuality was the stuff of legend.

He once threw a chalkboard brush, the old-fashioned kind with the wooden backing, at a kid coming through the doorway fifty seconds late. Knocked him flat.

"Next time you show up after the bell, Eryn," Phillips said, without glancing up from the intimidating, official-looking booklets in his hands. "You might as well go for coffee at the cafeteria. You won't get into my classroom."

The class *oooh*ed.

"That goes for the lot of you." Phillips turned on the others. "Is it too much to ask that you kids get to class on time, pencil at the ready? This is a test, people. A very important *test*."

I snatched the booklet he held out to me and shuffled, face burning, down an aisle to grab a desk in the back of the room.

I stared at the first question. *Use the following information to answer the next seven questions.* A detailed chart that looked like Egyptian hieroglyphs followed. I flipped through the booklet, looking for easy questions to answer first, hoping to build my confidence. Only there weren't any. Terms, formulas, and equations blurred before my eyes. *Fusion reaction, magnetic fields, repulsive force, mass of particles, and neutrons.*

The techy words made my head spin. Brit and I really should have started on that tutoring Mr. Phillips had insisted on. But it was a little difficult to focus on schoolwork with werewolves turning the town into a pan-fried breakfast and vamps scrambling my brains. I shut the booklet and put my forehead on my desk. I was royally screwed.

I tried to concentrate amidst a symphony of papers rattling, pencils scratching, kids sniffing and sighing in frustration. Desperation infused the air. I sat up, sniffing unobtrusively at my arm. It came from me.

From across the room, Brit cleared her throat, her way of encouraging me, to get me to at least *try.*

The pressure in my head intensified. I flipped the booklet face up once more. I stared at the first question, rubbing my temples in soothing circles.

And this time, things went down a bit differently.

The physics mumbo-jumbo made sense. Relief made the pain in my head fade into blissful nothingness, leaving me a bit light-headed. I picked up my pencil and circled my way through pages of multiple-choice questions. Then came the long-answer section.

Sketch the diagram showing the path of the scattered electron—state all necessary physics principles and formulas.

Okay, no problem.

I began to sketch, My pencil raced over the page as if it couldn't scratch down the answers fast enough.

In less than half an hour I'd whipped through the entire exam, answering each and every question in turn. I finished in a daze, stood, and handed my booklet to Phillips, who accepted it with a so-you're-giving-up-already sigh. His jaw fell open when he skimmed the first page. The writing on the page already looked like Greek to me as I slipped out of that-was-an-über-easy-exam mode.

Brit watched me leave the room, her expression saying she thought I'd bombed the test. I shot her a thumbs up and

a wink. Brit's pitying look shifted to a deep frown. She had no idea what was going on. I almost laughed aloud at her confused expression.

In the hallway I paused to take a few deep breaths and get my bearings. My spirits soared. Whoot! I'd kicked major physics butt and lived to tell about it. Knocking paranorms into the dust now had a close second on my list of favorite moments. I let out a disbelieving laugh. What the hell happened? Had Brit called in another magical favor? She had been studying me pretty closely in the classroom. Making sure the spell worked? But then why had she looked shocked when I finished so quickly?

"You're welcome." The voice came from behind me.

I whirled around, my heart in my throat. Wade leaned a hand on a locker close to my cheek, his wonderfully developed form outlined by his clingy T-shirt.

"God, you scared me." I flushed under his stare and shifted away from him, crowded by his unexpected proximity. I deflected his power, looking past the glamour to his real intent. Only at the moment I didn't smell any deceit on him, only a desire to please and his now-familiar scent of mint. "What am I supposed to be thanking you for?"

His strong, square jawline flexed as he flashed me his killer smile, drawing my gaze to his mouth—his teeth. The points of his incisors a bit too…pointy. Still, my heart jumped in response—and not from fear.

"The physics test." He jerked a thumb toward the classroom. "You were dying in there and I"—he paused meaningfully—"brought you back from the brink."

My pulse leapt in my throat, and Wade's pupils dilated, his grey irises almost completely blackened as his gaze dropped to my neck. Okay, *now* I was scared.

"What do you mean you brought me back?" I pulled my hair around my shoulder, hiding the curve of neck exposed by my collarbone-grazing sweater. "I did fine in there. Better than fine. I aced that test."

"I know you did," Wade said with a breathy laugh. His spearmint breath sent my long bangs into a gentle dance. I shivered. My skin tingled. Being this close to Wade was like being surrounded by an invisible field of menthol that stole my breath.

Wade watched me with knowing eyes. "I stood in the hall and fed you the answers. Telepathy, remember?" He tilted his head, his dark hair attractively disheveled. "You can find a way to thank me later."

I backed away from him, stumbled into the lockers. The air in the hallway curdled in my lungs. *Stupid.* How could I be so stupid? I'd been so worried about the test that I'd forgotten to protect myself. I'd left myself wide open for him to rummage through my thoughts like a bargain hunter at a garage sale. I squeezed my eyes shut, concentrated on the limestone wall I'd built to block him out, and then hastily slammed it into place.

Wade's eyes flickered. "I've felt that before." He frowned. "You shouldn't be able to…"

And just like that he was in my mind, testing the boundary I'd created. Weird sensations zinged through me, like biting on tinfoil, and I had no way to stop it. I clutched at

my sweater, my fingers locked in a spasm unable to reach my athame. Pressure built under my skull. My eyes pushed against my eyelids as if they were going to burst from their sockets. I mustered my strength and projected a single thought: *STAY OUT OF MY HEAD!*

The connection severed.

Wade jerked back. His jaw dropped in astonishment.

"I heard you," he breathed. His already pale skin blanched. "Impossible." He turned his head away, cursing. When he faced me again he was different, his teasing manner gone, his expression drawn. "That's why my father wants you," he said. "You're not human."

Before I could speak, he loomed over me. His grey eyes dared me to do something about it. "Human or not, you better be on your guard. When my father shows an interest…" He hesitated, then gave a grim smile. "Well, let's say he's not careful with his toys." His lowered his voice, a quiet, but ominous warning. "Speaking of games that might get you killed. Tell your friends thanks for the town tour, but they really shouldn't waste their magical resources on me." His breath iced along my cheek. "I won't enter your house again. Not without a very personal invitation."

I should have knocked him to the ground and pressed the point of my dagger to his throat. Yes, I should have. But I was fixed in place by my traitorous emotions, my body humming at the thought of inviting Wade into my bedroom. I bowed my head, afraid that if I made a move it would be closer to him, not away.

When the tension between us grew to astronomical

Judith Graves

levels, I looked up. Our lips almost touched. If I leaned a smidge forward… Wade's approving smile and watchful gaze sent a wave tingling in my stomach. Damn. My eyes fluttered shut. I shoved the desperate hunger Wade drew from me back into its Pandora's box. When I opened my eyes again, he was gone.

I choked back a frustrated groan.

Someone tapped me on the shoulder. I yelped and slapped a hand to my pounding heart.

"Easy does it, stressball." Brit laughed. "What happened in there?" The thick fringe of her black bangs half-covered her disgruntled expression.

"In where?" I asked, my brain not fully functional. My body wanted to take advantage of that fact and bolt after Wade.

Brit made a face. "The test. Did you give up or what?"

"Oh," I said. Right. The test I'd inadvertently cheated on. That was the proud cherry on top of the crap cupcake I'd been chewing on all day. "I did alright." I shrugged, then made a face and admitted, "Better than that, I think I aced it."

"You aced it?" Brit's expression cleared. "That's amazing! Really?" Happiness rose off her as if she'd bathed in it.

I winced. How could I ever tell Brit the truth? Once I told her Wade could shimmy into my thoughts whenever my guard was down, she'd know I walked the fine line between dark and light. Vamps could influence the weak-minded, but to completely read someone's thoughts—well, that became a matter of dark calling to dark.

Brit wrapped her arms around me in a crushing hug.

169

"This is fabulous. You must have a photographic memory or something. Nice." She released me and skip-walked toward her locker. "One exam down, one to go."

Thankfully, *I* didn't have another test. Brit was off to a chemistry exam, while I had a comparatively brain friendly art history class.

"Let's meet by the stoner doors at lunch," Brit said. "And then we'll head to Conundrum Café. Kate's not only a powerful witch, she can sling java that will take you to new worlds. I gotta say she has the best ginger cookies you'll ever have in your entire life." Brit twisted a strand of her poker straight black hair around her fingers. "Besides, Kate wants to ask you a few questions."

Questions. From a witch. Great. Things kept getting better and better. "I don't—"

Brit cut me off. "Kate's super nice." Her voice rose as her words rushed together. "So don't think she's got some grand inquisition planned, like she's working for the Hunter Council. She wants to know more about your dream and Wade's mother." She shrugged. "I guess a dream like that, back in time and so detailed, is kind of a big deal. Kate thinks you were magically transported through your subconscious or something."

Whoa. I'd have to keep my poker face on around Kate. She seemed to know more about my time travel experience than I did.

"Every witch in town will be jealous you got to experience magic at that level," Brit said. "You're like a witch's dream come true."

A wolven as a witch's dream come true? With my soul in flux and Wade meandering in my head anytime he pleased? The fact that he was a hybrid like me made it that much more difficult to ignore him.

"Plus Kate thinks if she sees you in person, she can amp up the anti-Wade spell. How cool is that?"

I didn't have the heart to tell Brit that Wade had sensed Kate's magic and only played along last night. Brit had a serious case of Kate hero/witch worship.

"Cool is overrated," I said, my skin still tingling from Wade's mentholy presence.

But Brit was already hurrying down the hall and didn't hear me.

In art history class I struggled to stay focused on Mrs. Stantial, who stood all of five feet tall and looked more like a student than a high school art teacher. A dynamo with a trendy fashion sense, she radiated intensity. Impossible to sit in her room without some of it rubbing off—unless you were a bit preoccupied with your life-and-death struggle against otherworldly forces.

I couldn't jot another note about Hellenistic and Roman statues. Why had I ever thought taking art history would be a brain holiday? Hello…comparative essays to write, dates, locations, and mythologies to memorize. Goodbye…paint-by-numbers trip down art history lane. Next time I'd read the fine print when registering. The class seemed entirely too…

ancient history after what had gone down between me and Wade.

My first attempt at a mental ward, and I'd blocked him, a vampire-witch, from scanning my thoughts. He'd discovered my paranorm abilities. Wade was far more powerful than the crew realized. More powerful than anything they—or I—had ever faced. And what had he meant when he said his father wanted me? Wanted me for what?

And how could I stop him? Or Wade?

Other than building a garlic moat around my uncle's house, how could I keep Wade out? Who knew if the usual vamp techniques would work against him? He could walk around in daylight and had witchy ways. He'd said he wouldn't enter the house unless I invited him. Could I trust him to keep his word? He was a vamp, for God's sake—one who was more than likely feeling up and feeding off my cousin.

Even more alarming—could I trust myself not to invite him in? Again, I relived that pull, that electricity surging between us. His darkness called to me in ways I couldn't explain. Ways that wouldn't be at all moral high ground or justifiable if I put the feelings into words.

And I had Alec to consider. We had kissed last night. We'd shared a moment. A hungry, raw, desperate moment. I couldn't deny it. Neither could he. But Alec was human. Worse than that—a hunter of creatures like me—he was ruled by duty and honor. Out to save his hometown from the paranorms.

We didn't stand a chance.

And what about Brit? She'd asked me to help the group

find out what happened to her brother. I understood what drove her. The not knowing was the most excruciating part. Exactly why I had made my bargain with the devil and followed Sebastian's go-hide-in-Redgrave order. He'd offered me a chance to discover what had happened to my parents.

For Alec's sake, for Brit's, and for the sake of my parents—on the slim chance that the Hunter Council might actually come through and dig up some information on them—I had to hold it together. Totally bad timing to be curious about my wild, dark, wolven side. Or to let it take me over, to give into Wade, no matter how strong the pull became.

My human will was stronger. I hoped.

Stantial flicked off the classroom lights and illuminated a PowerPoint presentation on the screen at the front of the room. I slid down in my desk and slipped into spectator mode as she described her one and only trip to Rome, giving us the nitty-gritty on each image. Most of the photos were blurry or underexposed. She blamed her camera.

The next slide came up, and I groaned. Wolves. Everything came back to wolves. They'd even taken over art class. About to biff my pencil at the screen, I forced myself to take the less dramatic route and slunk lower in my seat.

"Throughout the ages, animals have been worshipped as intermediaries between man and his gods." She used a laser pointer to highlight certain features of the bronze sculpture of a female wolf with two human boys reaching hungrily for her engorged…

The class gave a collective *Ewwww*, which Stantial ignored.

"As depicted in this sculpture, the Romans believed a she-wolf raised twin orphan boys, Romulus and Remus, who founded the city of Rome. Consequently, the wolf became a sacred animal within Roman culture. Here we see," she said, clicking to the next slide, "where I veered from the tour group and crossed into a restricted area." She held up her hand. "Not that I'm encouraging any of you to break the rules, but I had to see what they were working on." She gave a dreamy sigh. "And that's when I took this picture. Isn't it stunning?"

I'd practically fallen asleep when Stantial's coup de grace image flashed across the screen. The photo depicted a faded emblem painted on a crumbling limestone wall. Both the wall and the emblem were eerily familiar. My heart rocked in my chest. Up there on the screen, larger than life, stood the very same limestone wall and emblem I'd visualized to block Wade from my thoughts. I hadn't realized that my shield bore any distinct markings until I saw the wolf, snarling as it bit through a human skull.

I sat upright in my seat. My knees banged the underside of my desk. What had triggered the image in my head in the first place—or who had planted it there?

At the same moment, a deep gasp came from the next row of desks.

I twisted my head and met the tear-filled eyes of Olivia, the girl I'd seen crying in the locker room my first day of school. The one whose boyfriend, Travis—one of the missing guys from Wade's hockey team—had left her behind. Or so she thought. Alec had already written him off as a werewolf we'd eventually hunt down. The fact that Olivia suffered from

yet another public meltdown wasn't surprising. However, that she, too, had reacted violently to the image on the screen—the same instant I had—couldn't be a coincidence.

Unfortunately, our mutual wiggins woke up half of the class. Faces turned to gape at us, like ghosts caught on film.

Mrs. Stantial squinted at us through the darkness. "Is there a problem?"

Olivia's eyes overflowed with tears. She shook her head and shot me a panicked look.

"Ah, no," I stammered. "It's just that picture is…well, it's really….nice."

Stantial raised a perfectly shaped brow. "I hope *nice* isn't a reflection of the writing you'll submit for your final paper. True art is a lot of things, but it's never as tragically dull as nice." She looked back at the screen. "Although your instincts are good. This wall painting is an extremely rare find, salvaged from a late first-century house in Rome. The restoration work took years to complete. I can't believe I stumbled upon it before its official unveiling sometime next year. The scene is quite brutal, a complete contrast to the usual opulent landscapes found at such dig sites."

I swallowed hard as a knot formed in my stomach. Rare and brutal. Great.

"Despite the weathered stone," Stantial said, using her laser pointer to highlight areas of the image, "we can clearly see the human skull being savagely penetrated by the wolf's fangs."

"Savagely penetrated," a guy up front echoed. "That's cool."

No.

It wasn't.

Beside me Olivia scooped up her backpack and swung it over her shoulder, ready to bolt.

"So…ah, does it have any special significance?" I asked, earning another intent look from Stantial.

"Yes," she said slowly. "Scholars speculate that the residence may have been a meeting place for a fringe cult, a band of warriors who thought they could shapeshift into wolves."

"Nice," the same guy up front said. "Now this is art, man."

Stantial rolled her eyes and clicked to the next image. "In the next slide, we have…"

Olivia slid from her desk. "Washroom," she breathed as she passed me.

As Stantial lectured on, unaware of Olivia's exit, I sat at my desk, my pulse triple timing. What was going on here? Why had Olivia freaked out even more than I had at seeing the emblem?

I shoved my textbook into my backpack and snuck out of the room, heading for the girl's washroom down the hall from Stantial's class.

I'd expected the tears. I didn't think I'd ever seen Olivia without them. But nothing had prepared me for her pain, her sorrow. The salty scent of those bitter emotions fused into the bathroom walls like rock salt stuck in tire treads. Olivia was leaning over the last sink, her auburn hair hanging in a harsh, limp line as she stared at the cell phone in her hand.

"Olivia?" I crept closer. Despite being all blotchy and having T-zone shine, Olivia's beautiful face inspired a twinge of envy. Even at a major low point in her life she still looked better than I would after an extreme makeover. Wow. That was petty. I focused on the issue at hand. Olivia crying. Again. "Are you okay?"

"No, I'm not sure if I'll ever be okay again." She lowered the phone, her eyes bleak. "You've seen it before too. Haven't you?"

I raised a brow, but said nothing. Olivia was bursting to get something off her chest, and, if it was paranormal in nature I needed to look cool and noncommittal. Hunter training rule 7,876 or something like that.

"The wolf and skull," she said, frowning now.

I raised both brows. Noncommittal, noncommittal. "The what?"

"The picture Stantial showed." Olivia shoved away from the sink. "Travis had one like it on his arm." She thrust her cell toward my face, showing a closeup of a guy's muscular arm. The skull-and-fangs image had obviously been recently etched into his skin leaving his arm red and raw looking.

Olivia stared at her own waiflike arm as she traced the spot where Travis had his tattoo done. The girl was wasting away. All jutting bones and sharp angles. "He got it right before he disappeared."

I shifted my backpack. The art history text I'd stuffed inside jabbed into my shoulder. How did an ancient piece of art end up on the arm of some kid from a small town like Redgrave?

"Are you saying Travis had that thing carved into his skin?" I cringed. "Lovely."

Olivia's brilliant blue eyes flashed with anger. "He wasn't himself. He hated tattoos, never saw the point of jabbing yourself with ink. Then one day he said he dreamt about this awesome design and had to get one done."

I held my breath. Dreamt about it? Or had it flashed into his mind the way it had for me?

Her expression softened, and her eyes filled with tears again. "That was the last time I saw him." She sniffled. "You know, we were going to leave town together after graduation." She gave a sad laugh as she scrolled through the images saved on the cell. She held up one of her and Travis laughing in front of a locker. "Well, that was the plan." She showed me another, a closeup of Travis. "Wasn't he beautiful?"

"Uh, sure." I shrugged, then plunked my backpack on the counter, and fished inside for my makeup bag. I made a big show of putting on my lip gloss, covering up the odd blemish, and powdering my nose. This part of being a hunter bothered me the most. The evasions, the lies. But what could I tell her? That Travis might not be so pretty as a werewolf—with the molting human skin and matted fur? I'm sorry, Beauty and the Beast was hopelessly romantic...on paper.

"He wouldn't have left me here. We were getting out. Together." Olivia pushed the phone back into her backpack with trembling fingers. "So you can either tell me now, or I'll find out myself. That tattoo—you recognized it too. What does it mean?"

I stared blankly at Olivia, my thoughts like a pinball

gone mad, ricocheting around in my head.

Stantial had no idea the true value of the artwork she'd photographed. A tangible connection between the human and paranormal world. Lucky she worked in such an isolated community. I'd heard of humans stumbling onto proof of paranorm existence, but those unfortunate souls didn't live long enough to show anyone their finds, especially not a classroom of impressionable high school kids.

At my continued silence, Olivia sighed. "Fine. Don't tell me where you've seen it." She grabbed her backpack and made for the door. "But I know something's not right in this town."

Humph. She wasn't kidding.

STEREOTYPE MUCH?

Brit and I walked to the café only a few blocks from the school. Although it hadn't snowed, the grey sky and crisp air threatened the white stuff at any time. My wolf compensated for the chill as soon as we hit the outdoors, my internal temperature spiked. I started to take off my jacket, but with Brit shivering in her black canvas coat, wearing more layers than I was, I decided not to draw attention to my sudden tolerance for the cold.

Talk about premature hot flashes. Yikes. I lowered my zipper to catch some of the cool breeze. Uncomfortable and sweaty in sweater weather. How the hell was I going to survive a scorching hot summer day?

"There's something I've been meaning to ask you," Brit

said, hesitancy in her voice. "You might get mad, so I'll say it fast."

"Fire away." I shrugged. Whatever Brit had to say couldn't be as bad as the thought of me hiding in my room all summer because I'd started shedding all my hair. Now *that* thought made me mad—as in one-way ticket to bedlam mad. I squeezed the bridge of my nose, a de-stresser technique I'd learned from a school counselor. *Damn.* I rubbed away the dart of pain I'd self-inflicted.

Not only had my nose become a super sniffer—I couldn't even touch it without sensory overload. A sigh that could easily have slipped into growl territory rumbled in my chest.

Brit stared at me like I was about to go all Hulkish green. She took a deep breath and said in a rush, "You're sixteen. That's close to being legal. After your folks…weren't you given the option of going it alone? I mean, if *my* parents died, I'd hate to move out of our house, our town. You're so far away you can't even visit their graves. Wouldn't staying at home have made life seem more…normal?" She clapped a hand over her mouth. "That came out wrong. Ignore me."

I froze on the sidewalk, forcing Brit to stop as well, and studied her for a long moment.

"A normal life?" I said, once I could speak past the maniacal laughter that threatened to burst from my throat. "Now that's the real fairytale. What about my life has ever been normal? Sure, I wanted to stay home. But I didn't have a choice. My father was a hunter. My mom…"

Wait. What was I saying? I couldn't tell Brit like this. The right time would come, but this wasn't it. I took a second and

refocused.

"The Hunter Council doesn't let people like me walk away. They'll always be watching." My stomach lurched, but I said exactly what I'd been feeling since the funeral. "As for my parents—their graves mean nothing to me."

Brit lowered her eyes and stared at her Doc Martens, but not before I saw the shock on her face.

"Yeah, that sounds heartless doesn't it?" I choked out, striding forward once more. Brit kept up with me as best she could. "Wanna know why I couldn't care less about two boxes buried in the dirt?" My voice was too loud, but I couldn't stop the words from pouring out. "'Cause they're empty, Brit. We buried empty coffins. My parents' bodies were never found. I'm not even sure they're really dead."

"*Not sure they're…*" Brit grabbed my arm and pulled me to a stop. "What do you think happened to them?"

"That's what the Hunter Council is trying to find out."

"The Council's involved with your parents? But I don't understand, I thought they only dealt with the bigwigs…" She eyed me with new awareness. "Oh."

"Can we drop it for now?" I ground out. "I'm feeling a little not myself today."

"Dropping it, yup, we're dropping it…" Brit scuffed her boots on the sidewalk.

I shouldn't have told Brit, a *human*, anything about my parents, or my suspicions, or my sad little I'm-a-mutant-freakazoid life. I'd only put her in danger. I couldn't afford to get close to hunters, to people, period. Not now. Maybe not ever.

Uncertainty settled in my stomach as if it were moving in and ready to redecorate. Wasn't I already too close? To Brit, to Marcus, to Alec. Wasn't that the whole problem?

All I kept wondering was how Alec would act when he saw me for the first time since our kiss. Would he want to take up where we left off, or did he regret he ever met me? And really, what right did I have messing around with his life anyway? I couldn't get attached to humans—they were too easy to break.

"Isn't this place amazing?" Brit exulted when we arrived at the café, our tense conversation about my parents apparently well and truly on hold. I loved that about Brit. She didn't push, or prod, or try to guilt you into a confession. Probably because she knew I'd tell her the story eventually.

Conundrum Café. Wow, the name was larger than the actual building, a narrow two-story converted house that barely seated ten people on the main floor. According to a chalkboard sign on the wooden stair railing, the place had an art gallery on the second floor. I sucked in a breath when I spotted a bulletin board plastered with flyers about missing pets.

Someone had to get those werewolves in line. And it looked more and more like that someone was me.

Inside, a line of Zen-like hippie types stood to one side of a long, brightly painted counter. The counter's black surface glittered with gold-foil suns and a bevy of hand-painted stars and moons. A profusion of yellowing posters covered the cobalt blue walls.

Alec and Matt waved to us from a corner near a large

bay window. The window's thick covering of frost muted the daylight. The guys sprawled out on an orange plaid couch, the kind left on curbsides next to garbage cans, free for the taking. Alec had his long legs stretched out, his feet propped up on a heavy oak coffee table, his arms folded across his chest. My breath hitched at the sight of him, and I avoided his half-hooded gaze.

Brit waved to Matt and then pointed to the line. He held up his glass, silently asking Brit to get him another iced tea.

"Let's order first or we'll never get to eat before our next class," Brit said. "Time moves at its own pace in Conundrum. You get used to it or never come back. Personally, I like the atmosphere, the rustic charm. Plus there's Kate. Wait till you meet her."

The place was rustic all right, a blend of garage sale chic and vintage clutter. My feet scuffed across a lacquered plywood floor as we approached the counter. The twenty-something barista didn't appear in any rush as she worked around the various industrial coffeemakers and flavored syrup bottles.

Brit studied the menu board hanging over the counter while I counted the barista's facial piercings. Twelve. The sweet smell of cookies baking in the kitchen beyond the counter clashed with the jarring scent of silver. My athame's faint essence, muffled by the shoulder holster and my clothing, hardly registered, but the barista's piercings were right at nose level.

I covered my gag, clearing my throat loudly.

"Don't you think that's a bit much?" I asked Brit after

we'd placed our orders. "Getting your face filled with all that metal?"

Brit glanced at the barista. "I think she looks cool."

"Sure, now," I said. "When she's a grandma, those things will be hanging around her shoulders. How's that for a physics lesson? Gravity works, my friend."

"Ugh." Brit made a face and then stepped aside so a customer could pass us to exit the café. The steamer hissed and utensils clattered as the barista prepared our order. "No way. Kate will be a hip granny. Won't you, Kate?"

The barista laughed. "Someday, Brit. We'll see, I guess."

"Kate?" I asked. "This is *Kate*?" I leaned into Brit's shoulder and whispered, "As in the *witch*?" She looked way too young to have much magical power. No wonder her spell hadn't held Wade.

Brit shrugged. "The one and only. Believe me, she's older then she looks." Her eyes twinkled. "Wait," she said and then laughed. "You were expecting green face paint, a hairy mole, and an evil cackle? Stereotype much?" She scanned the counter. "You want chocolate sprinkles?" Grabbing a palm-sized metal shaker, she doused my latte's foamy topping with chocolate shavings.

"I gotcha covered, Kate." A young woman came from the back section of the café. She wrapped an apron around her slim waist. "Take as long as you need."

"Thanks, Beth." When Kate grinned, muscles flexed around a piercing in her cheek. She flipped up a section of the counter and draped her arm over Brit's shoulder. "Okay, girls, let's sit with your menfolk and talk shop. Glad you could join

us, Eryn." She gave me a conspiratorial wink. "I hoped that special brew I made up yesterday would do the trick, but I wasn't sure."

"Ah, yeah, thanks. Worked like a charm," I said, uncomfortable that I'd lied to this friendly, young witch. I couldn't bring myself to tell the others that Wade had been toying with them. Kate's magic was about as effective on Wade as control top pantyhose on a Sumo wrestler—some things couldn't be contained.

Kate didn't look a thing like the members of the coven my father had bartered with years ago. They had indeed lived up to the witch stereotype—except for the green face paint. An ancient coven was cloistered away in the foothills of the Ardenne Mountains. I had no idea what my father had traded to get my silver athame, but it was major. Well, not fork-over-your-firstborn major, obviously—but still, Mom always said Dad had made a huge error in judgment that day. Wolven and witches usually didn't get along in the paranorm world. They were both far too outspoken for their own good.

Kate was no exception.

"So, Alec," she said, dropping into one of the chairs across from the couch. "Did you give Eryn her present yet?"

Matt choked mid-gulp on the iced tea Brit had handed to him. She pounded his back until he could breathe and then squished between the guys to sit on the couch.

"It's not a *present*." Alec seemed to be choosing his words carefully. "It's supposed to give Eryn some protection. How many times do I have to tell you that?" He made a face at Kate and pulled his feet off the coffee table when she stabbed

her finger into his calf.

I stood clutching my latte. Confused. Embarrassed. Excited…

A gift that *wasn't* a gift? For me?

"Sit down here." Kate waved me into the chair beside her. "The other one wobbles." I sat down, appreciating the cool air radiating from the bay window behind us.

Kate laughed at Alec's dark expression. "This guy," she said, pointing at Alec, "came into the café five minutes after we opened this morning, asking me where he could get Eryn a…" She hesitated. "No, I won't ruin the surprise."

"Ignore her, Eryn." Alec met my gaze for a second as if gauging my reaction.

I gave a throw-me-a-bone shrug, hoping someone would fill me in on what was going on.

"Kate loves to make every little thing a big production." He reached into his jeans pocket and pulled out a small parcel, a few inches long, neatly wrapped in white tissue paper. "Brit told me you didn't have one, so I picked this up at the shop across the street. Every hunter needs basic protection. You can't do better than Christian symbols."

Alec was officially blurting. Usually I had that honor. The burnt toast scent of his uncertainty, his nervousness, started my own pulse racing. I unfolded the tissue paper, while Kate loudly insisted that if I liked it, *she* had told Alec where to look. The tissue rustled in my hands. My clumsy fingers ripped the fragile paper in a few spots. Something tumbled onto my palm—an antique cross pendant, its dark patina embellished with vines and a single rose resting in the

heart of the cross.

The silver cross etched itself into my palm as I examined it, but the burning pain barely registered. What Alec had said was true. We were lucky to have a few go-to defenses against vampires, all thanks to one of the original vampires, Judas, who'd betrayed his friend for a few silver coins. Ever since then, crosses and crucifixes repelled vampires. Holy water burned like acid, peeling away their preserved skin right down to the bone.

But the cross and its history wasn't what had me riding a wave of emotions. With the crew sitting around me, waiting for my reaction, and the gift in my hands, I could almost trick myself that these were my people. That I belonged. Cared for and cared about.

But as the silver singed into my palm, foreboding—dark and overwhelming—settled in my stomach, destroying my fairytale moment. This was going to end badly. For all of us. I knew it, and yet I couldn't walk away from Alec and Brit and Redgrave.

I could help. I refused to betray them in their hour of need. Loyalty could be so aggravating.

"So, do you?" Anxiety edged Alec's words. "Like it, I mean. You can exchange it if you want. The shop is across the street."

Our eyes met. I held his gaze. I needed to be watching him while I did this. More than a guy giving a girl a token present, this was acceptance on a silver cross platter. My heart on a spike.

"I love it," I murmured, then put the leather cord around

my neck, careful to hide the red welt in the center of my palm. The cross weighed me down like an oath, a promise I wore on my chest. It settled on my rust colored sweater in the dip between my breasts.

Kate and Brit made admiring noises, while Alec stared at the cross, watching it dip and slide with my every breath. Breath that came faster the longer he looked. He met my gaze again, his eyes dark with wanting. He flushed and grabbed his coffee mug.

"Like I said." He shrugged casually. *Too* casually. "It will give you more protection against Wade and his father."

Matt snorted. "Well, I'm glad that's settled. Since it wasn't a *present* or anything."

Okay, maybe Matt didn't exactly want me around.

Brit slapped his shoulder, her lips twisted in an exaggerated pout. "You know, you can get me *non*-presents like that anytime you want."

I tuned out their banter as my heart pounded deep in my chest, like it could shatter me into a million pieces. Alec had

given me a silver cross, an icon passed down through the ages from the ankh, the Egyptian symbol of life, to the Christian symbol of ultimate sacrifice. Meant to protect the innocent.

What protection existed for a creature that walked two worlds? Yet, belonged to none? Even now, with the heat of Alec's cross burning through my sweater, that beastly blood boiled in my veins. No symbol, no matter how holy and reverent, prevented Wade and his sire from pursuing me. They knew I wasn't human. Being half wolven ensured that in *my* case, the usual rules didn't apply.

I was paranormal fair game.

And Lord help me, around Wade, I couldn't think straight. Like I stood outside myself. Like maybe if Wade chased me, I'd enjoy getting caught. I had two hearts as well as two kinds of blood pulsing through me. I twisted in my chair, leaning heavily away from the crew, afraid Kate would pick up my emotions.

Crack. The wooden armrest of my chair split under the shift in pressure. My body jerked.

Kate reached out to steady me.

"Oh, *now* I remember." Kate laughed. "*That* one wobbles"—she pointed to the empty chair beside us—"and *this* one is totally falling apart." The armrest now pointed due south, hanging by a rusted nail and a prayer. I tried to pop it back into place.

"Whoa, what happened to your hand?" Kate grabbed my forearm and twisted it none too gently. The armrest slipped from my fingers to swing from the nail, exposing my palm. The imprint of the cross appeared as a raw, festering welt on

my flesh.

"Nothing." My chest tight with apprehension, I used some wolven strength, attempting to yank my wrist from her grasp, but Kate held on. The others, still razzing Alec about exactly what constituted a guy-to-girl present, hadn't noticed the tug-of-war over my hand.

Kate's amused expression faded. She studied me for a moment. Her power simmered in the air around us.

The hair on my neck vibrated with the mystical charge. My arm tingled strangely under her touch. I held my breath and braced for a blast of witch's magic. For her to denounce me to the crew. To Alec.

But the air stilled, and Kate only folded my fingers into a fist, hiding the wound.

"Liar," she mouthed and removed her hands.

I released my breath in a shuddering sigh.

"You know, boys," Kate said, interrupting Matt and Brit's fun, "it's too bad your mother doesn't come into town. Marie hasn't met Eryn yet, has she? I know she'd love her. Eryn seems like a real straight shooter, and Marie's so big on honesty and hunter loyalty."

I cringed at her pointed words.

Matt snorted. "Mom avoids Redgrave the way fugitives avoid donut shops." He angled his chin toward me. "Not even the chance to tell Alec I-told-you-so about Eryn lured her to town."

Alec shifted on the couch, glaring at his brother. I frowned. Matt had taunted Alec before about their mother. That she had revealed a secret about me. But what?

Brit tapped her watch-less wrist. "I hate to break up the Alec burnfest, but I can't miss my English midterm next period."

Kate made a face. "You're all business today." She glanced at me. "Eryn, I asked Brit to bring you here today to give you a warning. Your uncle has a reputation as a do-gooder. Lawyer, married to a kindergarten teacher, upstanding citizen, quick to lend a helping hand. But this time his do-gooding has landed him in the middle of a paranormal hailstorm." She took a sip of her black coffee. "Covens from all over the area are heralding a substantial increase in activity. It's like paranorms are relocating. Seeking untried ground."

"Exactly." Alec twisted on the couch, his face intent. "That's where your uncle comes in, Eryn, with his clients being run off their land. I did some checking at city hall, made like I was interested in working construction for the summer. They told me the real estate market was booming, so I'd get a job no problem. Seems Harbinger bought up most of the ranches and available properties surrounding Redgrave."

Matt shook his head. "What do they want with Redgrave? Most people can't wait to get out of this town."

"There's the appeal," Kate said. "An isolated population, miles of unclaimed territory…" She focused on me again. "Eryn, one more thing's been bugging me about your vision." She waved a hand when I started to protest. "I mean your *dream*. Did Wade's mother say anything to you? Give you some clue of her intent?"

"What do you mean, *her intent*?"

Kate's gaze locked on mine. "Did she give you a message?

A warning?"

I kept my face blank. "No," I lied. "She cloaked me so Wade and Logan wouldn't detect my presence, and then she…died."

Matt snorted, his face a mask of disgust. "You mean Wade killed her."

I shot him a dark look. "Yes, but he had no control over what he was doing."

Alec's head snapped up at that. I swallowed and pushed back the sudden rush of images—the witch demanding I watch her fate unfold, telling me only I could save her son. Wade feasting at his mother's neck. The torment on his face when he realized what he'd done.

"That's all I can tell you, Kate." I leaned on the chair's only secure armrest. "That's all that happened."

Kate sighed and shifted in her chair. Like she knew I was holding back and was disappointed I didn't trust her or the crew enough to tell the truth. How easy was I to read?

"For her to spend all that effort, use most of her magic, and then not communicate her will. It doesn't make sense…" Kate shrugged. "So, what's the game plan?" she asked Alec. "Tonight's the full moon, the werewolves will be at their strongest. If more beasts are going to be made, it will happen at midnight."

"The witching hour," I noted. "Why does so much of what we do come back to clichés?"

Kate smiled. "Well, all clichés originate in some truth. That's why they keep cropping up. At the witching hour magical energies and *other* paranormal strengths peak." She

paused and met my gaze. I could feel her willing me to tell the crew what I was. "You might want to make a mental note."

"Speaking of mental notes—" I tapped my finger to my temple, hoping no one noticed how unsteady that finger was. "I almost forgot. I had a bizarre bathroom confessional with Olivia today."

"You did?" Brit's eyes widened. "When?"

"After art history."

Brit leaned back in the couch, her black lined lips slanting down at the corners. "You have to learn to share. You never tell me anything good."

Kate shot me another pointed glance, I looked quickly away. She could hint all she wanted. I wasn't ready.

"Anyway, Olivia told me Travis got this weird tattoo right before he disappeared." I plucked a napkin from the metal dispenser. "Anyone got a pen?"

Kate handed me the one tucked behind her ear.

I sketched out the wolf-and-skull image from art class. "We both—I mean, Olivia wigged out when Stantial showed the class a bunch of slides from Rome. This was one of them. An emblem painted on a limestone wall." I omitted the part about the wall and the painting being exactly like the mental barrier I'd used to block Wade. They didn't need to know about Wade's stroll through Eryn-land. When I was done, I spun the napkin around so the others could see.

I expected the sketch to get a reaction—energy sizzled through my fingertips from drawing the image—but I didn't expect Brit to gasp and bury her face in Matt's shoulder.

"What?" Matt wrapped his arms around her. "Brit, what

is it?"

"My brother, Blake, had the same tattoo done a few days before he died." Brit said, her voice muffled against Matt's chest.

Kate examined the sketch. "This is old, powerful." She dropped the napkin on the table. "It's a brand. Those who bear it are marked."

"Marked?" Matt kept his arm tight around Brit's shoulders. "As in they didn't have those tattoos done willingly?"

I shrugged. "Oh, they probably got them willingly enough. Or thought they did. Olivia made it sound like Travis had gone from hating tattoos to being obsessed with them—with that one anyway." I avoided Brit's gaze as she peered at me from the haven of Matt's arms. "Stantial said scholars think it's an emblem for a warrior cult that thought they were descended from werewolves." I swallowed hard. "Lots of shapeshifters trace their origins to Rome." I didn't mention I knew this because my mother was one of those shapeshifters.

Brit tugged free of Matt and shifted to face me, her eyes swimming in black-washed tears. "Blake would never have gotten that tattoo if he'd known…"

I reached out and grabbed her hand. "I know. Whoever gave him and the others the design for that tattoo sure didn't show them the fine print."

"And that would be?" Alec raised a brow.

"Get branded with that thing, and you've agreed to become one of them. A werewolf."

Brit's face crumpled, and Matt glared at me as if

everything was my fault.

But he wasn't the one with gory images flashing through his head. Someone, or *something*, had beamed the werewolf mark into my mind. Why?

I made myself meet Brit's fixed stare. At least she'd stopped crying. I couldn't have asked her what I had to if there'd been tears. "I know this is a painful topic, Brit…but… your brother died about six months ago, right? And from what everyone says, that's around the same time peoples' pets started to disappear."

Brit nodded and rubbed her arms as if warding off a chill. "Blake died in a car accident, so everyone says. It happened during my dad's shift, and he arrived first at the scene. He said Blake was a mess. His body all mangled." She swiped at her running nose. "He said Mom and I didn't have to see him. We didn't want to. Who would want to see their brother, their son, like that? I wanted to remember him alive, strutting around the house with that huge ego of his, stinky feet and all."

Brit crumpled into Matt again. This must be crazy hard for her to deal with. It would be worse if I told her my father had been working on a cure for wolven that might have worked on werewolves too. How did I tell her there was a wafer-thin chance to save her brother when I had no idea where my father had stored his anti-were stash? After my parents disappeared, I found no trace of his work in the house or at the pharmaceutical company. Which accounted for the freaky things happening to me lately. Had the drugs only suppressed my wolf? Or had they altered it somehow?

The changes I'd been experiencing…were they normal for wolven?

Or was I different?

Was I evil? Why could Wade read my mind? Why the interest from Logan? Did he know about my father's drug?

I had the sneaking suspicion that Sebastian had a key role in Redgrave's current situation. His wanting me to come here, his assurances that he'd find out what happened to my parents…it all felt so contrived now. Like I'd been led by my nose.

Only now that I was off my father's drugs, I smelled the bitter scent of betrayal.

Brit stared down at the sketch. "If it's true, and the chief turned Blake into a werewolf, then he must have some dirt on my dad. That's the only reason Dad would lie about Blake's death." Her red-rimmed eyes met mine. "God, I hope he didn't lie. Please let Blake be at rest and not like those things we hunt."

"It's going to be okay, Brit." Matt gently brushed her hair back from her face.

Envious, watching them entirely too intently, I wondered what it would be like to have someone tell me things would be okay—what it would be like to actually believe them. I turned to find Alec considering me as if he was wondering what it would be like to reach out and tuck a tendril of hair behind my ear, to have the right to touch me and not have me pull away. The heat in his eyes made me breathless. Instinctively, I cupped my hand over the cross he'd given me, embracing the singe of my skin.

A customer left the café, letting in a gust of air and the scent of burnt cotton candy. Sickly sweet and far too perky for gloomy grey skies. Paige was close. I spun in my chair and placed my hand on the cool glass of the café's large window. The frost melted. My fingers slipped along the wet surface as I rubbed a spot clear so I could see outside.

"Oh, no…" I groaned. Across the busy road, a shop door opened and Paige stepped out, shoving her hands into her gloves. I pressed my nose to the glass. "Kate, tell me the tattoo parlor isn't that black building across the street."

"Actually, it is," Kate said, turning around.

"Why? What did you see?" Brit asked.

"Paige. She came out of there. She's peeking down her sleeve at her arm like maybe she got a tattoo."

"Oh, that can't be good." Kate rubbed her fist on the glass to clear her own porthole-sized view. She glanced at Brit. "Didn't you say she dated Wade?"

"Yeah, and she's totally obsessed with him." I pushed out of my chair and bolted for the door. The rattle of quickly abandoned spoons and coffee mugs rang out as the crew trailed behind me.

Outside, Paige had already sped away in her car. I screeched to a halt on the sidewalk. No way would I let her see me in the rearview mirror, chasing after her car like a dog.

"Should we go after her?" Matt asked. "The hatchback is parked around the corner."

"You'll never catch up," I told him. "She's given me a few rides to school, and let's say that Paige thinks of speed limits as more of a minimum requirement. She probably went back

to school to stalk Wade. It's her favorite pastime. Whatever glamour he used on her was a doozy."

Kate grimaced. "If her mind is weak, then, yes, a vampire's glamour or hold can have lasting effects." She quirked a brow at me. "I have a spell to reverse its effect. Being around Wade would make her ill. It's quite effective."

Brit's eyes widened with interest. "How ill are we talking?"

"Thanks, Kate," Alec cut in, "but I think we can use Paige's fascination with Wade to our advantage." He glanced across the busy street at the parlor. "If Paige has been marked, the werewolves will be after her. And we're already monitoring Wade's nocturnal activities. If Paige is glued to Wade's side, that makes our job easier."

One of the town's pint-sized buses slowed to a stop in front of us.

"You kids need a ride?" the driver called out, her voice rumbling like the diesel engine. "The designated pickup is at the post office, but you can hop on here."

"Hey, Janice." Kate flashed a wide smile. "We're loitering, sorry. I'll have a steamer ready for you after your shift. Be sure to drop by the café."

"Absolutely." The driver adjusted her hat and cranked the door shut.

"Wow," I said. "This really is a small town. Everyone knows the bus driver. Everyone knows my aunt and uncle…"

Kate gave me a brief hug. "It's a small, *fabulous* town. And we're glad to have you in it. But if we don't get this Harbinger thing figured out, it will be the last place anyone will want to live."

"You're right." Matt zipped up the jacket he'd grabbed on the way out of the coffee shop. "We should find out what Paige was up to at the parlor, so we know what we're dealing with."

"So far Logan has only turned *guys* into werewolves," Brit said. "Why would he turn a girl? They'd be weaker."

I laughed. "Oh no, they're not. Females are tough, unpredictable. I hate to say it, but the lunar cycle combined with PMS…that's something to be avoided at all costs."

"All right, *eww*." Brit made a face. "Point taken." She bit her lip. "Maybe Paige went inside to buy jewelry. Whip does sell other stuff in the parlor, right?"

Kate glanced at Alec. "That's true. He sells crosses, for one."

"Can we get past the cross already?" Alec folded his arms. "With Eryn's uncle causing all that trouble for Harbinger, who knows what Logan might do? Turning Paige would be the ultimate revenge."

"Let me go first," Kate said, taking the lead. "If you go charging in there with your faces all growly like that"—she nodded toward me, and I spent considerable effort smoothing my expression—"Whip will be diving for his shotgun before you can say *blood stains are bad for business*."

We jogged across the busy road—well, busy by Redgrave standards—ignoring the horn blasts. You'd think we were in downtown Vancouver the way these people drove. Alec and Kate discussed how best to deal with Whip, while Matt and I trailed behind. We were at the parlor door when I noticed Brit had walked to the crosswalk a half a block down.

I shot Matt a questioning look.

"She can't run like we can," he said defensively as if I'd called him a sorry excuse for a boyfriend, one who'd ditch his girlfriend and make her take the long way—which I hadn't, but I sure was thinking it. "She wouldn't have made it with all that traffic. Brit knows when to let us forge ahead. Sometimes she has to hang back and let others use their strengths."

"Speaking of Brit—" I groaned and dug in my pocket for my cell. "What time is it? She'll be late for her midterm and…" My words trailed off as I stared at the time displayed on my phone. Noon. How was that possible? We'd left school around noon, and we'd spent at least forty minutes in the café.

I was shaking my phone side to side when Brit walked up beside me and laughed.

"It's not broken. I told you time moves at its own pace in Conundrum."

I met her amused gaze. Then shot a disbelieving glance at Kate, who gave a sheepish shrug and pulled open the heavy metal door to the parlor.

"I told you she isn't as young as she looks," Brit whispered in my ear.

I revised my opinion of Kate's witchy powers as I followed her through the door. If she could wrangle time like that, the sky was the limit on her real age, not to mention her magic. Bizarre.

Whip's store bore all the trappings of a mystic shop. I'd certainly been in enough with my father to recognize the usual junk. Skulls, shrunken heads, dried bats—you name

it—hung from exposed rafters, and metal shelving held old leather bound books with taped-together spines. Scented candles and smoking incense sticks competed for airspace.

Talk about overkill.

The immediate war between vanilla and sandalwood made my head pound, but underneath, the deeper, darker odor of emotions set my nerve endings tingling. Grief, revenge, insecurity. Whip's customers each had their own reason for seeking out his services, and echoes of those motives lingered in the air.

A stocky guy with a red bandana on his head, wearing a black bowling shirt with red flames roaring across the chest, stood behind a glass display counter. His beefy forearms were covered in tattoos, and an actual bone jutted through his pug nose. A bone! Spurs jangled as he sauntered around the counter, revealing faded jeans, ripped at the knees. He was old-school rebel, complete with Harley Davidson boots.

He tugged Kate to him in a lingering hug that lifted her off the floor as he tossed a suspicious glance at the rest of the crew over her shoulder. "You brought the town outcasts. I tell you, I get all the best customers." His arm dropped to Kate's waist, and he tucked her against his side. He nodded to the younger couple. "Matt, Brit." Then he gripped Alec in a firm handshake. "Alec, I swear, if you're here to change your mind about that cross *again*—"

Alec tensed, and he twisted his head slightly back toward me. His tawny skin flushed a deep crimson that rose up his neck.

"I won't exchange it." Whip slapped Alec on the shoulder.

"You give her that masterpiece, and the girl's gonna be eating out of your hand."

Kate's shoulders shook with silent laughter.

"I think that's an overstatement." I stepped forward. "But, yeah"—I fingered the cross around my neck casually for a second, the silver rasping like sandpaper on my sensitive fingertips—"I like it."

"You *like* it." Whip snorted. "It's been blessed by a priest, sanctified by the local high priestess, and she *likes* it?"

"She's pulling your chain, Whip." Kate laughed softly as she smoothed Whip's ruffled feath...er, tattoos. "The Goddess knows it's easy enough to rattle. I don't think Eryn appreciated the 'eating out of your hand' comment." She made a face. "Neither did I. I hope you don't say stuff like that about *me*."

Whip gave Kate a cheeky grin, then eyed the cross around my neck. "Anyone who can put our Alec in the tizzy he was in choosing that cross is a friend of mine." He wore a conspiratorial smile. "Welcome, Eryn." He studied the rest of the group. "But I have a feeling this isn't a social visit. What can I do you for?"

"Eryn's cousin was here. Thin. Blonde." Alec wiggled his fingers near his head. "Lots of curls."

Whip snorted and shot me a look. "She's your cousin? My condolences. That one is a piece of work. Wanted some ink. I gave her a temp, but I don't think she'll be back."

Paige really had come in for a tattoo. Yikes. I wrapped my arms around my chest as a shiver of unease caught me off guard. "A temp? What's a temp?"

"I take the design the customer wants," Whip said, "and

make a temporary tattoo out of it—put it in the right spot so they can try it out for a few days before committing to the real deal." He shrugged. "I can tell when someone's serious or not. That girl was wishy-washy."

"What was the design?" Brit asked, her voice sharp. "Was it the one Blake had done? The wolf and skull?"

Whip's eyes widened. "You're right," he said slowly. "It *was* the same. Blake and a bunch of kids had the same ink done. I forgot about that." He frowned and rubbed his temples as if clearing a foggy memory. "I never forget my ink, that's odd." He shot Kate a look. "I may not know everything about what you do for this town, but even I can tell this isn't right. I never forget a tat. But I did." His face paled. "Have I done something wrong?"

"Not you, Whip. Never you." She patted his tat-filled arm. "But you might have been under a spell, or a compulsion, to do the tattoos and then forget about it. We've found a connection between the tattoos and all the terrible incidents going on around town. It's more than what you've heard on the news. *Our* kind of more."

From the resigned look on Whip's face, this was old hat for Redgrave.

CONVINCE ME

We left the parlor in a rush to get back to school for Brit's exam. The world had clicked along at its usual pace while we were in Whip's tattoo parlor. Brit said Kate could only manipulate time in the café, where her magic was strongest. Something about a preternatural time convergence in the crawl space under the java-sipping customers' feet.

When Brit started talking magicks and techy jargon I sorta didn't pay much attention. Did we have to kill it? Banish it with silver? Those were the details I cared about.

But I did wonder about one issue. If the timedoodle thingamabob existed in a fixed location under the café, did that mean Kate started to age whenever she left it? It had certainly seemed like she couldn't get back to Conundrum

fast enough.

I guess we all had our quirks.

Like Brit and her obsession with getting a decent education.

Back at school, Brit took off for her exam, Alec and Matt went to their classes, and I intended to go to mine, but at the last minute decided to skip. I shoved my Career and Life Management text back into my locker. Really, what could I possibly learn from a class like that? I didn't exactly see myself as career girl material.

I headed behind the school. The effort to blend with the masses drained me. Increasingly the perfumes, hairsprays, and body lotions grated on my nerves. I was in nose-ory overload, so I bolted for the great outdoors whenever I could.

A few picnic tables had been tucked behind a grove of spruce trees and out of sight of any windows. The perfect place to clear my head. Other students had abandoned the hideaway now that the weather was so cold.

Like I'd been abandoned in Redgrave.

I sat on a table, my feet resting on the bench, my chin in my hands.

I had to face facts. I'd been ditched by the Hunter Council after they'd promised to protect me, promised to find answers, promised they were on my side. I was done with their rules. No one had contacted me, not once since I'd arrived in Redgrave. Time for me to stop wallowing in woe-is-me-ville and take action. I had to find out what happened to my parents, maybe even go so far as to find my mother's pack and demand help.

But I had to save Redgrave first. I couldn't bail on my uncle's family now that paranorms had descended on the town—no matter how much Paige pushed my buttons. I refused to act the villain in the B-grade horror flick called my life. The Council had that role.

The bell rang for the last block of the day. It seemed like I'd been sitting there barely five minutes. I sighed, grabbed my backpack, and planned to slip back into the school via one of the teacher-only side entrances—a maneuver I'd performed often in my student career. But as I approached the darkened entrance, mint lit the air. I caught a flicker of movement in my peripheral vision.

In the shadows, shaded from the bright afternoon sunshine by a metal awning, Wade stood waiting for me. His shoulders rested against the solid metal doors. He had his arms folded across his chest. Taking a deep breath that sent the tingle of menthol into my lungs, I reached for the door handle, but he didn't move.

"Where have you been hiding, Red?" He gestured toward my rust-colored hoodie.

Why did it always come back to wolves and fairytales with Wade? Was he the one forcing the werewolf tattoo image down my mental throat? When he was in my head, did he learn what I was? Was he dishing out some cruel burn because I wasn't just Little Red, I was the Big Bad Wolf as well? I scrambled for my limestone wall, keeping my wards up against him.

"Hiding? Me?" I made an I-don't-think-so face. "I was just getting some air. You know the stuff that humans need to

survive?" Not great, but a lame burn still counted as a burn in my books.

Wade ran a hand through his shaggy dark hair and flashed me a grin. My heart sped up a bit.

"Don't be like that, Eryn. We both know you're not exactly human either, so let's stop pretending, shall we?" He pushed off the wall. "After our last…chat, I dug around in my father's office and found a file on you"—he held his hands about a foot apart—"this big." He shook his head. "My father's been watching you for months, even before you showed up in town."

I worried the inside of my cheek. Crap. *Months?* How was that possible? Before I moved to Redgrave, I was under the protection of my father's entire crew. It didn't make sense.

Unless…Sebastian…

"I don't know what he has planned for you, but it's not good."

Wade's intense gaze sent a familiar icy chill scorching along my skin. "I don't need to be a mind reader to figure out what the Delacroix have been telling you about me."

He studied my face while I struggled to keep my expression one of mild curiosity. If he only knew that I was the one filling in the Delacroix on Redgrave's resident hottie. Or should I say, resident evil?

"But they've got me all wrong," Wade continued. "I've been trying to get you alone to explain a few things. But you're hard to single out from the herd." His lips slanted. "Is that because you and Alec are getting touchy-feely? Paige said he's all you talk about at home."

Judith Graves

"What?" I snorted, ticked at him for thinking he had the right to question my friends, or speculate on my relationship with Alec, and at the same time, I was livid with Paige and her lies. Okay, the Paige thing bugged me the most. Her, I had to live with. "I barely say two words in that house." I wished my dear, darling cousin were within slapping distance.

She would be—as soon as I sniffed her out. "She's saying I've got the hots for Alec so you'll think I'm out of commission. Then she can have you to herself."

Wade's eyes glittered. "And are you?"

Tingles. Cool tingles danced across the nape of my neck. A warning that danger neared, and a sign I was a bit too into Wade. "Am I what?"

"Out of commission?" His brows rose. "Or are you still in the race?"

I gaped at him for a second. My face heated. "I only run when I have to," I said carefully, shrugging off Wade's bewitching charm, "and only if Alec's at the finish line waiting for me."

He sighed and shoved his hands in his coat pockets. "Yeah, that's what I thought." He gave me a sad smile. "Doesn't mean we can't be friends though, right?"

A vampire wanting to be friends with a wolven? "Okay," I said, my voice doubtful. "Friends. Sure."

"Good." Wade nodded. "Then as your friend, here's a bit of advice. Stop seeing Alec. He'll get you into a lot of trouble."

I rolled my eyes. "I think that's the cauldron calling the kettle black."

"I'm serious, Eryn. Hear me out. You're messing with

things you don't understand." Wade paused. "It's going to get you hurt."

His grey eyes darkened. I couldn't look away from his gaze. We were locked in a staring contest as he tried to access my mind, to influence me, and I struggled to keep him out. The energy he projected made me lightheaded. My barrier held, but it was shaky. I swayed on my feet. Wade's power squeezed my brain like it was in a garlic press. The thought of grey matter streaming out my eyes turned out to be a motivator.

I fortified the limestone wall, imagining steel beams driving up through the middle of the stones, locking them in place. The throb in my head eased. I stood to my full height, angry with myself for losing focus.

"Messing with what things?" I held very still so the world would stop spinning. How bizarre that this mental gridlock took place while we were having this nicey-nice conversation.

Wade blinked and the pressure in my head disappeared entirely. He dipped his chin, giving me this round.

"Well, for one," he said, "they think they can take on my father. *You* think you can take on my father." His lips twisted. "You have no idea what he can make people do."

Actually, I did. I'd seen firsthand what Logan had made Wade do—to his own mother. No matter how I sympathized with Wade at that moment, he was still a killer. He'd made his choice. He could have chosen death. He didn't have to be a monster.

Did he?

"Your father's making a big mistake trying to pin this

stuff on the Delacroix," I bit out. "And threatening Marcus? Paige? These aren't expendable crew members we're talking about. This is my family. Besides, I'm stronger than you think."

"Really?" Wade stepped closer, inches from my body. "Convince me."

His breath cooled my heated face. His silver-grey eyes focused on my lips, then drifted lower to my throat.

My instincts clamored at me to take charge, to become the predator, not the prey. Now that we'd put the mind games aside, other games were a possibility. It excited me to have Wade—danger—this close.

"I'm waiting," he said as he tilted in closer, whether for a kiss or a bite, I didn't know. Blood rushed in my veins. He drew a finger along the open collar of my coat. Part of me wanted to know what it would feel like to have him drink at my neck. He pushed the canvas fabric aside, revealing Alec's cross resting on my sweater.

"Cross-s-s-s," Wade hissed. Before I could blink, his body slipstreamed three feet away from me, but then returned to press even closer.

His features shifted. His eyes sank back in his skull, their almond shape morphing in the sockets, growing rounder. Wider. A dank, crude odor waffed off his skin replacing the scent of menthol.

"How beautiful," he rasped, another voice filling his mouth, overlapping his words like some lounge lizard ventriloquist. He glared at the cross, then reached out and stroked the silver form as it rested on my sweater. A sizzle and

the pungent scent of burning flesh wafted to my nose

Energy hummed around us, resonating through my body from my feet to the top of my head. Lick-your-finger-and-jam-it-in-a-light-socket kind of energy.

I couldn't move.

I trembled, willing my body to dive into action. This time it wasn't a crazy yearning for Wade that kept me from my dagger. I was literally frozen in place. Unable to do more than growl. Tucked under my jacket, my athame snapped with power, prodding me to put it to use. *Must reach. Got to try.* But my arms wouldn't move. Terror clawed up my throat. I ground my teeth together. No. He wouldn't get the satisfaction of hearing me scream.

"You're half paranorm, Eryn." When he met my gaze, Wade's eyes had darkened strangely, his pupils an empty blackness. "You're half wolven, so the file says. I read many things in that file. Enough to know you've learned that sometimes the pain is worth it." He pressed the cross against my chest, making us both cry out. Wade, in agony, and me, in fear and rage. I'd take mental gymnastics any day, over the total depravity blasting from Wade now. Was this his beast? The monster inside him that killed to survive?

He'd been taken over by the most base evil I'd ever faced. It oozed from his every pore. He had turned into someone else.

Something else.

His lips touched mine, then the pure essence of evil flowed from his breath as he spoke. "Don't you miss it? The cool slide of the blade against your warm flesh? The rush of

blood. Come on, you can tell me. Have you cut yourself lately, Eryn?"

A torrent of memories flooded my mind, tugging me down in a forceful undertow. The abrupt slice of the blade. I drowned as the metallic tang of my blood flowed. The release. The freedom. The beast pushed me down, churned for the surface. Helpless against the dual onslaught from Wade and my wolf, a sob tore from my throat.

The metal door behind us rattled.

Wade shoved me away.

I stumbled, my unfrozen limbs not quite stable. My heart slammed in my ribs like a battering ram. Wade's gaze held mine as Mr. Riggs opened the door.

"Were you kids locked out? Well, don't stand there. Hustle up, you two, there's an assembly in the gym. All teachers and students have to attend." He held the door for us. "And if I have to go…well, misery loves company."

Wade staggered as if his legs couldn't hold him upright. He held out his hand. "Eryn, please," he said, his eyes icy grey once more. "I can explain."

I elbowed past him and dove into the school.

"This isn't over," Wade breathed as I swept by.

My gut clenched. I hurried toward the gym to put as much space between us as possible. He was right, whatever "this" was—it was just beginning.

The squeaking gym doors earned us a few looks as we joined the assembly late. A mass of students sat on the impeccably polished wood floor. Teachers and other latecomers leaned against the gold-and-blue-striped cinderblock walls. I

scanned the gym frantically for Brit but couldn't find her. Mr. Riggs and Wade sidled into the gym behind me, keeping tight to the wall.

Someone tugged on my hand. I whirled around to find Brit at my side. Had she noticed my spastic reaction?

"Alec almost had a conniption when he saw you and Wade walk in together." She dragged me toward the back of the gym. Alec and Matt stood by the lopsided, five-foot-high tower of blue gymnastic mats—removed, in so many ways, from the rest of the student body. "What were you doing with Wade?"

"I wasn't *with* Wade." A flash of anger sharpened my voice. I'd gotten pawed against my will, thank you very much. "Wade was lurking at the east doors when I tried to get back into the building. The doors were locked. Riggs let us in." I couldn't tell Brit what had really happened, I was still digesting it myself. "And anyway, Alec doesn't look upset."

Alec had his gaze trained on the school stage, his face set in stoic lines. If only I could be that controlled. That focused. Maybe Wade wouldn't have gotten to me so easily.

Brit shot me a look. "Are you kidding me? Check out his hands, they never lie."

I scanned down Alec's broad chest—getting a bit distracted along the way, oh, my wolf lingered too close for comfort—to his strong arms. Preoccupied, I almost stepped on a kid and then growled at him for getting in my way. I shook my head, forcing the wildness back under lock and key. "Sorry," I muttered as I stumbled around him. "Brit, I can't see Alec's hands. They're in his pockets."

"Bingo." Brit lowered her voice as we got close to the Delacroix brothers. "A telltale sign our Alec is ticked."

She sure knew her crew.

When we reached the guys, Matt was all smiles. He shuffled over so Brit could join him and I could be near Alec. But Alec? Cold front. He kept his attention focused on the teachers setting up the podium and microphone on the stage.

"What's up?" I asked Matt, real chirpy like. "Somebody deface the principal's parking stall again?" At the last emergency assembly, the whole school got blasted because someone had spray painted over the *Reserved for Principal* sign to read *Reserved for Princess*. Mr. Fallsick wasn't pleased.

"You mean you don't know?" Alec asked, a bitterness to his tone I'd never heard before.

Jealousy. Waves of it rippled off him.

"No, I don't know. Why would I?"

Alec continued to stare at the stage. "I thought maybe Wade told you all about it, you being such good friends and all."

I shuddered. The empty blackness of Wade's eyes. The way he'd frozen me in place. With friends like that… "Wade and I did have a tête-à-tête." I paused. "More like a big bad *threaten*, if you must know. Not a pleasant experience, thanks for asking."

Alec examined my face. "You all right?" The hard lines of his expression softened.

"Yeah." I shrugged. "Nothing I couldn't handle." A boldfaced lie, but better than telling him that Wade not only waltzed in and out of my house but also my mind whenever

he felt the urge to scramble my brains.

Alec's body relaxed slightly. "Check out who he's with now."

I'd lost track of where Wade and Riggs had gone in the restless sea of students, who were getting crankier with every waiting moment, turning on each other like four-year-old twins fighting over the last birthday present. If the principal didn't get this party started soon, things would get ugly.

"There he is." Loathing seeped through Brit's voice as she pointed him out.

Wade stood at the door by the stage stairs, occasionally opening it to talk to someone in the hallway. Almost as if he were a part of the faculty—very in the know. Mr. Fallsick gave him a wave from across the stage.

Wade opened the door and escorted a beefy police officer up the stairs to center stage. A few other city-official-looking types followed, but stood off to the side. Cameras flashed, and I spotted a tall, leggy blonde woman snapping pictures of the entourage. Nina Clark, the reporter from the local TV station who'd been gushing over Logan that morning.

She really got around.

"Oh, God," Brit groaned as Mr. Fallsick greeted the officer and attached a wireless lapel microphone to his uniform. She ducked behind Matt. "Quick! Hide me."

Matt yanked me and Alec closer so Brit hid behind a wall of Delacroix and me.

"What's going on?" I tried to look over my shoulder, but Brit slapped my head.

"Don't look back here!" She poked me in the back.

"That's my dad onstage. If he sees me within forty feet of Matt and Alec, I'm dead. He's not around much, but that doesn't mean he'd agree to me dating one of the guys the whole police department thinks is killing everyone's pets. Another thing we have to thank Wade's dad for. If the chief of police says it's true, who can argue?"

Officer Hiels eyed the gym with a calculating gaze as if measuring each student's criminal potential. In seconds he focused on Alec and Matt. Even a whole gym floor away, his suspicions were obvious.

The guys suffered his attention with stoic expressions.

Pretty soon Wade tracked his interest and stared at the back of the gym. At me, standing with Alec. Kids spun around to see what the cop and the chief of police's son glared at.

"Yikes," I breathed. "Why do I feel like we're in a police lineup?"

Mr. Fallsick tapped his mic. *Thud, thud, thud.* The low beats hit my eardrums like bass drum kicks.

"Is this thing *on-n-n-n?*" His voice bellowed through the gym and ended with an ear-splitting squeal. I cupped my hands over my ears. My head buzzed with pain, still raw from Wade's forcible trip down memory lane. When the mic squealed again, Alec's hands closed over mine. My teeth ached from the reverberations.

Muffled screams rippled across the crowd, followed by relieved laughter when the feedback ended, but with Alec's warm skin pressed to mine, his body close, I didn't want to move. My eyes drifted shut.

Eventually, Riggs adjusted the mic volume.

Alec removed his hands as I lowered mine, but his dark eyes remained filled with concern. "I guess that was pretty loud."

I barely heard him through the ringing in my ears.

Fallsick tapped the microphone a few more times before beginning. "Thank you, everyone, for joining us. I know classes have been disrupted, but we have some extremely important information to share with you. Officer Hiels, from the Redgrave Police Force, is here to make an announcement." He gestured to Brit's dad.

Officer Hiels nodded and stepped forward. "Good afternoon." He dipped his chin toward the lapel mic. Then he seemed to think better of it. He took the mic off and handed it to Mr. Fallsick.

"Take this thing. I don't need it. I'm used to yelling at recruits." His gravelly voice carried easily to the back of the gym. "Listen up. I'm here to announce an official curfew for young people in our town, so that means life as you know it is about to change."

The gym rang with groans of disbelief.

Officer Hiels held up a hand, and the crowd quieted. "This is for your own good, people. We have several leads we're following on the pet situation here in town." He glared again at Alec and Matt, and this time half the gym turned to gawk at us. "But until we build our case, we're shutting you down. You all have to be inside your houses by 9:00 p.m. on weekdays and 9:30 p.m. on the weekends. That means no more movies, no night jobs, and most of all no one else is going to get hurt. Curfew starts tonight and is enforceable

by law. And the law is me. This is zero tolerance, people. Get caught out after curfew, and you'll be spending time in jail."

After a moment of shocked silence in the gym, Mr. Fallsick spoke into his mic. "On behalf of the students and staff of Redgrave High, we thank you, Officer Hiels, for taking the time out of your busy day to make this formal announcement. This won't directly affect us at school, but it might have some benefits for our test scores. After all, if you can't go out, you might as well study, right, kids?" He laughed at his joke. "Now let's give Officer Hiels a big Redgrave High thank you." He clapped, awkwardly, with the mic still in his hand.

A smattering of applause accompanied him, mainly from teachers and kids in the Axis & Allies club.

Officer Hiels gave Mr. Fallsick a nod and stalked off the stage. He patted Wade on the back as he exited the gym through the side door.

As it closed behind him, pandemonium broke out. Kids leaped to their feet, shouting, or gathering in furious huddles with their cell phones. But most glared at Alec and Matt for bringing the wrath of the cops down on their heads and at Brit, presumably for being related to the officer who'd ruined their social lives.

Mr. Fallsick gave up trying to get the students' attention and shouted into the mic at the teachers, "Take them back to class. Go back to class."

A curfew. With werewolves afoot and Wade all schizo.

Lovely.

CURFEWS OFFICIALLY SUCKED

That night I paced around my room, listening to Paige pacing in hers. Nine thirty on a Friday night. No self-respecting teenager stayed home at this hour. It was humiliating. It did make it easier to keep an eye out for Paige, though, in case she did anything stupid like try to sneak out to stalk Wade. But what if a werewolf attacked my uncle's house like they'd been doing the ranchers' places? How could I track it down if I had to worry about getting snatched by cops for being under eighteen and outside at a fourth grader's bedtime?

Forget vampires, curfews officially sucked.

Apparently Paige agreed with me. Earlier she'd pulled one of her diva fits and eaten supper in her room with her tunes blaring. If it had been anyone else, I would have pointed out

that country music didn't translate into I'm-full-of-teen-angst rebellion.

To stay sane, I tuned out the torch-and-twang wailing from our communal wall and focused on the myriad layers of sound around me.

Marcus chatted on the phone in his office on the first floor. At first I tried to keep up, but the legalese wore me down. Sammi holed up in the living room, reading bits of her kindergarten lesson plans aloud. I couldn't believe she even did lesson plans. I thought kindergarten teachers were glorified babysitters. Apparently they also have to teach kids a lot of stuff their parents should have already filled them in on. Not killing the class goldfish seemed to be at the top of tomorrow's agenda.

A muscle clenched in my stomach, like a stitch in my side after a long run. I groaned and leaned back on my daisy print pillows. After a few slow, deep breaths, the pain subsided. I sat up, rubbing my ribs. One of these days Sammi's experimental recipes would be the death of me.

A bunch of soft thumps from Paige's room caught my attention. My ears all but perked up and tilted toward the sound. My earlobes twitched. I touched the smooth skin to reassure myself I hadn't sprouted wolfy appendages. One month without my father's drugs, and my ears had lives of their own—how long before some other physical manifestation appeared? How long before I turned…

I slid my fingers around my still smooth, still hairless ears again. Not the time to let my wolven half roam free. Too much at stake. Like saving Paige from becoming a werewolf.

A scraping sound, like Paige dragging a chair across her laminate floor to her window, was followed by another loud thump and a muffled curse. I turned off my light, waited a second to let my eyes adjust, then bounded to my window. I eased the curtain aside to see Paige slink from her bedroom window and crouch on the roof.

My roof.

Paige was doing exactly what I planned to do in three hours to meet up with Brit. Sneaking out and busting curfew. I never knew my cousin had it in her.

Maybe she didn't. Maybe this wasn't Paige. Maybe this was Paige on thrall. Under a compulsion to become a werewolf for Logan's army. Like she needed an excuse to chew someone's head off. At least wolven only turned into wolves and not into muttly man-eaters like werewolves. I had a fifty-fifty chance I wouldn't crave human flesh. Not great odds, maybe, but better than my clueless cousin could expect.

Paige shinnied down the trunk of a large poplar tree growing alongside the house and scampered for the back alley.

"No no no," I mumbled as I grabbed my cell phone off my dresser and put on my shoulder holster and athame. I plucked my jacket from the back of my desk chair and then cranked open my window.

I phoned Brit as I swung my legs over the sill and checked the night sky. Backlit by the moon, a heavy cover of fast-moving clouds blocked the silvery orb from full view. The last thing I needed was a jolt of pure lunar action to excite my wolven side.

"Brit." I gave the area a quick look-see and then jumped.

"Listen, things are moving faster than expected." I hit the ground running, following Paige up the back alley. I suspected every vehicle parked along the empty street of being a ghost car lying in wait.

"What do you mean?" Brit asked.

"It's Paige." I sniffed the air for Paige's distinctive, trendy scent.

"Eryn, are you....snorting something?" Brit's voice was sharp in my ear. "You sound funny. What's going on?"

"Paige snuck out. She's on foot. I'm tracking her." My near infrared vision zeroed in on Paige's slight form. She stuck to the shadows and occasionally hid behind shrubbery. Mildly impressive. I kept well behind her. Not that I needed to be stealthy—she never once looked back.

"Er-ryn," Brit groaned. "What about the curfew? This is the first night. Cops'll be all over the place." She gave a frustrated sigh. "Don't get caught." She paused. "Don't let Paige get caught either."

"I think that's a given." We wouldn't get busted for breaking curfew. Bitten by a werewolf, maybe, but the curfew we could handle. I hurdled a mountain bike tipped over in the middle of the alley. Who rode a bike in this weather? "She's headed for town. Maybe she decided she wants that tat after all. When does the parlor close?"

Brit groaned. "Late, maybe around ten? I'm not sure, but I'll call Kate and tell her to go over to Whip's. She'll see that he's clearheaded and doesn't give Paige that awful tattoo."

"Sounds like a plan. Gotta go," I said as Paige bolted for a side street.

Brit's voice grew shrill. "Be careful."

I pocketed my cell. Another muscle cramp took me off guard. I folded over, breathing hard, willing the pain away. After a few seconds of rubbing my side, I straightened. Rotten experimental recipes.

Paige was nowhere to be seen.

A half hour later, my sniffer officially shot, I'd become heartily sick of Eden, the perfume that Paige and half the females in Redgrave bathed in. I'd tracked down a dozen false leads and nearly gotten spotted in the process.

I'd swung by Whip's parlor several times, but each time Kate had given me the Paige-didn't-show shrug through the window. I didn't want to get Kate or Whip in trouble for harboring a teen after curfew, so I gave them an I'm-heading-home wave and started down an alley toward my uncle's house. Maybe Paige had given up and gone home. I pulled out my cell to check in with Brit.

A scuffle at the entrance to the alley stopped me in my tracks. A low groan and a rasped call for help, so quiet I doubted a human would have heard it.

A guy in a …correction…a vampire in a black leather coat crouched over a human male, feeding in the darkness. The human was struggling weakly, his heels scuffing against the coarse road. My stomach rebelled, but this time it wasn't protesting Sammi's cooking.

My cell phone slipped from my slack grip and dropped softly onto a pile of overstuffed garbage bags by my feet. I grabbed it, shoved it back in my pocket, and tried not to scream. The leather coat, the hair. Ohmigod…

Wade!

No matter how badly he'd scared me back at the school. No matter how he'd hurt me with his taunts about the cutting habit I'd finally put behind me. No matter how much evil lingered inside him, every part of me cried out against what I was witnessing.

I wanted to run from the alley and pretend I'd never seen a thing, but I was my father's daughter—a hunter—so it was my duty to protect humankind. No matter who broke our laws. Muscles tense, I reached for my athame. Ready for action, I crept forward. Halfway down the alley, I tripped over busted pallets piled by the dumpster.

The feeding vampire twisted its head to glare at me.

I gasped.

Despite the blood dripping from his face, his gleaming fangs, and cold black eyes, I recognized the human this vampire used to be. I'd stared at his picture a few hours ago. An out-of-focus picture on a cell phone. A boy showing off his tattoo. *Travis.* Olivia's true love gone true evil.

"Get away from the human." My voice gravelly, shaky with relief. Not Wade, it wasn't Wade.

I gripped my athame. Not quite a wooden stake, but a single slice from the magic-infused knife would hurt Travis. A lot. And give me time to improvise a stake from one of the splintered pallets. It didn't have to be fancy, just functional. Plus I had Alec's cross for added protection, if things turned nasty.

I inched forward. The vamp growled and tossed the human aside. The human's heart still beat, but erratically. He

didn't have long. I had to get him to a hospital. I had to— I lost my train of thought as blood spurted over the concrete. The heat of it, his life force spilling out of him. The bursts, the pulses. My stomach knotted, doubling me over. The dagger slipped from my weakened fingers. I swayed on my feet. Drunk on the scent, the sounds.

The pain I'd felt earlier. Not from Sammi's cooking. From hunger. The beast under my skin called to me: *Shift. Embrace the darkness. Feed your bloodlust.*

My jaw ached. My teeth shifted in my mouth. I ground them together as they wobbled alarmingly. My face swelled, knees buckled.

I staggered.

The vampire laughed. His eyes glowed. He advanced, cocky, swaggering.

"Stay away from me," I said, my tongue too large in my mouth. I stuck out a hand to hold him off. An old nursery rhyme echoed eerily in my mind. My mother's voice breaking as she sang…*Ashes, ashes, we all fall down.* Was this it, my downfall? The wolf would take me over here in this alley? How much longer could I take the clawing at my insides?

Run. Get the hell out of there.

But I couldn't. Mesmerized. Blood pooled by the human's body. Maybe one lick, one nip. One tender bite. No one would see. Except the vamp.

I'd kill him.

After.

No! I stumbled backward. Another pain racked my gut. My knees shook. I was losing the battle. My beast was ripping

me in two.

Air gusted behind me. Then strong arms grasped me. Dragged me upright. A tinge of mint, familiar, welcome, overtook the tempting scent of blood.

Wade.

I clung to his solid, cool length, too dazed to care where he came from, how he knew I needed him. I only knew that he was there.

"Help me," I pleaded. And I didn't mean with the vampire.

The glint of pain in Wade's misty grey eyes told me he understood my internal battle. He'd fought it too.

"With pleasure." Wade extended a hand, his fingers splayed wide. A bolt of energy radiated from his palm. His vampire-witchy hold invisible, even to my wolven eyes. Power thrummed around us on a frequency I had felt before. The same electric charge Wade had used on me outside the school. And, like I had, Travis froze in place, his mouth twisted with rage, his fangs still bared. Immobile.

Painful gasps left my throat. For a second, I panicked. Wade. So strong. What if he and Travis worked together? Toyed with me? What if Wade shoved me toward the human, prone and bleeding on the ground? Forced me to feed?

What would I become?

But Wade merely held me at arm's length, so he could stare into my eyes. My vision blurred. His set features wavered in and out of focus.

"Think of something that calms you, something to soothe the beast," he said, his intense grey gaze holding mine.

I did as I was bid. The image of Alec formed in my mind. His unfailing belief that we would save the town. How he'd tried to be so casual when he gave me the cross necklace. The way his lips felt on mine when we kissed. The ache in my jaw receded, as did the puffiness in my cheeks. I relived the gentle pressure of Alec's lips.

The hands gripping my arms squeezed like a vise. "Of course, you would think of Alec." Wade bit off a curse.

A dull pain battered my head as Wade's rage and jealousy—images dark and violent, poignant and heart wrenching—bombarded me. How could I know his thoughts, feelings? How did he know memories of Alec had been my lifeline?

He's in my mind. And—OMG—I'm in his.

Wade thrust me away. A solid steel wall thundered into my mind from a vast distance. Wade had blocked *me.*

I blinked, coming back to myself, empty. Lightheaded. Lost.

"Play fair," Wade said huskily. "You're getting far too good at that. Sending a message when you're angry is one

thing, but reading my thoughts? A wolven twice your age wouldn't have that much skill, and you're only a half-breed." He laughed. "I'm beginning to understand my father's interest in you."

He shot a fierce glance over his shoulder at Travis's still form. "I have to take care of him." Wade turned back to me. "Close your eyes. Whatever you hear, don't open them until I tell you it's safe."

And the things I heard I will never forget. Terror kept my eyes squeezed shut. Terror at what Wade was doing. Terror at what might happen if I opened my eyes to watch. At last Wade's cool fingers touched my cheek.

"It's okay now."

I opened my eyes. The alley remained dank and filthy, but Travis and the human had disappeared. I inhaled, testing the air for that all-powerful scent of blood. Nothing.

Wade stood a few feet away. His speed amazed me. One second touching my cheek, the next... He stood there, eyeing me with concern. Heavy snowflakes the size of dimes drifted to the ground between us. Some caught in my bangs. Not a single flake settled on him—not on his artfully mussed hair, nor on his black leather-clad shoulders, as though he repelled their cheery, fat coldness.

He swooped down and picked up my dagger. He took a step toward me. Then stopped. His attention focused on the cross around my neck. Shakily, I fingered the silver cross weighing on my chest, Alec's gift.

The silver burned. I gasped and let my hand drop to my side.

Wade's lips twisted. "That's what caught my father's attention."

I frowned. Did he intend to take it from me? I zipped up my jacket, hiding the cross. Protecting it.

"At school," Wade told me. "He felt its presence and came to investigate." An unidentifiable emotion flashed over his face. "There's so much to explain, Eryn. I'm not what you think." He snapped his teeth together. "That's a lie. I am a vampire, of course. But today at the school"—his elegant features twisted—"that wasn't me. My sire, Logan, uses me as his vessel. I am of his making. He can see through my eyes, take over my body whenever he wants."

Wade turned away from me as if ashamed to be in my presence. Logan could take over his body. When was Wade ever himself? How did he dare to open himself to another being when Logan pulled his strings? Wade had let me see him as no other would. Vulnerable. In pain. I wanted to comfort him. But how?

"I knew what he was doing," he bit out. "How he touched you. I saw the hatred on your face, but I couldn't stop him."

"You changed so fast." I stuttered over my words, sympathy and regret caught in my throat. "Evil poured out of you." I swallowed hard. "But on some level, I knew it wasn't *you*."

The sudden brilliant silver gleam in Wade's gaze took my breath away. He approached, hesitant, cautious, as if scared I'd run away. "I can block him out for short periods of time. Like now. He's overconfident. He thinks I'm his willing slave." Wade's chin lifted. "He thinks wrong. I have my mother's

talent as well as his. I can act independently of him. I can protect areas of my mind that he can never gain access to."

Closer to me now, Wade held out my athame, hilt first. He didn't flinch as he held the blade. The silver blade would sting his flesh, not as much as a werewolf or wolven, but it wouldn't be comfortable. Nice that he could handle the touch of the rosewood hilt. So could I. That had to mean we had some good in us. I met his gaze, then took the dagger, and lifted my jacket to slide it back in the holster, flushing as I did so, aware of the sexual implications. Wade had followed my every move with an avid gaze.

Time for a mood killer.

"What about all this?" I waved a hand to the cleanup job he'd done in the alley. "Logan won't zap himself into your head and find out you kept me from going dark side?" How could Wade bear it when Logan took the helm? I'd come close to crying like a baby when the master vamp had confronted me using Wade's body. But at least Logan hadn't been in my mind.

"Did I help?" Wade nudged a chunk of crumbled concrete with his foot. His eyes fixed to the ground. "Or did Alec?" He held up a hand. "Please don't answer that." He scooped up the manmade rock and threw it into the dark alley. *Clang.* It struck the side of a dumpster. "My father caught me off guard today. Don't worry. He won't get that chance again. My protection wards are strong. There are parts of myself, thoughts, feelings, I won't let him…"

Wade fell silent.

I hoped he knew what he was talking about. I didn't

want to see him get hurt. He'd risked everything, telling me this stuff, knowing I could use it against him.

But I wouldn't. Wade and I were too much alike. Fighting the same battles with our inner demons. Speaking of which…

"The human, was he…" I let my words trail off, seeing the answer in Wade's grim face. "What did you do with the body?"

"What I had to." He ran a hand through his hair, his fingers clear of bloodstains, his clothing too.

Sterile. As if nothing had happened.

Oh, I really didn't want to know how he'd disposed of the body.

"I have his wallet." Wade told me. "I'll make sure his people are taken care of. This isn't the first time I've had to clean up another paranorm's leavings."

While I cringed at the comparison between a mess to be cleaned up and the loss of an innocent human life, I admired his efficiency. Every last drop of blood had disappeared from the concrete. The sudden image of Wade on all fours, lapping up the human's blood, flashed into my mind. Was I speculating, or did I still have a thread of my mental connection with Wade? Either way, my stomach heaved.

"What about Travis?" I had to focus on the other vampire before I gave into the urge to puke up Sammi's dinner after all. "Did you stake him or something?"

"I let him go. Eventually he'll lead me to his sire. Then I'll take care of them both, and any others."

I frowned. "Wouldn't that be *your* sire? Logan?"

"No, Travis is not of Logan's making," Wade responded

as if struggling to get the words out or scared to admit the truth. "My father has only ever sired one vampire. Me."

"Why do you—" I stopped. So weird that Wade kept calling the master vamp *his father* when he was really his unholy lord and master, but then Logan had fathered Wade into his vampire existence. Plus, Wade had been lying to humans about him for so long, he must have gotten used to doing it. Like he'd gotten used to feeding off humans and disposing of their bodies. I pushed the thought aside.

Wade ran a hand through his hair. "Logan Gervais is my father, my sire. He's old, wise, and evil." Wade glanced over his shoulder as if saying these things aloud would bring his father to us. "He knows the more underlings a vampire creates, the weaker their strength. He chose well when he selected me, a witch's son, to be his only progeny."

Grief flitted over his features. Did he remember the night he'd become a vampire and inherited his mother's power? He nodded to where Travis had dragged his prey.

"Travis had little strength. Enough to kill, to feed, but no mind-control skills, no glamour. Which tells me his sire has produced many. Too many. Even a savvy human could take Travis down."

"I guess you need to find his sire pretty fast then?"

Wade lifted a brow.

"Well, someone might stake him before you get the information you want," I said. "But Travis got marked with the wolf-and-skull emblem. Alec and his hunters—" I paused. I was one of those hunters. "*We* know how Logan is turning kids into werewolves. He compels them to get the tattoo,

doesn't he?"

Wade's face twisted again. "It's his roundabout way of following the paranorm rule that all who are turned require the mark. They turn at the full moon."

"But Olivia told me that Travis had one of those tattoos. So why is he a vampire?"

"His sire must have gotten to him before the full moon," Wade said, scanning the dark, cloud-covered sky. "Travis was marked, sure, but my father's not the only vampire in Redgrave. He's the strongest." Wade's stormy gaze traveled over my face. "All kinds of paranorms lurk in these dark alleys, in the woods, even in our school. And more are coming. Redgrave is popular with the paranorms. It's the last human outpost before miles of wilderness." Wade's smile was bitter. "Think about it, Eryn. With my father running the town, Redgrave is the ideal paranorm…vacation destination. If you want to be above the law, then you must be the law."

The law. I snorted. Logan wielded his power for personal gain. Sebastian and the Hunter Council were as guilty. Wade had it right. The town crawled with paranorms. Which meant the Council had sent me here to fail. They'd known Logan's power. Known that his witch child, Wade, increased his strength. They never meant for me to find out what had happened to my parents.

I'd been set up to die.

I never should have trusted Sebastian. Or let myself get close to the humans. My only choice was to help Redgrave get back to its bland, cookie-cutter-housing self and then get the hell out of town. The longer I stayed, the more people I put

If she didn't turn into a werewolf first. In my wolven meltdown I'd forgotten the reason I'd rushed out here in the first place.

"As much as I love to hate her, Paige is in danger," I told Wade. "We think Logan is after her too."

He groaned. "She haunts me, your persistent cousin. All I took was one little sip"—he held out his hands at my shocked expression—"forever ago. *Last year.* If I'd known she'd be so susceptible to my glamour I wouldn't have touched her." His eyes widened comically. "We can't let her be turned. She'd be a monster."

"That'd be a new look for her." My head thrummed as Wade found a hairline crack in my mental shield. I held up my hand. "Would you stop already?" How much more did he want to know? "I thought I told you to stay out of my head." I squinted at him as I sent out a mental feeler of my own to test our two-way connection.

"I will if you will." Wade let out a dry laugh. Then his expression hardened at the hum of a familiar engine.

A battered truck barreled down Main Street and passed the entrance to our alley at high speed.

"Alec's looking for you." Wade spun me gently in the direction of the street. A shiver went up my back as he pressed his hands on my shoulders and gave me a slight push. "Go now, before my father sees what I'm up to. Keep your mental wards high and strong. If my father ever discovered we've shared a link…" His voice lowered. "Go home now, Eryn. I'll find Paige and bring her to you. My father and his company

have some kind of heavy-hitting meeting tonight. I can't watch over you both."

"I can take care of my—" I jerked around. The empty alley held the subtle scent of mint.

Miffed, I shuffled from the alley and almost slid flat on my butt more than once on the icy sidewalk in my rush to locate Alec's truck. Getting busted by some curfew-happy cop because the cheap shop owners on Main Street refused to put out a little road salt was the last thing I needed.

As I reached the corner, the streetlights died on a sad sigh and left me standing there in the dark. My eyes, adjusting to the darkness, did a weird blurry/focus/blurry thing. A growl sounded behind me.

I froze. The hair on my neck did the something's-gonna-getcha-cha-cha, so I slapped a hand over them. *Down guys. You're weirded out because of the alley with the blood and Wade, and me nearly losing my mind, that's all.* But another growl rumbled, and this one sounded like my name. I whirled to face the threat. Dark forms in the distance moved closer.

I shifted on my feet, ready for action. I groped for my athame, prepared to fight for my life. The streetlights flickered back on with a series of snaps to reveal my pursuers—a parka-clad elderly couple, arm in arm, walking a small dog. They paused, frowned at my immobile form, and cautiously crossed the street, moving protectively between me and their dog. I must have been gaping like a fool. They probably thought I meant to pounce on the little mutt. As far as the town of Redgrave was concerned, kids had become the prime suspects. And here I was, out on the street past curfew, staring

down their dog.

"We've been looking all over for you."

I jumped again.

Alec—looking very dapper in a fleece hoodie, fitted jeans, and boots—stood not four feet away. "You didn't call Brit back. We were worried."

"I'm fine. Must have had the volume down." I flipped my cell open. Six missed messages. I navigated the slick sidewalk to his side. "So…did Brit tell you about Paige? Did you find her?"

"No. Kate and Whip are staying on the lookout, but my guess is Paige changed her mind about the tat and decided to find Wade." He shook his head. "Why are girls are so attracted to vampires? I know they can influence people with weak minds and dark souls, but that doesn't explain all the vampire movies and books out there. Women are so into vamps. I don't get it."

What could I say? I didn't have a weak mind, but I did kind of fall into the dark soul category. I certainly didn't want him to know how into one specific vampire I was, so I shrugged.

"Vamps are vile," I said, thinking of Travis attacking and killing that man in the alley. I shuddered. "Trust me, if women could see them without the glamour, they'd run the other way. Fast." Which made me a living, breathing contradiction to the average human female. A hunter and half wolven who could see through any glamour Wade radiated, and so far, I hadn't run anywhere.

"Girls are into the bad boy thing, I guess." Alec curled

his lip.

My throat dried. What would Alec say if he knew that I hid my wolven half, delving into dark emotions with Wade? When Wade wasn't around, I wanted nothing more than to fight at Alec's side, to be his partner—his everything. I was safe with Alec and wild with Wade. The light and the shadow. Each side of myself reflected in two very different guys.

An odd shift inside my gut wrenched a gasp from my lips. Did wanting Wade mean I'd turn evil? My two halves were snarling at each other. I had to prove to them, to myself, that I had a choice. That I had goodness in me and it reached out for Alec.

"Not every girl has a bad guy fixation." I coyly nipped at the top of my finger and then teased the glove off with my teeth. I felt really dumb with it dangling from my lips. After a panicked second or two, I opened my mouth and let it fall to the snow-covered ground.

Damn. That was so not sexy.

The wind danced in my hair as I embraced a seductress mode I didn't know I had on tap. My heart thumping in my chest, I reached out with my bare hand and tugged on one of the cords dangling from Alec's hoodie to bring him closer.

"Can you guess the kind of guy I like?" I asked.

"I have an idea," Alec said quietly, his eyes watchful, his lids half-closed. "But now's not the time. Matt and Brit are waiting in the truck around the corner. We can't be seen out after curfew."

"You're so *good*, aren't you? Such a dedicated hunter. So into this crazy job…" I sighed the words and leaned into him.

He gathered me in his arms and lifted me off my feet. I clutched his arm and angled my face so I didn't bump his cold nose with mine. We kissed like our lives depended on it. And maybe they did. Alec made me feel human, like I could walk in the light at his side instead of skulk in the shadows… with Wade.

And maybe I did the same for Alec. Pushed aside the duty, brought out the desire, the rebellion, the urge to break rules.

A horn blared in the distance. Once. Then twice fast. Alec reluctantly pulled his lips out of kissing range.

"We have to go." He picked up my glove and handed it to me, straight-faced, but with laughter in his eyes.

We headed for the truck. My shoes slipped on patches of ice so that I almost skated down the sidewalk. My balance off. My head spinning. First Wade, then Alec. Both hot, both dangerous.

I so had a thing for tall, dark, and dead wrong for me.

And it might get us all killed.

HERO, HEROETTE, WHATEVER

We'd been driving around for hours looking for Paige when I finally picked up her sickly sweet scent. She'd headed down the creepy, and usually avoided, dead-end road (pun intended), Blithe Way, that died at Crimson Cemetery. Lovely. A graveyard, a full moon, and closing in on midnight.

I made up a story about Paige rambling in her sleep about Wade and the graveyard. With my cousin's obnoxiously loud and whiny voice, it could have happened. And telling yet another lie was better than having Alec figure out I had the tracking skills of a bloodhound.

Alec parked the truck outside the locked gates, and we stared at the six-foot iron fence in silence.

"Eryn, you're sure she's in there?" Alec asked, his voice

neutral.

My nostrils flared. Sweet-smelling Paige was here all right. "Positive."

"Then I guess we better figure out how to get through that gate." Alec killed the motor.

Matt snorted. "We should wait in the truck. Girls like Paige don't do dead people."

I raised an eyebrow. "Did you just say what I think you said?"

Matt shot me a look and flushed. "You know what I mean. Can you picture Paige in a graveyard? Ten bucks says she comes bursting through the gate, screaming her head off."

Up until then Brit's only contribution to the conversation had been precise clicks as she bit her fingernails. But she slammed us with, "Aren't we going through the motions? If Paige is marked, she's done for."

Brit had issues with the graveyard excursion because they'd buried her brother there. But we could save Paige if we got to her in time. Frustration itched along my spine.

"There's always a loophole with lore if you act fast enough,"

I snapped. "A chance we can save Paige. Prime example? Travis was marked, but he didn't turn into a werewolf."

Everyone stared at me. I lifted my chin. "I saw him in one of the alleys tonight. He's definitely not one of the hairy backed and slobbery."

Brit gasped. "He's not?"

I hated myself for bringing that thread of hope to Brit's voice—hope that if Travis hadn't turned, maybe Blake hadn't either. Me and my big mouth.

"No," I clarified. "He's a vamp."

"What?" Brit slapped the back of my seat. "How is that possible? He had the mark. Olivia said so."

I shrugged. "A vampire must have gotten to him first."

Matt sneered. "*A vampire?* Don't you mean Wade got to him? I knew I should have staked that guy in English class."

"Not every horrible thing that happens in this town is Wade's fault." I shoved my door open and leaped out of the truck.

"And how would you know?" Matt yelled after me.

"I just *know.*" I shot an uneasy look at Alec's tense form behind the steering wheel. "Kate said it herself this afternoon. We've got a crapload of paranorms stalking this town. Bound to be more vamps than Logan and Wade."

I slammed the door on Matt's protests. Doors creaked as the others followed my lead and climbed out of the truck. We stood at the gate, pondering the six-foot-high fence. I was tired of waiting, tired of pretending I couldn't jump this fence faster than Paige could outline her practiced, come-hither smile with lip liner.

"Maybe there's another way in," Brit suggested.

Alec shook his head. "Matt and I have checked out this place before. Hearses, funeral processions, visitors all go in through these gates."

"This is stupid." My fingers had a stranglehold on the rusting chain. Sharp splinters of metal jabbed my palm, but I gripped harder, driving them home. I deserved the pain. What was I thinking? I'd come close to saying screw what the others thought and scaling the fence anyway. My wolf didn't take kindly to waiting for those who couldn't keep up.

"We should have a bolt cutter that can slice through that chain," Matt told Alec, who studied the empty road leading to the cemetery before nodding his okay.

Matt gave Brit a hanging-out-in-a-graveyard-won't-be-so-bad-you'll-see grin. "We'll be in there in a jiffy." He pulled a duffel bag from the back of the truck and handed it to Alec. Then he rummaged through the jumble of tools in the truck bed until he found a rusty tool.

A few quick snips later, we were inside. Huge trees, a quaint gravel road. Except for the sense of doom in the air, the graveyard had a peaceful Zen vibe.

We veered off the road and started our search. Respectfully walking a coffin's length distance from any headstone, we peered around markers and memorials with the flashlights Alec had taken from the gear bag.

"Way to show you care," Matt said as he shined his flashlight on a particularly fake-looking bouquet draped over a headstone. "Drop off some fake flowers and make it look like you're always visiting. Flowers shouldn't be eternally

cheerful like that. Not in a graveyard."

"At least they chose the right ones." Though a sugaring of frost covered the red roses, their vibrant color, their petals in full plasticky bloom, showed through. "Roses have power. You know, red for blood. Eternal life. My father used to stake them into the ground over a suspected vamp grave. To fix the vamps in place. If they couldn't dig their way out to make their first kill, they'd die. For good."

Matt blinked at the bouquet. "Huh, good thing there are plastic roses for the plastic vamps." Then he continued ahead.

I rolled my eyes. So much for bonding over a bit of lore.

Brit and Matt pulled into the lead as we searched the area for signs of life in this resting place for the good, the bad, and the rotting. Alec trailed behind me, glaring at every shrub as if it might attack. I spotted movement from the corner of my eye, whirled around, and crouched low.

With a slow flap of wings, an owl perched on a spruce tree behind us. The bird's talons circled a branch as it scrutinized the glistening snow. Narrowing on an infinitesimal shift under the surface, it swooped and, talons digging deep, swept up a mouse. The victim's thin jolt of fear pierced the night. The poor thing hadn't stood a chance.

My pulse raced with the owl's rush of victory. A smile tugged at my lips.

A touch on my arm startled me. Alec stood at my side and watched the owl soar off into the distance with its prey.

"They call it a Hunter's Moon for a reason." He pointed to the huge moon, no longer obscured by clouds that dominated the night sky. "The extra light gives the hunter an

unfair advantage, don't you think?"

"I guess," I said, blinking slowly.

His sharp-nosed profile looked a bit raptor-like in the moonlight. His black hair brushed his shoulders. Strong hands drew me close. His kiss was light and sweet, his lips cold. His breath heated my skin, warming me down to my frozen toes.

It was over way too fast.

"Guys," Matt called out. "Over here."

My lips tingled. I wanted more. But Alec had already started toward Brit and Matt, tugging me with him. I caught up and strode at his side, matching him step for step.

A series of howls rose in the night, echoing through the graveyard.

"Werewolves?" Brit's voice quavered. Matt pulled her close.

"I can double back and come up behind them," I told Alec as more howls ripped through the silence, seemingly all around us.

"No, we stay together and get these dogs." Alec grabbed the gear bag and pulled out two rifles. "Take this." He tossed Matt a gun.

Matt caught it with a ready grin.

I whipped out my athame, flipped it high so the silver blade glinted in the moonlight, and seized the hilt with a deft grip.

I laughed at Matt's disgruntled expression.

A twig snapped behind Alec. In a lightning-fast move, he cocked his rifle, whipped around, and pointed it toward

the sound.

Adrenaline pumped through my system. My teeth snapped together. A low growl worked its way up my throat.

"Did you just growl?" Brit shot me a sideways glance.

I tried to reply, but couldn't get my lips to form anything but a snarl. The muscles in my face twitched.

Alec stalked silently to a tall, gothic headstone, lowered the rifle, and reached behind the stone.

I caught a familiar scent. "Wait." I struggled to form the word.

"Come to Daddy," Alec called, then yanked a dark form from behind the stone.

"Come to Daddy?" Caught in Alec's grip, the collar of his black leather jacket bunched up at his throat, Wade managed a smile. "Do all self-proclaimed hunters sound that cheesy?"

Alec shoved Wade into the center of the circle we'd automatically formed.

Redgrave High's resident hottie—and the paranormal world's only vampire-witch—eyed Alec's taller, broader form and plaid fleece hoodie. "Your lumberjack bedside manner could use some work." He smoothed his black leather coat back into place as if he were stroking a cat. Or the thick pelt of a she-wolf.

My breath hitched. I shifted my weight, uncomfortable with the flood of heat that settled low in my stomach. The weight of my athame in my hands reminded me that Wade had given it back to me, had saved me from myself. I shoved the dagger back in the holster.

Alec flushed. "What are you doing here, Gervais? Aren't

246

graveyards a bit low rent for you?"

What *was* Wade doing here? Didn't he tell me he had some paranorm world-domination meeting to go to? Or had he shown up here to help us? Good luck trying to convince the crew of *that*. Deliberately goading Alec wasn't going to endear him to anyone. Especially keeping up this act. And an act it was. I'd seen the real Wade in that dark, dank alley, and he was nothing like the guy standing before us now. The real Wade had prevented me from giving in to the beast in the alley. Tormented, he wanted only to be redeemed.

Didn't he?

"I thought vampires liked their blood fresh?" Matt's innocent expression didn't fool anyone. "Hmm...unless Wade's experimenting with a freeze-dried diet?"

"Hardly," Wade said with feeling, glancing at a nearby headstone. "I was visiting an old friend."

Though we'd agreed to stay out of each other's minds, I concentrated on penetrating his ward. The steel wall he'd fashioned to block me out held firm. Dead-end central. I settled for physical signs that Logan might be using Wade's body again, acting through him via the blood vision he'd told me about. But Wade stood his ground, his grey eyes clear, none of Logan's darkness stewing in their depths.

A high-pitched howl pierced the night. A moment of quiet, and then a chorus of mournful bays echoed through the trees.

"Oh, God. I can't take this anymore. Where's my brother, Wade?" Brit spun in a circle, staring over the gloomy headstones to the woods beyond. "Is he out there with *them*?"

I stared at her, shocked. I had no idea she'd been that close to snapping, but the strain of not knowing about her brother must have driven Brit to the edge.

I'd been there a few times myself.

Wade lifted his hands, let them drop. "Brit, you must understand, Blake is no longer your brother—"

"Shut up," Alec cut him off.

"Blake?" Brit yelled, tears welling in her eyes.

"He won't recognize you," Wade said. "Don't do this. It's like you're calling him in to his supper." He paused, his gaze sweeping the group. "Which would be all of you, by the way."

"My brother told you to *shut up*." Matt turned in a circle, scanning the trees, watching for movement.

"Blake turned like the others. But because of the blood running through his veins"—Wade stared meaningfully at Brit—"the blood running through your veins, he fought my father's direct commands. And survived. He's rogue, Brit. He has no master."

Brit took a step closer to Wade. "Then what is he? Where is he?"

"I don't know." Wade addressed us all. "He can shapeshift like no other. He assumed the guise of one of my father's police officers and escaped from the cage holding the werewolves. Blake is like nothing we've seen before. But don't think that means you can save him. He's lawless."

"That's it," Matt ground out. He lowered his duffel bag and rifled through its contents. "I'm going to shut his hole. Permanently."

My pulse hammered in my throat. What the hell was

Wade talking about? What ran through Brit's veins? I studied her short, slightly rounded form. She couldn't run. Why? What was wrong with her? Her brother couldn't have had the same disability—he was a hockey player, for god's sake. They ran, didn't they? Kind of?

Matt withdrew a very long, very woody stake from the bag, his eyes trained on Wade.

"Matt, seriously, stop it," I said. "It's not funny anymore."

"I'm not laughing." Matt drew his arm back and fired the deadly missile at Wade like a quarterback throwing a perfect spiral pass.

"No!" The stake whirled toward Wade, who stood unmoving and watched it fly at him as if mesmerized. My body hurtling an impossible distance at an impossible speed, I dove into its path. Rolling in the snow, I snagged the stake moments before it plunged deep into Wade's…thigh.

The crudely sharpened poplar branch trembled in my grip, inches from his jean-clad leg.

"I appreciate the effort, Eryn." Wade's voice held a note of contrition. "But I think you sealed your fate by saving me from a minor flesh wound."

Oh, crap. What had I done? No human could have traveled that distance, or managed to pluck the stake out of the air before it struck home.

I jumped to my feet. The astonished expressions on Brit's, Alec's, and Matt's faces were exactly why I hadn't told them I was half-wolven. I waited for the disbelief on Alec's face to change to horror and for the horror to build to hating my guts and eventually chasing me out of town.

"I can explain…" I started.

Wade ran a hand through his hair. "I already tried that line on you, Eryn. Outside the school. If you recall, it didn't do much good then, and I don't think it's going to help you now."

Brit slapped her forehead and rounded on Alec.

"I told you she wasn't like other hunters." She groaned. "I could sense it. Why don't you guys ever believe me when I tell you I can sense other paranorms? Didn't I peg Wade months ago?" She rounded on Matt. "And you, always with the 'We can't trust her.' Think of the time we've wasted doing everything the *hard* way."

"You weren't there when my mother had her vision about Eryn," Matt said hotly. "You didn't see how it affected her."

The swirling snow and drone of the wind faded into the night. Visions? Meaning Alec's mother didn't have connections to the paranormal world, *she was one?* Humans could have intuition, that was true, but even that meant somewhere along the line they had paranormal blood mingled in their bloodline, but it had weakened over time. If Alec's mother had visions, she'd have to be first or second generation paranorm. Alec's mixed blood was comparable to mine. The question was—exactly what kind of paranorm lineage did the Delacroix have?

I tamped down my sudden excitement. So we had paranorm blood in common. Alec didn't seem too thrilled at my sub-par humanity. In fact, he seemed resigned, disappointed. Sad. Not the emotions I hoped for.

"If Eryn is the girl we *think* she is…" Matt's gaze slid

over my stricken form, then he pursed his lips and refused to complete his thought.

"Then she can save this town," Alec said, his voice devoid of all emotion.

Matt sighed impatiently. "And *destroy* you."

My fingers sought Alec's cross. I stroked its outline under my jacket. Even through the cloth the silver made my fingertips buzz. Had Alec's mother had premonitions that I was going to save the town, but would cause Alec untold harm? *Destruction* even? Because of my beast being set free?

"The only thing Eryn's going to help us destroy is Harbinger Properties," Brit championed. "Right, Eryn?"

I wished I could agree. I stepped away from the crew and pretended to scan the tree line for movement, my thoughts scattered. Under my high school girl sheep's clothing—I was wolven. A predator. And my father's tampering might have made me something much worse. Wade and I couldn't have communicated telepathically unless darkness burrowed in me. How could I reassure Brit of my harmlessness when the beast shifted restlessly under my skin?

"So, you didn't know about the Delacroix's talents?" Wade murmured at my side. "I thought Alec would have told you." He shrugged. "But then, you haven't been exactly forthcoming with him either, have you?" His eyes watchful. "What else have you neglected to tell him? Does he know I share a link with you that he can never hope to equal?"

Does he know about us, Eryn? Wade's voice a velvet whisper in my mind.

I stepped away from him. There was no *us*. A flare of

mint drifted off his skin, and I inhaled slowly, shivering in guilty pleasure. *Or was there?*

When I refused to speak, he sighed and grabbed the stake from my hand. "If you don't mind, I'll dispose of—"

Matt, misinterpreting, charged forward and tackled Wade in a spectacular, if unnecessary, move. Brit was impressed. Her eyes went all dewy.

"Get the duct tape from my bag," Matt ordered as he knelt on Wade's snow-planted form and twisted his wrists together behind his back. Wade held so still. Deliberately showing his good faith by not retaliating, although it was costing him dearly. He ground his teeth together hard enough for me to hear.

From behind a large cross headstone came a banshee-like wail.

"Leave…him…alone…"

Paige careened through the snow, her blonde curls snaking out from under a wool hat. She pounced on Matt, grabbing him by the throat, riding his back like a horse, and choking the life out of him as he hunched over Wade. Matt garbled out a few curse words as he clawed at Paige's hands.

Fortunately for Matt, Paige's pink foofy mittens didn't allow her manicured fingers to do much damage. Besides, she didn't hold him for long before Brit leapt on *her*. Brit ripped off Paige's hat and pulled on those curls like she was unmasking the big bad at the end of a murder mystery show.

"I don't believe this," Alec said, then sighed as I yanked the girls apart. Paige stalked away from me, snatched her hat, and dusted off the snow. Brit helped Matt to his feet. He

rubbed his neck and glared at Paige.

Wade stood in a blur of movement. His incisors extended slightly from the excitement of the scuffle. He eyed Paige with dread. Hmm, so she inspired fear even in the undead.

Paige, her eyes trained on Wade's fangs, stood trembling from her stalker-turned-avenging-angel line drive across the graveyard. Her lips parted as she tugged at the pink scarf around her neck and pulled it away from her flesh in invitation.

Wade's eyes darkened. Then he gave a low groan and twisted his body away from her as if repulsed by the easy conquest and appalled at his vampire body's instinctive response to the sight of her pale neck.

The rest of us shifted uncomfortably as if we'd stumbled upon a lovers' tryst. A bitter, hollow feeling settled in my stomach. Looked like a lot more between Wade and Paige than a case of vamp-control gone bad. More than a one-time feed.

"*Ewww*...awkward." Brit's face twisted in a grimace.

Matt and Alec stood tense, ready to bring Wade down if necessary.

Paige's expression hardened. She wrapped the scarf around her neck in angry jerks. Despite my inner turmoil, I sympathized with my cousin. Humiliated like that in front of us—the very people she'd never want to lose face in front of. But on the other hand, Paige obviously had a relationship with a vampire and had snuck out of the house despite the curfew—not to mention had almost gotten a tattoo that would have marked her as a future Werewolf Academy grad.

"Are…you…crazy?" I grabbed her shoulders and spun Paige around. "Graveyard stalking after curfew? Real smart, Paige. I can't wait to hear what Marcus says about this."

"Oh, that's rich." Paige laughed. She shoved her toque back on her head. "You'll be in as much trouble as me if my parents find out. Worse, because I'll say I followed you to make sure you didn't get attacked by the town dog killer. I'll come out sounding like the freaking hero."

"Um, Paige," Brit said with a smirk, "aren't you lacking certain physical attributes to be the *hero*?"

Paige rolled her eyes. "Hero, *heroette*, whatever."

Brit shot me an are-you-sure-you're-related glance.

"Doesn't look like your father's curfew had much impact, Gervais." Alec smiled. "All the people he wanted to confine are right here."

"Actually, the curfew was my idea." Wade grinned. Happily, his incisors had shrunk to their normal length. "At the very least I thought it would keep *her* out of the picture." Wade glared at Paige. "But I guess that was too much to hope for. I'd also hoped to keep you and your crew"—his gaze flitted briefly to me—"out of harm's way."

"So you've had a change of heart, is that it?" Matt jeered. He gathered up the duct tape as well as the makeshift stake and shoved them into the gear bag. "We're supposed to believe there's nothing to fear from you, a master vampire's minion, the only vampire-witch we've ever heard of?" The look he gave me was nothing less than withering. "Just because *she's* bought what you're selling, doesn't mean the rest of us believe your door-to-door sales pitch."

Paige sighed dramatically. "Good Lord, what's with all this *I'm going to kill you*, no, *I'm going to kill you*? And, I'm sorry, Wade may be a vampire, but he's one of the good guys. He and his father are trying to change. They don't kill, their desire is a gift," she intoned. Apparently the bond that had Paige stalking Wade also had her spouting off rhetoric like a good little vamp cult member. "They grace us with their need."

"Someone make it stop before I hurl." Brit poked a finger in her mouth.

Paige examined Alec and Matt. "You're not telling me those rumors are true? You actually hide in the woods and try to trap Sasquatch and stuff?" She laughed. "Vampires, okay. I get vampires—humans with a few extra teeth and a liquid diet. But werewolves? Why don't you post your hunts on YouTube?"

She hoisted herself onto a thick marble headstone. Her swinging boots tapped on the epitaph's engraved letters. She obviously had no qualms about waking the dead. "Go ahead. Catch something quickly." She waved her hands at Matt and Alec. "Let's see some action already. We're already busting curfew. We might as well have a little entertainment."

Alec rubbed at his head like Paige had given him a migraine. He did a slow scan of the graveyard's perimeter. "It looks clear. We'd better get back to the truck."

"Oh, goody. Movement." Paige hopped from her headstone perch. Brushing past me, she smirked. "I told you Wade was mine."

I sucked in a breath. "Are you insane? He's a VAMPIRE,

Paige. How long has he been using you, feeding off you like a leech?" Hurt and anger had me spewing out the words, not caring that Wade could hear me. "He's the walking dead. Unholy. Evil. He'll kill you."

"Maybe I want to die," Paige spat back at me. "Did you ever think of that?" She bolted after the guys.

I let out a harsh breath and elbowed Brit. "Can we get Kate to whip up some kind of anti-remembering spell for her when this is all over? Make her forget all about Wade?"

"Yup." Brit pursed her lips. "Kate could make her forget *a lot* of things." She glared after Paige. "Like the ability to speak."

We trudged through the snow, weaving around headstones. What had I been thinking, letting Wade get close to me? Trusting him? Wanting to help him? All lies. He'd been feeding off my cousin. Maybe he could read her mind too. She definitely had inner darkness.

I thought of Alec's expression after I'd saved Wade from Matt's stake. He'd looked….disillusioned. Like I'd disappointed him, not by being a paranorm, but because I'd risked my life to save someone as evil as Wade.

"I know I seem to be repeating myself, but me and Paige…" Wade said, catching up to me. "It's not what you think. She was willing to help me through some dark times, and I'll always be grateful. But this thing between you and me—" He grasped my arm, pulled me to a stop, and then brushed his knuckles across my temple. "Eryn, I've never felt anything like this before."

He tested my mental wards, trying to get inside my head.

For a second I almost caved, but then I knocked his hand away and dashed ahead to Alec's side.

"Alec, we have to talk," I said and reached for his hand, only to have him pull away.

"We've both been hiding things, Eryn. I get it." He shoved his hands deep into his pockets. "Can the details wait until we get Paige out of here? Now isn't the time." His voice was harsh. His body moved stiffly, his shoulders rigid with tension. His cutting tone grated on my raw nerves.

"When is it the right time with you?" I softened my voice. "Look, all I'm trying to tell you is whatever your mother said, I'd never cause you pain. And a word like *destroy*, that's pretty harsh—"

"Eryn, back off," he ground out and grabbed my shoulders.

"What?" I planted my feet. "I will *not*. If you'd let me expla—"

"Get out of here. Now!" Alec shoved me aside. He took the full impact of the werewolf that had launched himself at us.

Oops, I Did It Again

Alec absorbed the creature's impact with a grunt. He locked his arms around its chest, wrestling it to the ground.

Ohmigod. Alec. My wolf slashed to the surface. Alec was pack. *Mine. Fight for him.* But I could only sway on my feet. Muscles clamored as my human side baulked at the urge to shift.

If I let it happen, would I find myself again?

The hairs on my neck arched over like claws. The flesh on my back heaved and spiked, the hackles of a very ticked-off wolf.

Alec yanked out handfuls of fur, yelling bloody murder. The stench of rotting, snow-dampened werewolf overpowered me as he and the enormous beast tumbled across the snow.

Nostrils flaring with my harsh breaths, I growled low in my throat.

Hearing me, the beast wheeled and graced us all with a ferocious snarl, yellowed teeth bared, jaw morphing from vaguely human to wolfish, before it pounced on Alec again.

Have to fight. Have to do something. I struggled to command my fractured mind, to regroup. I was losing a tug-of-war between the beast under my skin and my soul. I was battling in quicksand, slipping down, soon to be submerged.

Paige let out a crazy girly scream at the molting mass of werewolf. The shrill sound brought my world into focus. A fusion of senses, of power. A firebomb went off inside me and melted all the flesh together.

She needed me. They all did.

And, Lord, Paige had some pipes.

I reached under my jacket and grabbed my athame from its leather holster. Beside me, Matt let out a string of curses. In my peripheral vision, he dropped to his knees and rooted through the gear bag.

The werewolf straddled Alec, crouching low over his squirming body. It snarled as if to say, *This kill is mine.*

My heart rocketed in my chest. We were beast to beast. Both out to win.

No way, Jose. Looks like you'll have to brown bag it.

"Don't settle for a measly human, Fido." I tucked my athame close to my side, out of view as Alec scrambled in the snow. I gripped the rosewood hilt, eyeing the werewolf's ribcage. I couldn't throw my athame without risking Alec. I'd have to get close and stab with a direct thrust. "Now there's

something meatier. And you're looking right at it."

The werewolf shifted its weight, uncertain. Snuffling and snorting, it tested my scent on the breeze.

That's it big guy, what am I? Food? Squeaky toy?

Or a bitch with a knife?

I sprang forward, launched into the air.

The beast howled with rage, leapt for me. Alec rolled out from under its morphing limbs. Over his body, the beast and I collided in a mass of fur and flesh. I stabbed my blade again and again.

The creature reared back, snarling in pain. It knocked me to the ground with a brutal hit to my neck and shoulder. I tumbled to the snow. In a flash of movement, I tried to right myself. A small crimson dot marred the pristine snow. I ran my fingers along my neck. They came away wet. *That mutt scratched me.* My athame slipped from my bloody fingers.

A gunshot pierced the night. Matt? Was he protecting Brit? Grunts and shouts of battle erupted all around us. Was Logan back? The stench of werewolf increased. More had arrived. Where was Wade? Was Alec okay, or had I done too little, too late?

Paige was screaming nonstop, spurring me into action.

The weight of the werewolf on me, my fingers plowed into the snow, searching for my athame. Finally, I grasped the rosewood hilt. Thrust the dagger into the beast's jugular. Wereblood, dark as oil, gushed from the wound. Freaked, I shoved the creature off me. With another forceful stab, I struck the beast's black heart.

The silver worked fast. A dead boy stared up at me with

soulless eyes. *What a waste.* Logan would pay for each and every death. A flare of white light, and he was gone.

I spun to see Alec and another werewolf crash into the base of a marble headstone. *Good. He was still fighting. Still alive.* Huge chunks of polished stone exploded into the air, glittering in the moonlight like shards of glass. The werewolf recovered and lurched to all fours.

"Alec…" I stumbled forward, my heart galloping in my throat.

A metallic burst of silver permeated the air as a shot rang out. My long layered bangs danced as the silver bullet rocketed over my shoulder. Too close. But I'd take that up with Matt later. If there was a later.

The bullet scorched a trail along the beast's back, ricocheted off the demolished headstone, and embedded itself into a tree twenty feet away.

Rumbling its displeasure, the beast dug two claws into Alec's hood and dragged him through the snow, caveman style. They disappeared behind a large crypt.

Matt shouldered me out of the way. "Stay with Brit," he ordered, reloading his rifle. "And keep your eye on Wade. I don't trust him."

I made a grab for his arm, about to shove him out of *my* way. *Silly human, you're more breakable than I am.* He bolted after his brother, roaring bloody murder as he rounded the crypt.

A shot. A muffled curse. Another shot. Silence.

I sucked in a breath.

Then Matt's voice. "I got it."

A blinding white light flashed from behind the crypt.

"Alec's fine," he yelled. "We're going to scout around. Stay put. We'll be right back."

I scoured the tree line, the tombstones, for signs of activity. The area was clear of weres, for now. How many had we killed? How many more innocent kids had Logan forced us to slaughter? Pulse erratic, I whirled to face the others.

Wade was struggling to unclasp Paige's hands from around his neck. When he did, Brit shoved Paige behind her, following basic hunter field strategy—keep humans safe at all costs. Nice, but what was Brit's real value to the crew? Staying behind to protect a human was one thing, but in battle, not being able to run was deadly. Possibly the death of any human she tried to protect. How could I use her to our advantage?

And Wade's enigmatic expression, his lack of emotion, the way he straightened his leather coat and avoided my gaze—not what I wanted to see.

"Why didn't you do something? Alec could have been ripped apart!" I charged toward him. "You could have put your *Mr. Freeze* on the werewolves. That might have been an idea."

Wade crossed his arms. "You're talking suicide. If I use my magic on creatures my father made, forged from my own power… That could backfire in very painful, deadly ways." He met my gaze. "At the very least, I'd be weakened. You need me fighting fit."

I snorted. "That's convenient." I shot a glare at Brit. "And *you* could have warned me Matt was about to blow my head off! That last shot trimmed an inch off my bangs."

Brit's eyes were red-rimmed, her concern for Matt clearly overriding everything else.

Wade pursed his lips. "Frankly, I'm surprised it took all of us to put those dogs down. With odds like that, I don't see how the infamous Delacroix brothers have lived this long."

"We aren't all immortal, Wade," I shot back. My mother's kind were vulnerable to silver poisoning, plus all the regular human illnesses. They had increased healing powers, true, but they didn't live forever. I rubbed at my nose with the back of my hand. The stench of werewolf lingered. "We don't have the benefit of unlimited do-overs."

"Er…yn…." Paige singsonged.

I wrinkled my nose at the increasing stench. "I can't be the only one who smells that."

"ERYN!"

"What?" I whirled around. Paige stood frozen, her trembling finger pointed toward the edge of the cemetery. Fine snowflakes billowed around the graveyard's tombstones and crosses, glistened in the moonlight, giving the graveyard an ethereal vibe. The light diffused in the mist and drifted over the tributes to the dead, illuminating the pack of werewolves storming our way. Some launched over the terrain on all fours, others on two grotesque versions of human legs.

The rest of Logan's fleabag, foaming-at-the-mouth army had arrived. Bloodlust emanated from their hulking forms in bitter waves.

Paige's mouth opened and closed like a goldfish's, but no sound emerged.

"Alec, Matt," I yelled, even as I realized we could never

fight them all off, even with the Delacroix's stash of silver bullets. "Um…help."

Shots rang out from the far side of the crypt. The brothers were fighting their own battle. We were on our own. Without the aid of silver bullets.

Brit, Wade, and I formed a circle with Paige in the middle—all that stood between her and certain death. I tried to gauge our odds, but lost count after twenty beasts. Their unpredictable shifts and leaps too hard to track.

"Wade, are you sure about that freeze of yours?" I asked. Logan must have ventured far and wide to amass such a pack.

"I'm sure. An attack would fire back at me threefold, but I can put a ward around us," Wade said. "It might hold them back—or they may slip through unharmed." His hands moved quickly, sketching fiery symbols in the air. "These creatures share my father's essence. That can contaminate my magic." A whoosh of energy blasted over our heads, shimmering in the air like heat waves over sunbaked asphalt. The werewolves closest to us backed away, hissing, from the surge of power.

"It's working." Relief tinged Brit's voice.

Paige inched behind Brit, then me, to wrap her arms around Wade.

"I'm scared, Wade," she said in a little girl voice. "Hold me."

Oh for the love of— I grasped the back of her coat and hauled, but she held firm.

Cursing, Wade lowered his hands to shove her away, and the ward he'd built weakened. He resumed his work, more symbols kindled to life but his concentration had weakened.

His shoulders strained, his arms trembled. The air above us lost its pulsing energy. Three werewolves snapped and snarled. The ward smoked and sizzled, then dissipated into the snowy air. The creatures paused as if puzzled they weren't injured.

Wade, Brit, and I glared at Paige, who retreated a few steps.

"Well, sor-rry," she drawled, then blanched as the beasts neared. "Aren't you going to do something about them? They don't look very friendly."

"Ya think?" Brit snorted. She drew in her leg like a slingshot and released a powerful sidekick. *Smash.* She leapt in the air, linked her fingers together and crashed down, whomping the beast on the head. Foam spewed from its jowls.

Brit stunned me as she pummeled the werewolf into submission. She might not be able to run, but, by all that was holy, she could kick paranormal butt. The beast slumped to the ground.

"Use silver to kill them," Brit yelled. She held up the medallion I'd returned to her. "Or they'll keep coming back for more." She plunged it deep into the werewolf's chest, ripping through muscle and sinew. How was such strength possible from a human?

The other werewolves howled in rage as their fallen brother morphed to human form, then disappeared in a flash of light.

I gripped my athame and assumed a battle stance as a werewolf thrashed toward me.

Wade nodded his approval.

I scanned his hands. Empty. He could fight, but had no

way to vanquish the weres.

"We need more silver," I yelled.

"Sorry, Red, don't have time to knock over an antique store," Wade sniped.

I stumbled over Matt's gear bag, open on the ground, and kicked it toward Paige. Her eyes glazed and panic stricken as she stared at the circling beasts, Paige didn't move.

"Find some silver," I shouted as I stabbed my athame into a werewolf's throat, then struck again directly in its heart, settling into the rhythm of battle as my father had trained me. "Wade needs silver to kill them. Throw him something."

Wade was the magic word. Paige shot a concerned glance at her vampire love, who was wrestling a werewolf. His face twisted with rage as a claw tore a foot-long gash in his leather coat. Paige ducked and rooted through the gear bag. She tossed items randomly at Wade's back.

A wooden cross glanced off his leather coat.

He hissed.

"Sorry," Paige called.

She tossed porcelain relics, a vial of holy water.

Wade roared.

"Oops, I did it again," she sobbed apologetically, then yelled at us, "I don't work well…under…pressure. I'm strictly an indoor girl."

Two more beasts charged. I had no time to supervise Paige's antics. The air filled with evil. The stench of carrion caused my throat to tighten. I gagged. My thighs twitched. My legs dug into the earth, claiming this ground as my own.

The beast in me awoke. Ravenous. Frenzied. *Let them*

come. My pulse thundered in my ears, drumming out the grisly, yet thrilling, grunts and snarls of the werewolves all around us.

Wade leapt in the air, landed on a molting back, and sank his two-inch fangs deep into its neck.

I roared my approval into the night. The cry that left my throat wasn't human. A few werewolves halted mid-step. Their heads swung toward me.

Behind me, Paige squealed her success. An antique silver serving spoon whizzed through the air at Wade. He snatched it and with one hand ripped the molting flesh from the beast and with the other plunged the silver spoon into its heart.

I'd heard of silver spoons in people's mouths but… whatever worked.

A werewolf leaped at me with a drawn-out snarl, incisors dripping with stinking saliva. My nose scrunched up at the smell of recent kill—canine. How these creatures defiled themselves. Slaying such weak prey. I dodged his charge, then waved my hand to get rid of the fumes.

"Whew, someone's been eating their dogs raw again."

The creature froze as if stunned I hadn't cowered in fear. But I was no longer plain old Eryn—I was Eryn with some serious wolven attitude. The hands gripping my athame now had claws and tufts of silver fur. My jaw extended, bones cracking and shifting to make way for a wicked mouthful of teeth. This should hurt like hell. But only my teeth ached, elongating—scraping against my bottom lip. I swiped my tongue out to collect the blood.

"How 'bout a snack with a little more kick?" I said

thickly, through a mouthful of fangs. I shot out a sidekick and struck the beast with such savage force its head lollygagged on its shoulders. I laughed. Before he could recover, I launched myself at him. With my strange wolfish hands, I grabbed him by the scruff of the neck and the snout. Purely on instinct, I snapped his neck with an awesome wrench.

Black blood spattered my chin. Breathing hard, I wiped it off on my sleeve and met Wade's openmouthed stare.

I bared my teeth, riding the rush of adrenaline and wolven strength. But it was new, untried, and all too quickly ebbed. I gulped in air as the pressure in my face faded and my teeth resumed their normal size. I stared down at the boy I'd killed. His face etched into my mind, his pale skin dotted with freckles. Another lost soul. Then he burst into a ball of white light.

I had no time to feel anything more than a twinge of regret.

Wade, Brit, and I worked as a team, slaying and cataloguing the dead, committing their faces to memory even as they disintegrated. We killed many, shielding our eyes as werewolves imploded around us, leaving us vulnerable, blinking away spots in the night.

The werewolves began to retreat, slinking back through the graves and into the woods.

My athame trembled in my hand. *Gotta rest a bit.* I slumped against a granite angle, using the stone as a prop to stay upright.

"Father must have called them back." Wade met my gaze, his expression bleak. "They'll tell him I helped you protect

Paige. That I killed their brothers. There's no good way to spin this."

Sucking in gulps of air, I stared at Wade. My wolf worked overtime, revving through my veins, healing me from the inside out. *Helped protect Paige?* Was that what all this was about? If Paige hadn't been with me, would he have stayed to help? Or had he jeopardized his standing with his father to protect her? I shoved the sharp stab of jealousy aside and pushed myself from the tombstone. The core of my body rejuvenated, my muscles aching, but steadfast.

I turned to see how my cousin was holding up.

Nothing but a pink foofy mitten rested on the snow.

"Oh no—" I lurched forward, clutched the mitten to my chest.

"Where'd she go?" Brit cried. "We need to put that girl on a leash."

Wade pointed, his face grim. "There."

Twenty feet away, near the woods that edged the cemetery, a werewolf reared onto its hind legs with a roar. Paige knelt in the snow, her arms shielding her head as the beast towered over her. In the after-battle quiet, sound carried to my sensitive ears. Cartilage snapped as the werewolf changed from walking on four legs to standing on two. Its torso shifted to normal proportions. The more human it started to look, the more evil it seemed.

With a single long howl, the werewolf slung Paige over his shoulder and slipped into the woods.

"Don't." Wade made a grab for my arm as I leaped forward. "They want you to follow. It's a trap."

But I was already running a zigzag slalom around tombstones and crypts, my nose high, trailing the horrid perfume and rotting werewolf blend into the forest. When I had Paige safe, I'd kill her myself.

"Eryn, wait for me-e-e…" Brit's voice echoed around me.

"No, Brit, wait for the guys," I shouted over my shoulder. Brit broke into a run. I slid to a stop as her legs gave out and she stumbled. Magical energy sizzled in the air. Her body shimmered and trembled, her face shifted, her skin darkened.

"Brit!" Frantic, I reached for her, but grabbed only a fistful of air.

Gossamer wings, iridescent yet glossy, like black licorice, arced behind her as Brit jettisoned over my head into the night sky. Ohmigod. A dark sprite. No wonder she never ran in front of humans. The urge to break into flight would have been maddening.

"Where did they go?" Brit screeched, hovering in the air above me. "I don't see them. *I don't see them.*"

I stifled my own panic and opened the door to my wolven side.

I inhaled deeply. Beyond the beast's gloating stench I picked up Paige's lingering fear. Fear was easier to track. It called to me. My skin stretched taut over my bones, barely kept me from splitting in two.

The whooshing thrum of Brit's wings above me kept time with the pounding of my feet as I ran. Branches flew at my face, but I barely felt the stings. Deadwood, thickening brush—nothing slowed me down. I moved, fluid, without conscious effort, at an incredible speed. Outside of myself. This Eryn wanted blood, wanted to wage war.

I couldn't help but like her.

My lungs—cavernous. My ribcage popping and then expanding as I took in both air and the scent of my prey. And the saltiness of fresh blood on the air, Paige's blood.

Paige was pack…I couldn't let Logan have her.

"I see them," Brit yelled above me. Then she tucked her wings into her body and dove into the treetops.

Ignoring the pain twisting my guts, I sped up and followed Brit into a small clearing. In the middle of the snow-covered field, the werewolf stood a few feet away from my cousin, snorting and gnashing its teeth. *Why wasn't it ripping into her already?* Paige held out her mittenless hand. A torn gel nail dangled from her finger. Blood dripped from her hand in slow motion, staining the snow crimson like a cherry snow cone.

The coppery scent of her blood traveled fast across the clearing, brought to me by the wind. My jaw ached, my face

swelled from the pressure.

"Look what it did," Paige raged. "I'm bleeding!"

The werewolf, having morphed back to its walking-on-all-fours state, stared at Paige, its jaws hanging open.

In the throes of full-on bloodlust, hardly in the position to appreciate the humor of the situation, I couldn't get any closer to Paige. In my semi-morphed state, I might be more of a threat to her than the werewolf.

Brit knocked Paige into a thick shrub, then swooped at the beast. She glommed onto his back, immobilizing him with her arms and the four-inch long talons at the tip of each wing. *What I'd give to have those babies.* She yanked his forelegs back, snapping his spine, leaving his ribcage exposed.

At his roars of pain, I ran forward, gripping my athame, then hesitated. Brit looked so foreign in her dark sprite form. Her eyes flickered strangely, glowing gold like a cat's.

"Do it," she snarled, thrusting the werewolf's exposed belly toward me.

I hauled my arm back and fired my athame straight into the werewolf's heart.

Bulls eye.

Brit let him go as he morphed to human form. The boy who slid from her grip was the rancher's son. His parents had been on the news that morning, pleading for information on his disappearance. How long ago that seemed.

We shielded our eyes when his body shimmered. The light faded, leaving a melted snow imprint of his body on the ground, like a crime-scene chalk outline, with Paige's other mitten resting in the center. Paige dove for it as evil's sour

stench drifted across the moonlit clearing.

My nose wrinkled. My lips twisted into a snarl. Logan stalked into view, flanked by two of his wannabe-vamp rent-a-cops, who hissed at us like poorly costumed actors in a B-grade horror flick.

Well, Wade *had* tried to warn me.

THERE'S A PLAGUE IN THIS TOWN

I stroked the thin leather string around my neck that held Alec's cross, promising myself that *next* time, if there was a next time, I'd count to ten and recall this exact moment of sheer panic before chasing after weres, or vamps, or anything else. The silver cross flashed in the moonlight as if taunting Logan to come and do his worst.

I grabbed Paige's arm and yanked her behind us. The cool night vibrated with the paranormal energy fogging the air. Brit's dark wings twitched behind her, fanning back and forth like an angry cat's tail.

"Hey…" Paige batted at the iridescent wing blocking her view. "Get a grip on that Halloween costume, you freaking ghoul."

Logan glided forward, a fine mist of snow drifting in his wake. He exuded evil in a black suit and scarlet tie, his hair slicked back with product, probably some formaldehyde-like preservative. I couldn't look into his refined, gaunt features. Knowing death came for you was one thing, watching the smirk on its face as it swaggered your way—quite another.

Logan's police officer henchmen kept pace with him. I identified the ever-ready minion, Officer Flutie. And the other...

"Is that...?" My words trailed off.

Brit's features fell into shocked lines. "Not *him*, not now," she said, her breath catching.

Officer Hiels, Brit's father, moved swiftly alongside Logan as the trio stalked toward us. First her brother had been turned into God-knew-what kind of monster by the very thing moving toward us, and now her suspicions about her father's role in Blake's death had been confirmed. Officer Hiels must be high up in the ranks to be Logan's escort. Either that, or Logan relished doling out as much misery as possible.

Wade had said Logan hadn't created any other vampires, but his sire had certainly created a police force of enthralled humans. Mindless. Mere husks to do Logan's bidding. Their eyes, empty. Savage.

I searched the clearing, looking for an escape route. What was keeping Alec and Matt? Were they hurt? And had Wade abandoned us now that his father was here? I couldn't project any questions his way and risk Logan overhearing me tap into our mental line. Besides, no matter how convincing Wade's performance, how sincere he seemed, I knew better

than to trust the bad guys. Didn't I?

Paige hopped up and down, trying to see over me and around Brit's wings. "Over here." She shouldered between us with surprising strength. "Chief Gervais." Her voice had the reverence of a cult member toward her leader.

"You've come to save us!" Paige stumbled forward, holding her injured finger aloft as if asking him to kiss it better. "Like they said on the news, you're Redgrave's only hope."

Brit grabbed Paige's arm and dragged her back. "Reality *bites*, Paige. Do those look like the teeth of Redgrave's only hope?" She gestured to the inch-long fangs that had sprouted from Logan's incisors at the sight of my cousin's blood.

"Get your freakage off of me." From out of nowhere, Paige whipped out a silver fork that she must have pillaged from Matt's gear bag and jabbed it in Brit's arm once, twice… like she was prepping a potato for the barbeque.

Brit shoved her away, and Paige ran straight for Logan. Seriously, you'd think the daughter of a teacher and a lawyer could take one look at the fangs, the hollow cheeks, and Bible-paper-thin skin and do the math. Her almighty Chief Gervais = evil.

Logan actually *did* kiss Paige's finger when she threw herself into his arms. He licked at the semi-dried blood and grinned at my audible gag. Thankfully Logan's surprise appearance had jolted me from bloodlust to survival-lust, and I no longer wanted to make a snack out of Paige. Oh, the *ick* factor. A few minutes ago, however, Logan's provocative actions might have sent me over the edge.

Paige pressed herself against Logan and sighed, "There's more where that came from."

I wanted to hit something. Brit would have to do. I slapped at her shoulder. "Are you seeing this?" I demanded, ignoring her pointed glance from her shoulder to my hand. "She's acting like that news hound. First Wade, now Logan. She must really have some nasty evils in her."

But then, I'd always known that, so why was I surprised?

The officers circled us slowly while Logan wrapped his arm around Paige and gave her a comforting, creepy hug.

"Tell me you've got a hidden power that's going to come in really handy about now," I said out of the corner of my mouth, trying to recall what other talents dark sprites had. Sprites usually kept to themselves. Most of what my father had told me about them—pure speculation. "You can spit fire, right?"

Brit shook her head, never taking her golden eyes off her father's hard features.

So much for hoping he'd snap out of it at the last second and help us take Logan down. His half-hooded gaze skimmed over Brit like she was part of the scenery. He didn't recognize his own daughter, even though she looked the same except for the freaky eyes and the wings.

"You can turn invisible and attack them from behind?" I guessed.

"You've seen it all. There's nothing more," Brit ground out. "My father," she spat the word, shooting him a dark look, "is human. I'm like you, half-blooded." Her eyes sliced over my human form. "What about *your* wolf? Why hasn't

your wolf appeared?"

What could I say? *I don't know how to control her? I wish my father had never tampered with my natural state?* Otherwise right about now some heads would be rolling.

As if finished with her, Logan shoved Paige backward into Officer Flutie, who made an inhuman sound low in his throat. He staggered, then gripped Paige's arms. She struggled against his hold. Fear flashed across her pale face.

A snarl ripped from my throat, but Brit's roar drowned it out. Energy zapped through the air like static as her fury built. Grief and rage emanated from her like waves of heat, and her golden gaze never left Logan as she lunged forward.

Logan must have felt her power too.

"Another time, my dear," the master vampire said with a grin. With a sweeping wave of his hand, my dark sprite BFF became an instant ice sculpture, immobilized by the same freeze magic Wade had used on Travis. A fine mist of fog rose off her skin as the scent of mint struck the air. Wade's scent. Wade's magic.

My breath came in shallow, panicked gasps. *Whoa.* We'd known Logan must feed off Wade to gain his immunity to sunlight, but apparently Wade's blood contained all kinds of magical goodness.

Logan's freeze outperformed Wade's. Brit's eyes remained open and unblinking, her wings, so still they looked computer generated, too fantastical to be real.

Paige screamed, high and shrill. Logan cut the sound short as, with another wave of his hand, her pretty face became trapped mid-cry, her upper lip stuck on one tooth. The officer

holding her solidified mid-cringe. His partner, covering his ears, stood frozen also.

Even snowflakes hung suspended in the air.

I swallowed hard. So why was I still able to move?

The master vampire glanced around at our strange group, Paige and Flutie, Brit and her father, then back at me. "I told my son curfews were a bitch to enforce." He adjusted his suit coat. "Makes the already-borderline types, like you and your friends, rebellious."

He glided over the snow to Brit's immobile form, sending the white stuff into whirligigs under his black boots. He stroked a finger down the frozen, dark line of Brit's cheek, but she stayed as stiff as a store mannequin. "There's a plague in this town. A resistance to my will being spread by the Delacroix family and the half-breed paranorms like yourself that they recruit. But their mutiny is only busy work. A waste of their time." He gestured to his minions. "If my friends weren't otherwise occupied, they would reassure you that I'm a fair man. A just master."

I so doubted that. "Did Ethan consider you a fair master? Or Blake?"

"Ah, Blake." Holding up a hand, Logan pointed a finger to my neck. His nail lengthened, looking seriously gross and deadly sharp. "Now, he was a special case."

I willed my heart rate to slow, struggled to pace my frantic breaths. Anything to pull Logan's dark gaze away from the pulse hammering in my throat. Was he going to execute me vamp-style, with a single swipe across the neck and then let me bleed out? Vamps considered that the ultimate insult,

to drain enemies and refuse to drink their blood, to waste their life force.

But he simply crooked his finger. Alec's cross levitated off my coat as if magnetized and strained toward that long-nailed finger.

"Such a lovely piece, my dear," he said drifting to me.

I took an involuntary step back. *No, I can't run. I have to see what the bastard wants, strike him down if I can.* I lifted my chin and planted my feet in the snow to stop my knees from trembling.

In front of me now, Logan eyed the cross with something akin to fascination. "I hope you don't mind my taking a closer look."

"I'm sorry. I have a no-ogle policy." I shoved his freakish finger aside. He might be about to drain me dry, but I'd be damned if I'd simper and coo at him like Paige had.

Logan yanked his hand back, held it up as if to strike me down, then laughed dryly, and relaxed his stance. "Good to know. Now for the other McCain who's been causing me trouble." He slipstreamed away.

Paige and Flutie, frozen together, rocked like wooden statues as Logan tugged Paige's canvas coat down to reveal her upper arm, decorated with the temporary wolf-and-skull tattoo.

"Ah, your cousin set me on a merry chase. Resisted the call for quite some time." His black eyes met mine. "But then, you also resisted my efforts. Must be something in the McCain blood, wolven influence or no."

Oh, hating him was in our blood all right.

He examined Paige's tattoo with a deep frown. He licked his finger and rubbed at the marking, then hissed in annoyance. "So that's why the beast didn't turn her. It's not real." He cocked his finger, his nail poised over her flesh. "The rules of engagement say that blood must be drawn for the mark to work. Then any of my pets can curse the victim with a single bite."

I inched forward, grabbed my athame from its holster, and held it behind my back. I didn't have a wooden stake handy, but beheading…

"I'm not much of an artist," Logan said, tilting his head, "but this shouldn't be too difficult. All I have to do is carve along the lines. Unless you'd rather do the honors?" He shot me a questioning glance. "Now don't look like that. I know it's not the same as tracking her down and letting her wriggle a bit before you dig in–" He paused. "But I also know how you like to cut."

Someday I'm going to banish his ass. I promised myself. *Someday real soon.*

"The only thing I want to carve into right now is you." I surged at him, jammed my athame, stained black with werewolf blood, under his throat. The dagger hummed with infused magic, glowing in the night.

Logan hesitated. For a second.

Then he disintegrated in front of my eyes. Black mist, cold and suffocating, surrounded me, blinding me. I stabbed at it, but Logan had disappeared. When the mist cleared, I twisted to find him watching me, his arms folded across his black suit coat, his elegant features set in a smug smirk.

"We don't always get what we want, now do we?" he said. "But you get an A for effort." He eyed me approvingly. "I think the Hunter Council is right in casting you out of the way. You're quite something when your back's up. Strong, aggressive. I see your potential." His smirk slid into a sneer. "But then I've always said a little backyard breeding improves the stock. My son is living proof. As are you, my dear."

My head reared back. *How dare he compare my parents and their love to a clinical breeding program?* I growled against the pain as a rush of memories flooded my mind. My father teaching me to always be on guard; my mother telling me to open my heart. They'd wanted the best for me. They hadn't wanted my life to end like this.

"Feeling a bit…wolven?" He raised a brow. "You might want to hear me out before you show your claws."

I fought to contain the beast under my skin. My mind fogged over. The clarity I'd had minutes ago faded under a haze of wolven rage. My eyes burned with the effort to focus on his face and not see him as a delectable raw steak sandwich. The wolf brought such craving, I struggled to make sense of his words. "Talk now. Die later."

"See, you're already down to two-word sentences." Logan laughed. "But you're right, I should get to the point of tonight's appearance." His dark eyes gleamed. "I'm here for you, of course. The Hunter Council has placed a substantial bounty on your head."

"A what? On my what?" Dumbfounded, I squeezed my eyes shut. Logan was right. I could barely think straight.

"Your perky wolven ears heard me." Logan sounded

bored. "The prize is too big to ignore, and I intend to collect. Of course, the Council couldn't kill you outright. Against their code." He laughed. "So they sent you to my town, knowing I'd finish you."

My eyes flew open. I expected to find him at my throat again, but he hadn't moved. He'd totally underestimated me—thought he was safe here in this clearing. But I might surprise him.

He gave me a terrible grin. "The Council gave you a fighting chance. Their first mistake. Look how long you've lasted. You've even surprised me. Then they got tired of waiting and sent their demons to do their dirty work. Lesser vampires invaded my territory, turned my chosen pets before my beasts could get to them." He looked unimpressed. "I can hold them off, of course. I can give you the time you'll need."

"Time for what?" I glanced at the tree line. Why hadn't Alec and Matt found us yet? And where was Wade? Would he risk his father's wrath and join their attack, or had he found a way to keep Alec and Matt away until his father was finished with me? Were Wade and Logan working together after all?

"To acquire something for me. I'm prepared to spare the lives of your friends, as well as your interfering uncle and his family, as long as you do so."

The master vamp had iced my friends. His hounds were crawling over Redgrave, and he was bargaining with me?

"What's the *something*?" I gripped my athame as I observed his smug face.

"I've been tracking your father's progress for years. His work could forever alter the paranormal world. This interests

me." His sculpted lips slanted. "Then he disappeared." He jabbed his finger at me, his eyes darkening to black holes—his thrall, his power kicked in, but thanks to the wards I already had in place against Wade, he couldn't touch me.

"Get me his notes, get me every last scrap of his work, and I'll let your family live. Fail and I'll make you watch as I turn them into my willing slaves." He made a sweeping gesture with his arm. "Now, I have a meeting to finish."

"Wait," I called out, and Logan paused, raising a brow. "I get the notes, you never make another werewolf again. Not in this town. Not anywhere."

Logan tsk-tsked. "You're hardly in a position to make demands, my dear. Perhaps you need some clarification." His eyes blackened. I shrank back, scrambling to fortify my mental wards. "Do as I have asked. Or you'll all die slow, horrible, vile deaths." His smile said he looked forward to them. "My specialty, ask around."

As I sucked in a trembling breath, Logan released his men from the freeze hold with a wave of his hand. The officers stumbled for a moment, then righted themselves, apparently unconcerned that they'd been trapped, petrified. Too under his rule to care. The trio, suspended in the air, glided back the same direction they had come, retreating into the woods as if on rewind. Logan's hand waved once more before they disappeared in a puff of mist.

His suspended animation broke, and the world returned with a vengeance. I stood stunned. Life, brutal and cold, swirled around me. The smell of death seeped into the air.

Brit woke with a gasp. The energy she'd built before Logan

zapped her whistled through the air, then *poof*... Gonzo.

Where'd he go?" Her wings fanned, caught the wind, and lifted her upright.

"Vanished." I tried not to look as freaked out as I felt. Rubber legs. My breath shallow.

"I hate it when vampires pull that crap." Brit glared around the clearing. "Dad and Flutie too?"

I nodded.

Brit's yellow eyes flickered with anger and pain. Seeing her father at Logan's mercy could only have fueled her bitterness. She'd tasted defeat at her failed attempt to take Logan down. I understood because I was swallowing nasty emotions of my own. Sure, Logan had let me live, but the encounter had left me wanting a three-day-long shower under a sandblaster.

Behind us, a spine-tingling howl cut into the night, followed by a brilliant flash of light. Alec rushed into the clearing, his rifle at his shoulder. Wade followed with Matt at his side. Behind them, the stuff of nightmares. A league of werewolves snapped at their heels, their shadowy forms gaining on the guys, as relentless as a storm-blackened wave crashing toward shore.

With a shout, Brit charged into the air and crossed the clearing in a blink. Hovering over the molting, shifting mass, she swooped and dove at the beasts. The werewolves jumped and clawed at the air, too slow to catch her, but it distracted them enough for Alec to take aim and fire off rounds of silver bullets without fear of retaliation.

I had to follow my heart. No more obeying orders— things always ended badly when I followed orders. If I'd

cut poor Cujo loose when I'd wanted to, the mutt might still be alive. If I'd told Sebastian to screw off and stayed in Vancouver, asked questions, tracked my parents down, I might have found them.

I tore across the clearing to intercept a werewolf eyeing Matt like a raw slab of meat in the middle of a veggie buffet. As I blindsided the werewolf, Logan's words echoed in my head. *They sent you to my town, knowing I'd finish you.*

I'd been thrown to the wolves in Redgrave. Literally. By the very council who'd promised to uncover the truth about my parents' disappearance even as they'd betrayed me. Put a bounty on my head. Told me lies.

The werewolf tumbled across the snow, righted itself, and came back for more. The sky exploded in a white cloud as it leapt for me. Pain radiated through my chest as the beast smashed into me, pinning me to the ground. Its fevered breath roasted my neck. I opened my eyes. The werewolf's grill-like teeth and glowing red eyes were inches from my face, its claws sinking into my ribcage.

"Eryn, don't move." Matt jumped to his feet and scrambled for his rifle. Fear, for me, for all of us, vibrated in his voice.

My breath left me in a rush. The beast crushed me to the ground. My bones collapsed, about to perforate my lungs. Incisors tore through my coat, ripped at my flesh. Searing pain, immediate and cruel. Tears blurred my eyes. Shock fogged my mind. The hard, slick feel of teeth scraped my fingers as I clawed at the jaws snapping at my shoulder.

He has me. I'm dead.

My body went numb. My hands dropped to the ground. I stared past the frenzied body writhing on top of me and focused on a clear bit of night sky.

Mint, pungent and sweet, filled the air around me. The weight on my chest lifted. Above me, his head bowed, Wade staggered to his feet, his mouth dripping with black werewolf blood. Beside me, the ravaged beast morphed into a young man. Then his blank face dissolved into light.

Wade took a shuddering step closer and stumbled over the scorched earth and melted snow where the beast had disappeared. Long gashes in his coat left strips of shredded leather dancing in the wind and even the scent of werewolf couldn't disguise the sour stench of evil surrounding him. Wade had been in Logan's presence, and recently. Which meant one of two things: he'd been dragged to his sire, or he'd gone willingly.

Had Logan freeze-framed the world again? Had hours passed before Wade had joined us in the here and now? And Lord help me, could Wade resist the scent of my blood? Surely the master vampire knew Wade had helped us. What had he done to him as punishment?

Wade?

I lifted the limestone wall, opening myself up to him, wanting to feel our connection again. I built another wall so huge it encompassed everything around us. *Wade? You're safe now. Tell me you're okay.*

With a low moan, Wade lifted his head. Eyes greyer than the sea, with no hint of Logan's darkness. But they held no joy. Only sorrow.

You shouldn't do that. His husky voice filled my mind. His words came in a rush. *Don't ever let me in like this again. If my father discovers our link, he'll get inside your head. He'll find your weaknesses, dig up things you've blocked out—things about your parents.*

So what? I wouldn't be in this mess if I knew what happened to my parents.

You know more than you think. Wade's face set in hard lines. *Once Logan gets in your mind, he can do things. He could be miles away and do this—*

My chest ached. I couldn't get enough air. Couldn't take in a single breath.

WHAT ARE YOU DOING? I screamed into Wade's mind.

Exactly what Logan will do. If he uses me to connect with you this way.

The pressure ebbed. While I sucked in gulps of air, the thoughts Wade sent to me became fractured, disjointed.

I can't be trusted. There's not much time. I can destroy my father. If you get the information he wants. I know your parents are alive, Eryn. They're alive. My father's been trying to track them. But you have to find them first. I won't let...

He stopped using words. They didn't come through fast enough. Wade projected a flood of images at me. Dark. Evil. Things I had to do to help him kill Logan. Choices only I could make.

The images stopped. Only Wade's voice remained. *I'm sorry. I had to show you. You had to know.*

Logan's malicious laughter echoed in the dark depths of

Wade's mind.

He's coming. Wade's eyes filled with a black death that swallowed his soul. Darkness swirled in the whites of his eyes.

I edged away, fire burning in my shoulder as I twisted in the snow.

Fight back, I told Wade. *Shut him out.*

I will, Wade assured me. *When you're ready. When it's time.*

A gentle, cool touch on my lips. The kiss of a ghost.

With a tremendous roar, savage, with the force of a jet engine, Logan closed in on Wade. Then Wade's voice raw, determined. *I won't let him touch you.*

Wade severed the link between us. Nothing but silence. His absence hit me like a sucker punch to the heart.

I'd never felt so alone.

The battle went on around me. Screams from my friends rang in the distance. The singe of silver meeting werewolf. The brilliant flash of white light.

My legs twitched. I should try to get up, but I was so tired. Trees tilted wildly with the wind. Their bare branches superimposed over each other. Blurred. Dimmed. The cool comfort of the earth cradled me. I didn't want to fight. Only sleep. Let go. Drift.

Warm air beat against my body in powerful gusts and then, as quickly as it had flared up, it faded into a whisper in the trees. A gentle touch on my hand made me open my eyes. Brit knelt beside me, her face wet with tears. A weird iridescent glow surrounded her. I squinted. Arcing from her back, the faint outline of wings.

"You're so beautiful, a beautiful dark angel…" I breathed.

"What are you talking about?" Brit sniffled, her gaze focused on my shoulder. "I'm no angel. And you're not going to die, so don't even think you can leave me to look after Paige. She's your problem."

"Matt, can you heal her?" Raw and hoarse, Alec's voice came from somewhere behind me.

Then Matt leaned over me, his expression bleak. "It will take more than I've got. We need Mom."

In my mind, a distant voice. Like a whisper. Like a dream. Wade's voice.

Hold on, Eryn. Remember what you need to do. I'll help as much as I can.

With the words came the warmth of being cloaked, protected—made safe.

Brit's concerned eyes morphed into stars, and I slipped into darkness.

The fire burning a hole in my shoulder flared up my neck and through to my back. Frightening tremors wracked my body. My muscles contracted, pulsing without pause. My teeth ground together so hard I feared they would shatter. What happened? Where the hell was I? Lightheaded, outside of myself. *So much pain.*

Werewolves...

Teeth...

Blood...

Wings...

Images flashed through my mind like firecracker flares. Brilliant and shocking. *Logan.* A groan escaped my lips.

"Shhh. I've got you now." Strong arms locked me against a solid, warm chest. "We're almost home." The words rumbled against my ear. Not the voice I'd heard in my mind telling me to hold on—that he would help.

So then…"Who?" I asked.

"Matt, hurry. She's losing too much blood." Brit's shout answered my question.

I twisted in the arms holding me close, but my deadened limbs had little strength. My skin was clammy. Beads of sweat slid along my forehead into my eyes. I squeezed my lids shut. Alec gingerly supported my weight. I lay in the front seat of the truck, resting across Alec's lap as Matt drove. Brit sat between the brothers, pressing on my wounds with cloths already saturated with my blood.

Where was Paige? Huddled in the back of the truck, staring at us through the glass.

The pain in my shoulder spread across my chest like black ink spilt on white satin, sinking deep. I panted, unable to take in a breath without feeling like my lungs might shatter. My eyes grew heavy. I gave in to the darkness.

Clouds gathered over the mountains. Sensing the storm, a large grey wolf called out to his mate. She ran to him, her jet-black coat in stark relief against the fading sun. Midway through the clearing, the first shot rang out.

The wound in her side forced her into an awkward lope. She fell. Heedless of the danger, the male raced to her. He stood above

her, keening low in his throat. The second round took him down.
  All was quiet.
  A gentle mist descended from the heavens.

I woke on a sob. The wolf's sorrow lingered, even as I tried to open my eyes. I fought the weakness. A desperate panic smothered me.

"You're safe, Eryn," a woman's hushed voice said. "You're safe." A gentle hand touched my shoulder. Fingers smoothed my hair.

"Mom?"

There was a pause.

"A friend."

Then she murmured words so beautiful, yet foreign, rhythmic. A spell? My eyelids grew heavy. Thoughts swirled as I tried to process what and where. Alec's mom, not mine…

And I remembered my parents were gone, and I was alone.

Always alone.

I wept and fell into a dreamless sleep.

Break It To Me Gently

Morning sunlight cast gold and ruby patterns on my closed eyelids. Birds trilled in the distance. The delicious scent of freshly baked cinnamon rolls drifted around me. My eyes flew open. An everything's-right-with-the-world way to wake. Comforting. Soothing.

So freaking scary.

Above me a sharply peaked ceiling glowed with sunlight. I lay tucked under a heavy, multicolored quilt. To the left of my narrow brass bed the source of the bright sunlight, a dormer window framed by sheer lace curtains above a small writing desk. Lavender paisley wallpaper and a dried flower arrangement on the nightstand completed the picture.

I eased into a sitting position, gasping at the pain in my

side. I glanced around the room. Tasteful furniture. No lime green paint. No lava lamp.

Where the hell was I?

Footsteps, like someone tiptoeing across a hardwood floor, approached the bedroom door, then stopped. The door inched open.

Brit's head peeked around the door. Her long black bangs obscured her face. She swiped them out of her eyes, watching me, tentative, cautious as she entered the room. Her skin glowed with health. You'd never know she'd spent the night fighting for her life.

"Hey, you're awake." She ran a finger along the dresser as she approached my bed, stopping a few feet away. "How are you feeling?"

I sat up, letting out a year's worth of curses as pain snagged my ribs in a death grip. "Need I say more?"

Brit dashed across the room, wrapped an arm around me, supporting my weight.

"You are so ridiculous," she snapped, though her touch was gentle. "I told them we should have put you in a drug-induced coma or something, but does anyone ever listen to…"

Brit's concern washed over me. My fingers clawed into the quilt. I stared at my white knuckles, drawing in a long, slow breath. I called on my wolf. Strong. Powerful. A quickening in my veins brought her to me. The burning pressure squeezing me in half began to ease. I released my death grip on the quilt's quaint little squares.

"I'm okay." I shrugged Brit's arm off. She reached for me

again, and I knocked her hand aside with a flick of my wrist. At the hurt in her eyes, I let out a frustrated sigh. "Sorry. I'm not the greatest patient. But no coma required. Seriously, I'm fine."

Brit's frown should have turned me to salt, but she backed off and perched on the side of the bed, the air over her shoulder, calm and still. No more iridescent wings. No more golden eyes. Still…awkward. If I grilled Brit about the whole dark sprite thing, she might ask me about my own duality issues. What had I looked like out there in the woods? What had I turned into?

My legs shifted restlessly under the covers. "Where are we?" Was Paige okay? Alec? Wade? My eyes flew to Brit. "Where is everyone?"

"Here, at the Delacroix ranch. You don't remember?"

I shook my head. The stab in my shoulder forced me to suck in a breath. "The graveyard. Alec's truck. The werewolves. But it's all pretty hazy. Did everyone get out okay?"

"Sure, nothing to worry about." Brit gave a vague nod, her gaze fixed on a neatly folded bundle of clothing at the end of the bed. I guessed I wasn't the only one weirded out by our mutual…weirdness. "And Marie fixed things with Marcus and Sammi so don't stress over them either."

I groaned. "Oh crap, I didn't even think. Marcus, Samm… They must be so worried." My eyes widened. "They must be pissed."

"No, you're golden. Marie called them, said you and Paige were out cruising and ran into car trouble. She told them it was safer for you guys to crash here instead of getting busted

for breaking curfew." Brit snorted. "Ironic that the curfew actually worked in our favor." She handed me the bundle of clothes. "We found some stuff for you to wear. Your clothes were pretty much trashed."

"Thanks." I threw back the quilt and swung my legs out in what should have been a lightning-fast movement. Instead, I wobbled to my feet. *Damn, I hate being all feeble. Come on, wolf, heal faster.* I teetered my way across the room in a dizzy haze and took the clothes. Every breath sent stabs through my side.

"The jeans might be too short for you and too big, but it's better than going around in *that*," Brit said, nodding toward me.

I tilted my head down carefully, wary of jarring my shoulder. An oversized T-shirt covered me to mid-thigh. I inhaled. Earthy, fresh. Alec's T-shirt. A flush of warmth spread over my skin. I stepped into the jeans, hissing at the flash of pain in my chest as I bent over.

"Maybe you shouldn't be moving," Brit said.

I glared at her and eased the black sweater over my head, my shoulder stiff and resisting. Alec's plain white T-shirt hung down about a foot lower than the sweater, but I didn't care. I loved the feeling of him all around me. I didn't, however, love the ache in every muscle of my body.

"Marie thought you'd sleep all day. You should take it easy for a while longer." Concern tinged Brit's voice. "You know, have a morning, noon, and night snooze-fest."

"Not necessary." I scowled into the dresser mirror, my ponytails slanted weirdly, the ends of my hair kinked up. I

straightened what I could, my muscles already more fluid. My wolf kicking in. I ran a finger down the smooth skin at my neck. Not a sign of the scratch that werewolf had given me. I slipped the T-shirt collar down over my shoulder. No gaping wound where the other had fed, just deep bruising. My skin an ode to every shade of black and blue.

Silver glinted in the glass. Alec's cross dangled above me, looped around the top of the mirror's ornate moldings. Someone must have taken it off me when they were patching me up. I grabbed it and quickly put it on. The weight of it resting safely on the cotton T-shirt...

There. That makes me feel human again.

"You might as well come downstairs, Miss Vanity-in-the-Aftermath-of-Battle." Brit rolled her eyes. "Marie and Matt will be amazed at your recovery. They're healers, shamans. They did their best, but weren't sure how much they could help because you're...anyway, your ribs were bruised, you had a hole in your shoulder so deep we could see bone." Her laugh was hollow. "I thought you were a goner."

I made a face in the mirror. "I did too." I lifted my arms, stretching my torso. "Whatever they did probably saved my life, but I heal pretty fast."

Brit snorted. "Yeah, I can tell." Since she'd entered the room I'd gone from barely able to sit up in bed, to strolling around the room and conducting personal appearance damage control.

She yanked the bedroom door open, and a tremor of unease snagged up my back as I followed her down the stairs. About to meet Marie, Alec's mother, who even Kate deferred

to as the woman who'd predicted I would destroy her son. If she really believed that, why had she bothered to patch me up? Because she loves her son, and her son loves… Whoa… maybe my noggin took more of a beating than I thought.

At the bottom of the stairs, we followed a narrow hallway to the back of the house where a tabby lay curled peacefully in a doorway. As we approached it lifted its head, fully alert. Its eyes tapered into slits. Fur puffed up and out three times its normal size.

"Nice kitty, kitty," Brit cooed, but the cat yowled and darted away. She watched it go, her lips in a pout.

"Well, we definitely won't be crazy cat ladies when we're old and haggard," I told Brit as we entered the sunlit kitchen.

"If we live that long." Brit snorted.

In the kitchen, Alec, Matt, and Paige looked up from a long farmhouse table. The freshly baked cinnamon buns I'd smelled earlier sat on a tray, cooling in the center of the table. My heart lurched. The scene could have been right out of a family sitcom, if it weren't for the scratches and bruises on the guys' faces, arms, and hands. Obviously, they hadn't healed as fast as me and Brit, the paranorms. The outsiders. I cringed at the shell-shocked look in Paige's eyes.

And the arsenal of paranormal battle gear spread over every available bit of counter space. Shotguns, disassembled for cleaning. Silver bullets packed in sandwich bags. Knives. An ax with the handle modified into a sharp pointed stake. The scent of garlic and sweetgrass hovered in the air.

It was too much. They'd all faced too much.

"You're awake." Alec crossed the kitchen in two strides.

"You're more than awake. You're up and walking and talking." He ran his hands down my arms, patting me like he expected to feel broken bones.

I reached out and traced a purplish bruise on his high cheekbone.

"Yup, just like a real girl." My breath came fast when his touch slid to my lower back, the warmth from his hand spread to my whole body.

He twisted to face his brother. "Matt, you and Mom… this is amazing."

"Oh, that wasn't all us." Matt took a bite from a cinnamon bun.

"Oh, right." Alec's gaze shot to my hand suspended between us, still reaching for him.

It fell to my side. Damn, he remembered my claws, the fur. How did you make small talk after something like that?

I flushed at the intensity of his stare. Like he tried to see inside, to how I ticked.

"I feel fabulous, considering." I made a point of catching Matt's eye. "I guess I owe you, big time."

Matt nodded. A bit anticlimactic, but at least he didn't snort or roll his eyes or glare at me like I just skinned the cat on the stairs. Nice. We were beyond outright animosity.

A door latch clicked, and a woman wearing a salmon-colored zip-up hoodie and jeans stepped into the kitchen. She carried a handful of dried herbs and a ball of string. I could see where Alec and his brothers got their good looks. Mrs. Delacroix had an exotic, ageless beauty. Her sable hair was cut into a sleek bob, and she wore a fashionable pair of glasses

perched on her nose

At her side stood the large, grey wolf-dog that had been running in the woods the first time I encountered Alec. The dog's head tilted, ears cocked in my direction.

"Welcome to our home," Mrs. Delacroix said. Her eyes, a deeper brown than Alec's, were soft as she clasped my hands in hers. "We're so happy to have you with us, Eryn." Her gaze traveled over my torso like a practiced physician. "Now that you're feeling better perhaps, we should discuss why the Hunter Council wants you dead, and how we're going to save this town?"

I blinked, shocked by her sudden commanding tone.

The room erupted as Matt surged to his feet, and everyone began to talk at once. The wolf-dog began whining and padding in a circle by the kitchen door

Alec frowned at his mother. "I thought we agreed to break it to Eryn gently?"

"The time for gentle has passed." Marie eyed her son calmly. "I spoke with Kate. The high priestess of the Littan coven warned her that paranorm bounty hunters are sniffing around, looking for Eryn."

Bounty hunters closing in. Just what I didn't want to hear. Hadn't we been through enough? The werewolf attack. His fierce bite. His stench. God, he'd been *chewing* on me. My bottom lip trembled, and I bit down hard. I couldn't freak out now.

It was over. And everyone accounted for. I looked over the room again…almost.

A fist squeezed my heart.

"Where's Wade?" I asked Alec, who suddenly found the back of a nearby chair absorbing.

The room fell silent.

From the open window, frigid morning air blew through the kitchen. I shivered. A feeling of doom settled over me. The happy, sunshiny, birds-are-chirping morning had been a sham. Hadn't seemed right from the start.

"Okay," I said into the silence. "I get it. Something went wrong." I crossed my arms. "Did Wade take off? Go all evildoer again?"

Matt and Brit exchanged a look. "Someone tell me." I turned to the only other person in the room who might care if Wade lived or died, even if he had her hyped up on his thrall. "Paige, come on. Spill."

"We don't know where he is," Paige said, her tone bitter. "But it's not like you think. He didn't do anything wrong." She lifted her chin and glared at each member of the crew. "We wouldn't have gotten out alive if he hadn't helped us, and they all know it." She pressed her lips together and stared out the window. "He could be injured, or dying…"

My pulse raced. Putting my fingers to my temples, I closed my eyes, concentrating. I reached out with my thoughts, searching for Wade's frequency, but came up blank. Tiny comet-like squiggles darted willy-nilly behind my eyelids, but no matter how hard I squeezed my eyes and drew on the power, Wade wasn't there. Not like when he'd blocked me out. This was worse. A black hole. A void of nothingness.

I swayed and fell into Alec's arms.

He touched his forehead to mine. His concern washed

over me, soothing the lingering pain in my body and the ache in my heart. He lowered me into a chair. I was in another world. Separate from them. Different. Tainted.

I relived the images Wade had bombarded me with in the clearing. My father smiling at me, my mother at his side. Brit sandwiched in a bear hug between Blake and her father. Logan's death. Yes, he'd shown me that. But the blood. So much blood.

And then he'd left me.

"Don't leave," I cried, my voice loud in my ears.

"We're right here," Brit said. "We're all in this together, Eryn. You're not alone."

I blinked, coming back to the world and looking around. Alec's face pale and strained as he knelt beside me.

My muscles tensed, urging me to run from the weight settling on my shoulders. The burden of friendship. Of love. But the time for running was over. I had to tell them the truth about Wade—how Logan could take over his body, his mind, and how Wade could never really be trusted. But I also had to tell them the truth about myself. Human and wolven—and thanks to my father—something much more.

Something dangerous.

But maybe that's what they needed.

What this town needed. Because nice wasn't going to get the job done, and it certainly wouldn't bring down the Hunter Council.

Wade had shown me the way to win this war.

I had to give up my mortal soul—
Give in to my wolf.
Find out what lies under my skin.

So far, I'd only scratched the surface.

The SKINNED Series

A normal life?
Now that's the real fairytale...

SECOND SKIN

JUDITH GRAVES

FRIENDS DON'T LET FRIENDS FLY DRUNK

The cool night air ghosted my breath as I tore through the trees, dodging their heavy, snow-covered branches. I leapt over the randomly placed tombstones scattered throughout Crimson Cemetery like a pro whipping through a round of mini-golf. It sucked that I was becoming familiar enough with the cemetery's terrain to charge forward on automatic. That I was doing so for the third night that week was just plain irksome.

The hair on the back of my neck trembled. Not a good sign. I inhaled sharply, the pungent scent of hungry, drooling werewolf drifted on the breeze. I was heading right into its path.

It seemed I was always running straight toward the stuff any normal person would be running from, screaming their heads off. But then I wasn't normal. I wasn't really a person either if you wanted to get picky about the details. I shot a look up at the starry sky, tracking the dark form that dipped and swooped over the graveyard like some ginormous half-baked prehistoric bat. In her dark sprite form, my best friend's wings sliced through the trees, causing mini-snowstorms to dump down on me with each impact.

My thighs worked harder as I bolted up hill, keen to take the advantage of the higher ground. Brit was closer now. Reachable. Physically at least. I knew she was hurting, no one doubted that. She wore her feelings like a shroud, blocking us out. She wouldn't even talk about it to Matt, her boyfriend. But going all clammy wasn't the extent of the problem.

On a nightly basis, Brit drowned her sorrows in her mother's liquor cabinet. She was out of control, self-destructing.

Unfortunately, a lot of her pain came down to choices I made.

"We don't have to do this tonight," I called as I sprang into the air, swiping at the jean-clad legs hovering five feet above me. "Let's just rent a tear-jerker and bawl our eyes out. We'll both feel better."

"Leave me 'lone!" Brit glared down at me, though her eyes were slightly unfocused. Her long black hair whipped around her, twitching like the tails of hundreds of angry cats. "I'm just goin' for a walk."

Still running at top speed while Brit flew above me, I had to laugh at her interpretation of *walk*.

"I hate to shatter the illusion," I told her, "but this ain't your average evening constitutional." I leapt up again. Once. Twice.

"Stop that!" Brit's expression changed from rage to shock. "What are you doing?"

"Friends don't let friend fly drunk," I shouted. I gripped a hand around her calf and hung on for dear life. Brit dipped at the change in weight, then surged upward and banked hard all at the same time, pinwheeling us in space.

I looked down.

I shouldn't have.

We'd cleared the hill and were now soaring twenty feet over the graveyard. My stomach rolled. Werewolves, vampires, and other beasties I could handle, but heights? Not so much.

Dizzy, my Aunt Sammi's burnt chili supper crawling back up my throat, I struggled not to black out. My grip slackened, and my fingers slid down Brit's jeans. Terrified, my body flailing in the air, I grabbed at her ankle with both hands. Fear made me a bit testy.

"Brit," I screamed, my hands now sporting three-inch claws that dug ever so slightly into Brit's flesh. "Take us in for a landing or, so help me, I'll gut you right now!"

My best friend let out an eerie, dark sprite wail. I'd only heard her make that sound during these little freak out episodes, and each time my sensitive wolven ears threatened to bleed.

A howl rang through the night. A reply to Brit's call. Fantastic. Now I'd have drunken master Brit AND a werewolf to deal with. Brit's high-pitched screech caused pressure to build in my head. I couldn't stand it and covered my ears with my hands, trying to block the sound that echoed down from the sky, ricocheted off the trees, and then faded into the distance.

I didn't even realize I'd let go of Brit until I struck the snow-covered earth with enough force to shatter a few bones—if I'd been human, that is. Being half wolven, I merely let out a pained groan, thankful I hadn't landed on top of a tombstone. *That* might have been really uncomfortable.

I rolled to my feet and with a little shimmy of my hips, like a dog shaking out its fur, cleared snow from my shoulders and butt. I pulled off my hat and slapped it hard against my thigh to get rid of the white stuff caked onto the rust-coloured wool.

A sudden gust of wind at my back announced Brit's presence. I spun to witness the crazy flapping of batlike, iridescent wings, a jumble of waist-length black hair, and Brit's arms and legs as she crash-landed a few feet from me.

Jerking my hat back on my head, I heaved my way through knee-deep snow and hauled Brit upright.

"Aren't you getting tired of this?" I shook her none too gently. "He's not hanging around his grave waiting for you to appear!" I said the words the rest of our hunting crew feared to tell Brit. "Blake isn't your brother anymore, Brit. He wouldn't even recognize you."

Brit pressed her lips together, her black-rimmed gaze focused over my shoulder, eyes narrowed with pain.

My heart lurched. I hadn't meant to hurt her, but I couldn't keep watching her hurt herself. I was the key to saving our small paranormal-infested town, Redgrave. And, just maybe, I could save Brit's brother, Blake, who had been turned into some freakish sprite/werewolf hybrid against his will. My gut clenched in frustration. Sure, I had a marginal possibility of gaining access to a drug that might reverse what had happened to Blake. But Brit had no concept of the things I'd have to do to get it. That my very soul would be a bargaining chip in a game I'd likely lose. Was it too much to ask for a little time to adjust to the idea?

A strange mixture of odors blanketed the night. I lifted my chin, inhaling deeply. Dank earth. Blood. Werewolf. The same burnt rubber smell that came from Brit's wings when she overused them.

Brit's whirled me around. My jaw dropped in amazement. I met her triumphant look with my own stunned expression.

"Wouldn't recognize me, huh?" Brit whispered into my ear. "Wasn't waiting for me?"

Blake crouched before us in his morphed werewolf/dark sprite form, his wings three times the span of Brit's and sporting dagger-like hooks at the ends that arched high over his back—ready to strike.

Whether he planned to take us both out, or just me, I wasn't sure, but the shifting breeze brought another scent into the equation. We turned to stare at the two massive werewolves thundering toward us from the trees.

Lovely.

About The Author

Judith reads as much as she writes, devouring at least two books a week. She loves heated debates over character motives...she's been kicked out of several book clubs for just this reason. With her faithful sidekick at her feet—that'd be, Willow, a yellow lab—Judith remains unfazed by book club drama and is furiously writing more paranormal stories. Which hopefully, you'll read.

Working in a school library, Judith is surrounded by children's and young adult literature (there's no escape!). She fosters the joy of reading in students and staff at her school. She helps out with the school choir and drama club. If it has to do with words or music, Judith is around. A singer/songwriter for more than ten years, Judith often writes songs about her characters—since they are beasties of the night, this makes for interesting listening.

Thank you for purchasing this Leap Books, LLC publication. For other fabulous teen and tween novels, please visit our online store at www.leapbks.com.

For questions or more information contact us at info@leapbks.com

Leap Books, LLC
www.leapbks.com

Watch for other exciting releases from Leap Books...

Kenzie didn't expect her first summer in the Florida Keys to be murder. Cute guys, awesome boats, endangered species, gun-toting thugs...

When city girl Kenzie Ryan moves to a Florida wildlife refuge, she plunges straight into an eco-mystery. Kenzie trades New York streets for Keys pollution cleanup, and now, instead of hailing cabs, she's tracking down a poacher of endangered Key deer.

Her new home does have some benefits—mainly Angelo, an island native, who teams up with her to nab the culprit.

Island Sting
Bonnie J. Doerr
ISBN-13 978-1-61603-002-5
ISBN-10 1-61603-002-X

But will they both survive when the killer turns from stalking deer to hunting humans?

Island Sting includes notes on the endangered Florida Key deer and the National Key Deer Refuge.

Every woman in the Maxwell family has the gift of sight.

A talent sixteen-year-old Kasey would galdly give up. Until Kasey has a vision about Josh Johnstone, the foreign exchange student from England. The vision leads her into deep waters...a lead in a play and into the arms of Josh. But Josh, too, has a secret. Something that could put them all in danger. To solve a mystery of a supernatural haunting, they must uncover the secrets of the haunted theater when they are trapped on the night of the full moon.

Freaksville
Kitty Keswick
ISBN-13 978-1-61603-001-8
ISBN-10 1-61603-001-1